Pastor Pete,
Great book my
girlfriend's uncle a
A character feels totally
by you 😊 Church in O u
totally has a Pentecost
vibe. Hope you enjo
deserved sabatical
this read!
Blessings,
Ryan Daley

SOUTHIE'S LITTLE ANGEL

Paul Donovan

This is a work of fiction. Names, characters, incidents, and dialogues are products of the author's imagination and are not to be construed as real. Any resemblance to actual events or persons, living or dead, is entirely coincidental.

Copyright © 2014 Paul Donovan
All rights reserved.

ISBN: 1495364798
ISBN 13: 9781495364792
Library of Congress Control Number: 2014904287
CreateSpace Independent Publishing Platform
North Charleston, South Carolina

Dedication

This book is dedicated to Thomas W. Taylor, a true friend who taught me how to have compassion for everyone. Thanks for watching my back and always keeping me laughing. We miss you, rest in peace.

Acknowledgments

To Jesus, my Lord and Savior: Thank you for your unlimited grace and mercy you have bestowed upon me.

To Norman Jones: My brother in Christ, how I cherish the times sitting at your kitchen table studying scripture and helping me better understand them with your vast knowledge.

To Matthew McGuire: A friendship I will always cherish.

To Jim McIsaac: Thank you for the hospitality you always provided to me.

To my siblings: Richard, Michael, Eileen and Janet, I feel so grateful for having you in my life.

To my parents: Richard and Claire Donovan, thank you for all your sacrifices you made for us and always being there for me when I needed you most with your unconditional love.

To my daughters: Debralee and Danielle, you have grown up to be amazing, wonderful, young women. I am a very blessed man and proud father.

To my wife: Virginija, your continued loving support and loyalty made it possible for me to write this book. I love you with all my heart.

Disclaimer

This is a work of fiction. Names, characters, incidents, and dialogues are products of the author's imagination and are not to be construed as real. Any resemblance to actual events or persons, living or dead, is entirely coincidental.

"Pride is concerned with who is right. Humility is concerned with what is right."
- Ezra Taft Benson

Thank you Brutus for 17 years and 4 months of unconditional love and abundant joy! You'll live forever in our hearts.

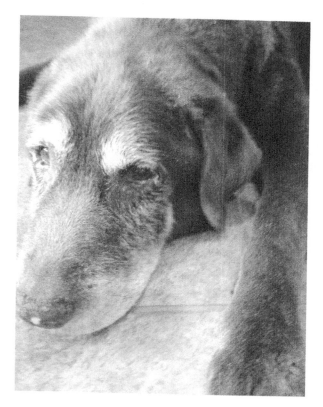

My daughter Debralee and I at her wedding.

My daughter Danielle, rock climbing in Mexico.

1

It was a beautiful summer evening as Libby (short for Elizabeth) stared out the window, waiting for her dad to arrive home. He was supposed to be there by nine o'clock. He had promised her that he would be home right after his Alcoholics Anonymous meeting to tell Libby her favorite bedtime story. The babysitter kept looking at her watch because she had an early exam in the morning and needed to get a few hours of studying in. Libby remembered how the wall clock's chimes used to ring every hour before it had broken two years earlier. She wished she could go back to that time when everything in her life was different. Ten-year-old Libby knew exactly what this meant. She hoped her dad was just running late, but in reality, she knew that whenever he broke a promise to her, it meant that he was drinking again.

She said good night to Danielle, the sitter, and walked up the stairs, disappointed one more time. Danielle could see Libby's eyes welling up with tears as she walked past. Danielle wondered how a father could do this to his child, especially after she had lost her mother in a car accident one year earlier. Libby loved her dad so much; it was difficult for Danielle to witness this. She went from sadness to extreme anger. She wanted to report the situation to child services, but she knew how much Libby's dad meant to her.

When Libby reached her room, the tears were streaming down her face. Before she got into her bed, she looked up at the beautiful painting of Jesus that hung above it. As she did every night, she knelt down to say her prayers. But this time there was an urgency to it. As she wiped the tears from her face, she put her head down and her hands together. It took her a couple of times starting and stopping because she was so upset. When she regained her composure, she said, "Dear Jesus, I know you needed Mommy in heaven, but I'm asking you to please help Daddy. Can you let him know that you love him as much as I do? He's been so sad since Mommy died. I don't know what I'll do if something happens to him. He loved Mommy so much. Can you please heal his pain? I don't know how you'll help him, but I do know that you can and you will. I know you are taking care of Mommy. Please tell her that Daddy and I miss her very much. Amen."

2

It was now almost midnight. Danielle was awakened by a familiar sound. It was Jim, Libby's dad. He was singing, and she could hear him from a block away. She wasted no time meeting him at the door. As Jim was trying to pull his keys out of his pocket, Danielle swung the door open, which startled him for a moment. He had seen this look on her face before. He was about to try to explain himself when she cut him off. She said, "I don't want to hear excuses from you anymore. I'm tired of hearing them." Jacket in hand, she started to walk out the door. He tried to pass her some money for watching Libby. She looked at him and then down at the money. Then she knocked it out of his hand. He looked down at the money on the ground and leaned against the house for support. Danielle demanded that he look at her. When he did, she said in a firm voice, "Mr. Davis, I know what you've gone through. But it's time you stop playing the victim here. You have an adorable, ten-year-old daughter up there that needs you in her life, and all you can think about is yourself. Stop focusing on what you lost, and start focusing on what you still have."

He was about to defend himself as she turned to walk away, but suddenly he stopped and realized that what she had said was true. Deep inside him, he knew she was 100 percent right, and if he wanted his life to change, *he* had to change. This was a terrifying thought: to face "life on life's terms," the saying he had heard so many times in the halls of his AA meetings, but now it resonated with him. He turned and put the key in the door.

As he walked in, the first thing he saw was the family photograph on the wall. It was of Libby; his wife, Susan; and him. It had only been taken eighteen months ago, but it seemed like it had been an eternity. He put his coat on the sofa and walked over to the picture. As he stood there and looked into Susan's eyes, he said, "Honey, if you can hear me, please help me. I've made a mess of my life. I know Libby deserves better than this. I don't know what's wrong with me. Every time I think I'm moving forward with my life, I can't help but look back at my mistakes. I can't do this alone. I need you more than ever. Please, Sue, please." Then he took the portrait down, grasped it against his chest, and sank into the recliner. He leaned back and passed out. The clock struck midnight for the first time in two years. Those chimes rang out, but Jim didn't hear them. He was fast asleep.

3

Libby was in her room, sound asleep. Then she was awakened by a soft voice calling her name. She sat up in her bed and saw a light across the room, unlike any she had ever seen before. She tried to make sense of it, thinking it was a streetlight, or maybe it was Danielle checking in on her with a flashlight. As she looked at it, the light kept changing color: from white to orange, then white to yellow, and it moved constantly. She knew that she should be afraid, but she was feeling a tremendous amount of emotions—peace and love went through her whole body. Libby asked, "Who's there?" The light seemed to stop moving, and in the center of it appeared the figure of an angel. Libby asked, "What do you want?"

A soft voice replied, "Libby, Jesus has heard your prayers." When the angel of the Lord spoke, the words sounded like they were in a musical form, but she understood them so clearly. The angel said that Jesus was deeply saddened by the people of this world and the choices they had made, and that He wanted to use Libby to help redeem them. "The Lord is going to give you special gifts so you can show them what will happen if they do not change their ways. Do not be afraid. He will always protect you and be by your side." Libby was about to reply, but the light faded away until it disappeared.

Libby didn't know if this had all been a dream, so she pinched herself on the arm and shrieked in pain. As she let out a loud "Ouch!" she lay back down in her bed and tried to fall asleep, but she tossed and turned. She wondered how she, a ten-year-old girl, could possibly help so many people. She then remembered what she had asked Jesus to do and how important it was to her. She would do anything to help her dad whom she loved so much. Almost instantly, a calmness came over her, and in just a few minutes, she was asleep.

4

Libby woke to the aroma of blueberry pancakes. This was often the way things were when her dad had a slip. He would try to make things as normal as possible, like nothing ever happened. He would clean the house like a madman. It seemed he thought that if everything else was in order, his life was in order. It couldn't be further from the truth. Jim had the mind-set that if he didn't talk to Libby about what had happened the night before, somehow she would forget all about it—thinking that he was protecting her from the truth—but he didn't realize that it is more devastating to a child not to talk about problems.

Libby sat down at the table but didn't have an appetite. Jim was singing and whistling like everything was OK. He asked, "What's the matter, honey? You're not hungry?"

Trying to avoid eye contact, Libby replied, "I don't feel so good."

As Jim touched her forehead, he said, "You don't feel like you're running a temperature."

"What's hurting me, you can't see or feel." That was like a knife going through Jim's heart. He didn't know what to say. There was a dead silence that seemed to last forever.

The doorbell rang. It was Maria, Libby's best friend. Maria's family was Latino and lived in the projects nearby. Her parents were hardworking, just trying to make a better life for their children; each held two jobs. There was only one week left of the school year, and they were both eagerly looking forward to their summer vacation. Libby grabbed her schoolbooks and started toward the door when Jim said, "Whoosh, no kiss good-bye for Dad?" Libby tried to stay mad, but she just couldn't. She thought the world of him. She managed to smile and gave him a strong hug as Jim leaned down and kissed her. When he started to let her go, Libby held on even tighter. His heart just sank with remorse. When they separated, Jim noticed a welt on Libby's arm and asked, "Hey, what's this?"

Libby looked down and saw the red bump and suddenly remembered about her experience the night before. She said, "Oh, a spider probably bit me."

Jim replied, "Well, it must have been a big one." Jim leaned down and kissed it and said, "Love you."

Libby said, "Love you too."

As Libby and Maria went out the front door, Jim's best friend and coworker came walking up the driveway. He yelled out to Libby, "Hey, kiddo!"

"Hey, Uncle Lucky."

Maria asked, "Why do you call him Lucky?"

"My dad says if it wasn't for bad luck, he wouldn't have any luck at all."

5

Lucky and Jim worked for a construction company and drove to work together every day, often having long conversations on the way. Lucky had been sober for ten years. He had always been there for Jim whether Jim was drunk or sober. But today, when they got into the truck, Lucky could smell the odor of alcohol on Jim from the night before. Lucky was about to confront him on it, but figuring Jim felt bad enough, he decided not to say anything for now. So they drove to work, not saying a word the rest of the way.

Libby and Maria passed Maria's apartment on their walk to school. Maria's mom and dad were just leaving for work at the local meatpacking factory. Maria's family were devout Christians, and whenever Libby was over there, they seemed to be praying together all the time. She had always admired how close the family was. Libby loved the framed saying on their wall: "It's not a house that makes a home; it's the family that makes a home."

In school at her desk, Libby felt somewhat strange. She wasn't sick, but something was different. She knew everyone in the class, but when she looked at any of them, it was as if she knew what they were feeling. As she glanced around the room, she knew who was feeling sad, angry, upset, joyous, happy, or fearful; which kids felt superior; which ones felt less than; and everything in between. It was overwhelming for her.

Just then, Mrs. Stanton walked in, and everything stopped for Libby. Her teacher had always seemed to have a certain sadness about her, but today, Libby could not stop feeling what Mrs. Stanton had inside her.

As the bell rang at the end of the day, Libby waited for everyone to leave. Once all the other students were gone, she walked up to Mrs. Stanton and stood there for a few seconds. The teacher looked up at Libby and asked, "Is everything OK, Libby?"

Libby looked right into her eyes, put her hand on Mrs. Stanton's, and said, "Jesus wants you to know that He forgives you and that your baby is with Him now." Then Libby left the room, having no idea why she had said what she did; she did not even know what it all meant.

Mrs. Stanton sat frozen, her eyes tearing up. She looked up and said, "Thank you, God, thank you, God, thank you." Eight years earlier, Mrs. Stanton had become pregnant when she was seventeen. She had tremendous pressure from her parents to save the family from embarrassment, and she aborted the pregnancy. It had haunted her ever since.

6

Libby met up with Maria, and they walked to their after-school program. They had signed up for it so Libby could wait for her dad to come home from work and Maria could wait for her older brother and sister to get home from high school. Libby could not stop what was happening to her. Everybody she looked at, she knew what they were feeling. Her head was spinning all over the place. She felt she was supposed to say different things to different people; she had to force herself to keep quiet. She really thought she was going crazy. She was afraid to tell Maria about all of this, not knowing if she would believe her or not.

At the construction site, Jim, Lucky, and Charlie (who they referred to as their "third amigo") were just finishing up for the day. Though Charlie was a good friend of Jim and Lucky's, his only problem was that he was one of "them born-again Christians." It seemed like every conversation they got into, Charlie talked about Jesus, his lord and savior, which pretty much broke up any beer drinking, cussing, and foul-mouthed-construction-worker conversation. But still, they were the three amigos, and they always watched each other's back. Charlie knew the issues Jim was going through and often tried to talk to him about God. Jim never wanted anything to do with that stuff. He had such guilt and shame that he never imagined even God could forgive him. He would say to Charlie very respectfully that he should try to help someone who really deserved help from God. Charlie had been in prison when he gave himself to the Lord. He was a down-and-out drug addict then. Today, he lived his life for the Lord, and it was wonderful and abundant. But Jim still didn't think he deserved that, which frustrated Charlie to no end. Being a true friend, though, he would never give up on Jim.

When they were just about to leave for the day, Joe, the foreman, called Jim aside. He said, "I'm sorry, Jim, but I have to let you go."

Jim replied, "Joe, what's this all about? I've shown up every day and put in a good eight hours."

Joe said, "Jim, it has nothing to do with that. The numbers people in the office said we had to cut labor costs by ten percent, which means the last ten guys we hired have to go. And, sorry to say, you're one of them. I wish I could keep you on, but I can't."

Lucky and Charlie were watching from a distance and knew exactly what was happening. They tried to console Jim, but he would not have any of it. He felt the world was against him and that God was punishing him for taking away Libby's mom. Worse than that, he felt he deserved everything he got.

It was very quiet on the ride home. When they were about four blocks from his house, Jim said, "Pull over. I want to walk the rest of the way."

Lucky said, "Jim, it's starting to rain, and we'll be home in five minutes."

Jim ordered, "Pull over." Lucky knew what that meant. He was going to the package store to buy some liquor. Jim got out of the truck without saying a word, and Lucky drove off. He went into the store, bought a bottle of Jack Daniels, and then walked the rest of the way home.

7

Even over the short walk, Jim wrestled with the demons in his head. He tried to justify why he could have a drink. After all, the forces of evil were against him, and he felt he had been cursed for the rest of his life, so why not enjoy what he could? This was self-justification, the worst enemy for any recovering alcoholic.

As he walked in the front door, he purposely did not look at the family portrait, remembering that he had asked for Susan's help the night before. He sat down in his favorite recliner, put the glass and bottle in front of him, and opened up the bottle, knowing what was going to happen if he took the drink. He tried as hard as he could to think it through. He reached over, opened the bottle of Jack Daniels, and poured himself a shot. His hands were trembling. When he finished pouring, he picked up the glass and held it to his lips. Suddenly the front door opened, and Libby walked in. He had been so upset over what had happened at work that he had lost all track of time. Libby's look of disbelief was matched by Jim's look of deep shame. He put the drink down on the table. Libby walked over to him. She always knew he was in deep emotional pain, but this was the first time she actually felt all his guilt, shame, and remorse. She now knew what her dad had been going through over the past year.

Libby stood in front of him and said, "Dad, when I touch your hand, you are going to see what will happen to you if you choose to live this way." She gently reached over and held his hand.

Jim sat there like a statue, not moving or even blinking his eyes. He was mesmerized by Libby. She told him to close his eyes. When he did, she closed hers. Then Jim saw himself in a gutter on a street corner. The next vision was of child services removing Libby from the home, both of them screaming and holding on to each other for dear life as the police took her. Then he saw Libby in a state home for children, sleeping on a mattress in a freezing cold room. Next, he saw a man making sexual advances on Libby. By this time, Jim was screaming out, "No! Leave her alone!" The last vision he saw was of himself in a casket, with Libby, Lucky, and Charlie looking at him. They were the only people at his funeral. Then he saw Libby crying uncontrollably and her new foster parents walking away from the casket with her. Knowing another man would be her dad, Jim pulled back as hard as he could and broke free from Libby. Then he was in the fetal position on the floor, crying, sobbing, and saying, "I'm sorry, Libby, I'm sorry." They just held on to each other as close as possible, both saying, "I love you, I love you." This was what one could call a spiritual awakening on a grand scale. From this point on, they both knew that nothing was ever going to be the same again.

8

The next day was Saturday. Lucky had called Charlie because he was concerned about Jim. "I think we need to go over there whether he wants to see us or not. He's our friend, and we can't let him destroy himself." So Charlie picked him up to head over to Jim's.

When Lucky got in his truck, Charlie put on some gospel worship songs that he had on a CD. Now, Lucky knew he'd gotten sober by the grace of God, but he'd never claimed he had a strong personal relationship with Him like Charlie did, who was always on fire for God. Charlie knew how Lucky saw things, and when they drove past a bunch of guys they knew on the street corner, Charlie rolled down all the windows and cranked up the song "How Awesome Is Our God," which had everyone's heads turning. If Lucky could have climbed into the glove compartment, he would have. The more Lucky tried to hide, the more Charlie turned up the volume.

When they reached Jim's house, they had already made a game plan. They would play "good cop, bad cop." They had to convince Jim that if he wanted his life to get better, he couldn't ever take another drink. When they got to the front door, not knowing what to expect, it whipped open before they could ring the bell. There stood Jim with a big smile on his face. They had not seen him laugh, or even smile, since Susan's death. "What's up, guys? Come on in. Do you want some coffee?" Lucky, who was never at a loss for words, was speechless. Jim didn't even wait for a response. He had already started to pour three cups. "Here, sit down."

They all sat at the kitchen table. Charlie asked, "How you doing, man?" He looked directly into Jim's eyes to see if he had been drinking.

Jim said, "I haven't felt this good in years. Something happened to me last night that I can't put into words, and it's changed my whole perspective on life."

Lucky said, "Well? Tell us what happened!"

"I know this is going to sound crazy, but here goes. I was sitting right over there with a glass of Jack Daniels. I was raising it to my lips, ready to take the first drink, when Libby walked in." Lucky and Charlie immediately dropped their heads down, but Jim said, "No, wait, I didn't drink it." They both looked up and then looked at each other. "Libby came over to me and said, 'I'm going to put my hand on yours and show you what your future will be like if you keep on drinking.' When she touched me, all these horrible visions kept coming, things I don't even want to talk about. I was shaking with fear. For the first time in my life, I was able to see, and feel, what would happen to me, and more importantly, Libby. I don't know, man, when Libby touches you, she has this gift of allowing you to see into the past or the future. Not only see but also feel it, like I said. We had a long talk after this happened last night, and she told me about a dream or epiphany she had the night before. She said that an angel of the Lord came to her and said that Jesus was going to give her special gifts to help people redeem themselves of their sinful ways."

Lucky leaned back in his chair behind Jim, and while looking at Charlie, put his finger to his head to insinuate that Jim had finally lost his mind. Charlie was so intrigued with the story, he didn't even respond to that. Charlie, being more spiritual, yelled out, "Hallelujah, hallelujah, praise God!" Lucky looked at him and just rolled his eyes.

9

Jim got up to go outside, with Charlie following close behind. "I don't know what this is all about, Charlie. I don't know what I'm supposed to do with all of this—"

Charlie interrupted. "Look, man, you are blessed. God is working through Libby. He has a great plan for your life and Libby's."

"Well, what's that?"

"I don't know, only He knows. And it's your job to follow it." Jim went to light up a cigarette, and Charlie pulled it out of his hand. "Hey, what are you doing? Your body is not yours, it's the temple of the Holy Spirit, and you better start treating it that way." Charlie was a prime example of this philosophy. He was a physical specimen, watching everything he ate or drank. This was the opposite of Jim, who ate and drank whatever he wanted and had a two-pack-a-day smoking habit. Charlie said, "I got an idea. Why don't you come to the gym with me today? You've been neglecting your body for a long time, and besides, it would be good for your head."

"I can't, I have Libby."

"Bring her with us, and she can swim in the pool." Jim was out of excuses and finally agreed.

Lucky was still inside at the kitchen table finishing his coffee when Libby came down for breakfast. "Hey, kiddo."

As Libby prepared a bowl of Frosted Flakes, she noticed that Lucky couldn't take his eyes off her every move. Realizing what was happening, she yelled out to Jim on the patio, "Dad, you told them!"

Jim yelled back to Libby, "Lucky and Charlie are family, honey. We shouldn't hold any secrets from them." Libby responded by letting out a big sigh, shaking her head, and rolling her eyes, while Lucky kept watching her.

Libby snapped, "Do you want to take a picture?"

"Sorry, kid." Lucky looked out at Jim and Charlie, and then turned back to Libby. "Hey, kiddo, you wouldn't happen to know the numbers for the lottery tonight?"

Apparently Jim heard that and yelled, "Lucky, what are you doing?"

"Hey, you can't blame a guy for trying," said Lucky.

"Even if I gave you the winning numbers," Libby said, "you would probably lose your ticket." Jim and Charlie busted out laughing, and Lucky turned two shades of red.

Lucky looked directly at Libby and asked, "Why am I always the butt of the jokes?" But then, thinking Libby would feel bad, he added, "I just call them like I see them."

Jim and Charlie were really laughing now, holding each other up to keep from rolling on the ground. Lucky broke his own record and turned three shades of red. When all the laughter settled down, Jim said to Libby, "Do you want go to the gym with us? You can go swimming at the pool."

Libby loved the pool. She jumped up, not even finishing her breakfast, and responded with a big yes. "Is Lucky coming?"

Lucky replied, "Why? Do you need someone to make fun of?"

"No, we already have you." Now she was also laughing.

Lucky said, "I'm leaving," and all three of the others said no, no, no, they were only kidding.

"We love you, Lucky." He threw his hands up in the air as they all hugged him.

10

When Libby got to the pool, the local high school boys' swim team was practicing. There were six lanes, but they were only using four of them. Libby had fond memories of coming here with her mom for swimming lessons, so it was bittersweet for her. She climbed down the pool ladder but jumped back; the water was too cold. Libby decided just to jump straight in instead. So she squeezed her nose, closed her eyes, and leaped in. As soon as she hit the water, she felt as if she had made a mistake, but soon she became used to it. The swimming coach shouted orders at the other swimmers. They all looked pretty tired and seemed like they just wanted to go home. The coach told them, "You have to practice longer and harder than any other team in your conference! Your record is zero wins and three losses."

One of the team spoke up and said, "Yeah, but Coach, we've been in the pool for two hours and we're tired." The rest of the team agreed with him. Just then, there was the sound of an electric motor coming from the boys' locker room. Out came a sight they had never expected to see: a man in a wheelchair who had no arms and no legs. He just had this little stub of a foot on his left side. They all stood there in shock. However, that was nothing compared to what they were about to see. The man had his friend lower him into the water, and he started to do laps in the pool.

There was complete silence, and all the boys had their eyes fixed on the man. He was doing the backstroke, turning over and doing the breaststroke, diving down to the bottom and coming up for air. Slowly, one by one, all the boys got back into the water, feeling embarrassed for saying they were tired. They swam faster than they had all day and broke their own personal and team records, even after already practicing for two hours.

After all the boys left the pool, the coach went over to Nick Vujicic, who was just getting back in his wheelchair. He patted Nick on the back and said, "Thanks, Nick, it works every time."

"You're welcome, Coach." Nick looked at Libby and said, "Hi, my name is Nick."

"Hi, I'm Libby." Libby had felt somewhat stunned since she'd gotten the gift of feeling other people's emotions. All the homeless, all the people in the soup kitchens, the long unemployment lines, the abortion clinics she passed on her way to the gym: she could feel the pain of their sorrow, despair, humiliation, hopelessness, and so on. This was what she expected from Nick, but from him she only felt joy, peace, and happiness—and even more important, a sense of purpose, an overwhelming feeling of gratitude. She thought that this kind of peace could only come from God, and it showed all over his face. Libby noticed his accent and asked him where he was from.

Nick replied, "I'm originally from Australia, but I'm staying here for the summer with some friends." Nick sensed that there was something bothering Libby, so he came right out and asked her if she was OK. Libby said that she was, but that her dad was going through some difficulties and she thought that he might want to meet Nick someday. Nick said, "Anytime." Nick had his friend pull out his card and give it to Libby. He said, "Tell him he can call me anytime, day or night." This request was not surprising to Nick. He had people from all over the world always wanting to talk to him. He was very in tune with people's emotions because of the astronomically difficult roadblocks he'd had to deal with in his life.

Libby said, "Thank you. And by the way, you're a really good swimmer."

Nick replied, "Thanks, Libby, you are too." They kept looking at each other as they said their good-byes.

11

When Jim arrived at the gym, at least a half dozen guys came over to greet him. They asked, "How's Peter doing?" Peter was Jim's brother and was about six years older. Peter had had a reputation growing up in Southie as one of the toughest guys you never wanted to mess with. He never looked for trouble, but there were always some out-of-town gunslingers trying to make a name for themselves. The joke in Southie was, if Peter hit you, you'd wake up with a beard. When these guys came in and started with Peter, people would immediately start laying money on the bar, and the bartender would be taking bets. The guys weren't betting on who would win, but rather whether the guy would be knocked out cold before he hit the ground. Peter still was a gentleman after they were unconscious. He didn't keep hitting them. Usually he would pick them up and set them in a booth and order a drink for them for when they came out of it.

The only guy who could give Peter a run for his money was Danny O'Shea. Danny ran a crew from the D Street housing projects. Peter's crew was from Mercer Street, and let's put it this way—they didn't receive Christmas cards from each other. Danny wasn't a gifted fighter like Peter, but he was the type of guy that you would have to almost kill before you stopped him. His nickname was Crazy O'Shea. If there was ever a nickname that fit someone to a tee, it was Danny's. They were archenemies that had many battles over the years.

That all changed one night when Peter and his best friend, Mattie, got off the train at North Station going to a Bruins game. They heard a big commotion on the platform. When they looked over, there was Danny getting pounded by four guys. Now, like Peter, he was as tough as they come, but these guys were putting a real hurting on him. Without any hesitation, Peter yelled over to Mattie, "Come on, that's O'Shea over there." They charged the assailants and the tide quickly changed. In a few short seconds, the four of them were on the ground. If the police from the MBTA hadn't shown up when they did, those guys would have been taken out of there in an ambulance. You see, it didn't matter if a guy was a friend or foe. If he was from Southie and in trouble with anyone from out of town, you had to step in and help him. They called it "principles over personalities."

After that, Peter and Danny became close friends. That's what often happened growing up—the guy you had a fistfight with ended up as your best friend. The two became so close that you could say they not only had respect for each other but also actually loved one another. Whenever the crews met up at Castle Island, Peter and Danny always walked alone in front of everyone else. Jim was the only one allowed to be with them. He had fond memories of listening to their conversations. They seemed to let their guard down with each other. He remembered one conversation in particular. Danny asked Peter, "Why do you think we are the way we are?"

Peter asked, "What do you mean?"

Danny replied, "Well, why are we the ones in charge? When there's a threatening situation, why do we step up and take care of things even though we're outnumbered?" This got both of them thinking, and they would have many long conversations about it.

They both felt they were different from anyone else, which made them closer to each other, even more than to their own crews.

They often talked about their futures. Peter would say he wanted to get out of Southie someday and see other places. Danny, like Peter, had a little sister. She was three years younger and happened to have the same birthday as he did. He would always say that all he wanted to do when he was twenty-one and she was eighteen and off to college was to move up to northern New Hampshire to a town called Colebrook where their older cousin Skip had inherited a small campsite. He dreamed of living a simple life and not having to deal with all the violence and craziness in Southie. Sadly, that day would never come. On his twenty-first birthday, he was in a nightclub downtown, where a guy was grabbing a young girl inappropriately while nobody else said anything. Nobody except Danny. Before you knew it, four shots rang out, and he was on the floor. He took all four to the chest and collapsed, where he died alone. This saddened Peter greatly. The one thing Danny always would talk about was that his only fear was to die alone. Peter could never get that picture out of his mind: Danny looking up at everyone, knowing he was dying, and not recognizing anyone there.

Jim always knew when Peter was thinking of this. He had an expression on his face that he had never seen before Danny died: a little bit of Peter had died too. Danny's family had asked Peter to give the eulogy. It moved people to tears because it truly came from his heart, and when something comes from your heart and isn't scripted, well, people just know it. And on that day, everyone in that church knew it.

Somehow, when Jim, Lucky, and Charlie got in a scrape (usually because of Lucky's big mouth), amazingly, Peter would walk around the corner and save their asses. Jim had always idolized his older brother. When Jim and his friends hung down the park, all the older kids hung on the wall. If you were allowed to hang on the wall, well, then you'd made it. Jim was the only one in his crowd to be allowed on the wall because of Peter. Even when Peter wasn't around, he could still hang on the wall with the older guys. Jim's friends were in awe when they saw him being allowed to hang with the others. It was a rite of passage that every kid couldn't wait for. Of course, Lucky figured that since he was Jim's friend, he had a right to be there. That lasted about thirty seconds. Then the guys on the wall grabbed Lucky and duct-taped him to this huge oak tree in front of the wall. This was to be a lesson to anyone who tried to make it on the wall without first being accepted. Word spread real quick around Southie, and everyone ran to the park to witness it. Even all the cops on patrol were coming by in their cars. They all stopped and had a good laugh for themselves.

Sergeant Donovan came by. He rolled down the window and yelled over to Mattie, who was Peter's best friend and second in charge. He said, "Mattie, how long are you going to keep him there?"

Mattie looked over to his friends and then said, "We're figuring to let him go on Groundhog Day." Everyone, including Sergeant Donovan, got a big kick out of it. All the guys really respected Sergeant Donovan. He was a local cop who had grown up in Southie and knew all the kids by their first names and really looked out for them. I don't think there was a kid in Southie who hadn't got one or two whacks from Sergeant Donovan's billy club. You just had to take it. If you ever went home and told your parents that the sergeant whacked you, you were sure to get a worse beating from your old man.

Just then, Peter had walked into the park. He first didn't notice Lucky taped to the tree. He walked over to the squad car and said, "Hey, what's up, Sarge?"

"I just asked Mattie when they were going to release the sacrificial lamb over there."

Peter looked over and saw Lucky tied to the tree. He then looked at Sergeant Donovan, grinning, and asked, "How long has he been there?"

"I think long enough. I don't want anyone who's not from Southie to drive by and report it. Too much paperwork for me. I'll take care of it." He gave the chop sign to Mattie to cut him down. Sergeant Donovan said to Peter, "How's your mom?"

"She's doing well."

"Great, tell her I said hello, and try to control these numbskulls. God knows I can't."

Peter tapped on the roof of the squad car and said, "You got it, Sarge."

It was always difficult for Jim when someone asked him about Peter. Jim hadn't talked to Peter in years. When Jim turned eighteen and Peter gave him his part of the inheritance, he had felt wronged. He'd figured that there should be more money. After a night of drinking, Jim showed up and confronted Peter and said some horrible things, and neither one of them could let their resentments go.

Peter had had real talent as an athlete. He was an all-scholastic middle linebacker with Southie High. Scholarships had come in from schools all over the country. He also was academically talented. He loved Southie but always wanted to get out and have a better life for himself. Those dreams had ended when their mother passed away in his senior year. Their dad had passed eight years previously. Peter had had to put college on hold so he could be a legal guardian to Jim, who was only twelve at the time. He had had to take a job as a longshoreman until Jim turned eighteen.

Jim and Charlie were dressed in their workout clothes, lifting weights. Lucky, however, was dressed like an Irish gangster, with his scally cap, jeans, work boots, and sweatshirt that said "Southie" on it. "Southie" was short for South Boston, where they had all grown up and still lived. Growing up in a tough Irish neighborhood, these guys were as loyal as they come, and it was all about loyalty. Any one of them would have taken a bullet for another—and almost had on several occasions during the racial tensions of forced busing. It had been an ugly time for Southie, but they all got through it.

Charlie was working Jim real hard on the weights. Jim's arms were starting to feel like Jell-O. No matter how hard it was, he wasn't going to let on he was hurting. Lucky hadn't lifted a weight all day. He was just spotting these guys and constantly looking around at the cute girls. This always baffled Jim and Charlie because he hadn't had two dates in a row with the same girl (hence the name Lucky). The only time he had was at their senior prom, and that was only because his date had had to pay for everything that night, even his tuxedo. So she went on a second date with him to recover her expenses.

Now Charlie was yelling to Jim, trying to pump him up for his last bench press. Charlie added on some extra weight, and Jim asked, "What you are doing?"

Charlie dismissed Jim's comment and said, "Come on, bro, suck it up. You can do this. This is God's plan for you today; I can feel it. Come on, Jim, God's behind you on this one." By now, people were starting to look around. Lucky was playing off like he didn't know them. "Get ready and pump yourself up. Remember God's plan, hallelujah." Jim positioned his hands on the bar and counted to himself, *One, two, three.* At this time, a gorgeous girl walked right by Lucky, and his head turned 360 degrees, like an owl's. That's when Charlie turned quickly behind himself to get a drink of water from the cooler.

At the exact moment that Jim lifted the weights off the bar, he knew he was in trouble; he barely got the bar off the bench. Arms shaking, tipping the bar from one side to the other, he was able to get it to the top. Now was the hard part. He lowered the bar about two inches. As soon as his elbows started to bend, the bar came crashing down on his chest and rolled toward his throat, cutting off his windpipe. He couldn't say anything. He could feel himself turning red and then blue. He didn't know why his friends weren't spotting him. Feeling as if he was just about to pass out, he saw a huge right hand grab the center of the bar and pull it off of him, setting it on the bar holder. He thought it was the right hand of God saving him from certain death.

Thinking, *Wow, two spiritual experiences in one week,* he felt the air return to his windpipe. He saw Lucky turn around toward him and Charlie walking back from the water cooler wiping his face, saying, "Are you ready, bro?"

12

"Am I ready? Where were you guys? I almost got killed."
Charlie said, "I told you to count to three."

"I did, to myself. Was it God's plan for me to die here today?"

Charlie said, "Well, what are we, mind readers? We didn't hear you count to three."

In all the confusion, Jim looked up at an enormous man with muscles coming out everywhere on his body. He must have been about six foot four and 375 pounds of solid muscle. He had picked up that bar off of Jim like it was a toothpick. They were all astonished at his size and physique.

In a hoarse voice, Jim said, "Thanks, man, you saved my life. I'm Jim."

Charlie said, "Hi, I'm Charlie, nice to meet you."

Lucky said, "Hey, bro. I'm Lucky."

The hulk of a man said in a very soft, calm voice, "I'm Pastor Pete." They all looked at each other. Pastor Pete told them he had already finished his workout ten minutes earlier and was about to leave when something told him to go back into the gym and make sure he hadn't forgotten anything. "I was working on this bench earlier and thought I might have left my towel. As soon as I got here, I saw you pinned down."

Just as he said that, Libby walked over, all changed and ready to go. She said, "Dad, I want to tell you about someone I just met in the pool."

"Not now, Libby. I want you to meet Pastor Pete." Libby's hand was swallowed up by Pete's enormous one as they shook. As they did, the expression on her face changed from blank to a huge smile. She saw that Pete had once lived the life that her dad did, and she knew instantly that God had put him into their lives for a purpose.

"Dad, can we invite Pastor Pete to our house for a cookout?"

At first Jim thought it might be a little inappropriate, having just met him, until he looked at Libby. He knew right away that she had seen something she liked about Pete and had a feeling that he would somehow play a huge role in their lives. Jim said, "Sure, we would love to have him over. Pete, would you like to join all of us for lunch?"

Pete didn't look like the type to turn down a meal and said, "Sure, I would love to."

Jim said, "Great, you can follow us to our house."

As Jim was preparing the food on the grill, he knew it was just a matter of time before Lucky said the wrong thing. Lucky said, "So, Pastor, how do you keep the members of your church from leaving the congregation? Do you put them in a full nelson, or do you prefer the headlock?" Jim and Charlie just raised their eyes to the sky and shook their heads.

Pete replied, "I don't know, I've always wondered which one worked best. Come here, let me try them on you and let me know." As Pete moved toward Lucky, all you saw was an ass, elbows, and those big ears under a scally cap fleeing the scene. Everybody got a good laugh from it, even Pastor Pete. Unlike Lucky, he always seemed to say the right thing at the right time. That's just what pastors do.

After they all ate, Jim approached Pete nervously and asked, "Pete, when you have some time, can I call you about something that is going on with Libby and me?"

Somehow Pete seemed to be expecting that question and responded with a gracious "Of course you can. Here's my cell number, call me anytime." This made Jim feel real comfortable with the pastor, like he had someone in his corner.

13

It was now Saturday evening. Jim and Libby were watching cable TV, and Jim was flipping through the channels one after the other. Libby, frustrated, said, "Dad, why can't you just watch one channel at a time? Why do you keep flipping through all of them?"

Jim, looking puzzled, thought for a moment and then said, "I don't know. That's just what guys do."

As soon as he said that, Libby said, "Stop." There on live TV was a preacher screaming and yelling. He was touching people on the forehead, claiming they were cured from all kinds of diseases. The wheelchairs started flying across the stage as people jumped up out of them and walked while loud music played. When everything settled down, the preacher went into a song and dance about how "you can have all this if you sow a seed" of a thousand dollars to his ministries. They would send you something in the mail and all your financial problems would go away. You would suddenly start receiving free money. This really angered Libby. She loved watching television ministries. There were so many good churches out there helping all the charitable causes that really needed it. But she also knew that there were many more who preyed on people who were hurting and desperate. Especially since she received this gift from God. How could these wolves in sheep's clothing tell people that somehow God would favor you if you sent your money to this preacher? And if you didn't, God would see you as disobedient toward Him. What if you didn't have a thousand dollars, or five hundred, or even five dollars? Would He not show you His love? Libby knew God's love was not for sale. It couldn't be bought. She knew that His grace and mercy were free to anyone who asked for them.

The more Libby watched the preacher, the angrier she got. She walked over to the TV set and knelt down in front of it. By now, there was a close-up picture of the preacher making his appeal for viewers to send their money to him. Libby reached her hand out and put it directly on the man's face, and in an instant, he stopped talking. His face went from calm and focused on his scripted speech to confusion, then to nervousness, then to sheer terror. The man fell on the floor, screaming for his life and saying, "I'll send all the money back! God, please, make them stop!" As all the preacher's people came running over to him, the TV camera suddenly shifted to the choir, which was instructed to start singing.

Jim jumped off the couch and sat next to Libby. He said, "Libby?" Libby was still looking at the TV. Jim said, "Libby, look at me." Libby turned and looked at her dad. "Libby, what did you do to that man?"

Libby paused for a moment. "Jesus said, 'There will be many who will come in my name.' False prophets, wolves in sheep's clothing. I just showed him what his future would be. I showed him entering hell." Jim realized that Libby's gift was something more than a gift. It was more like a calling...like a mission for her life. Jim thought, *I better strap myself in; this is going to be a heck of a ride.*

Just then, the phone rang. It was Charlie. "Hey, bro, how you doing?"

Jim, still feeling stunned from what he had just witnessed, said, "Ah, ah, ah...good, good."

Charlie said, "I just want to know if you and Libby want to go to church tomorrow morning." Charlie had asked Jim a thousand times before, and he had always respectfully declined. Because of all his recent losses and disappointments, Jim was angry with God, and Charlie never expected him to say yes.

Jim responded, "Church tomorrow?" Libby turned around and nodded. Jim said, "Yeah, sure."

Charlie was stunned for a few seconds. Then he said, "Jim, you feeling OK?"

"Yeah, just fine."

Charlie, letting out another "Hallelujah, praise God," said, "Great."

Jim asked, "Is Lucky coming?"

"No," replied Charlie. "He went to his church for confession today and is exhausted."

"Why is he exhausted?"

Charlie said, "Because he was there for seven hours."

Lucky was surely not a criminal in any sense of the word, but he was always looking for an angle on everything. For instance, when they worked in a ditch on the road on their construction job, Charlie and Jim would be there with shovels in ninety-degree heat, while Lucky's job was to stand there in an orange vest, waving traffic along. The thought of Lucky in a confession booth for seven hours made Jim crack up.

Charlie said, "I'll pick you guys up at eight forty-five. And after the services, we can go down to Sully's at Castle Island for lunch." Castle Island, on the waterfront in South Boston, is a beautiful place to walk around and look at the scenery while jumbo jets fly right over you from Logan Airport, seeming so low that you can almost touch them.

By now, Libby was jumping up and down for joy. Libby had been to Charlie's church many times with her best friend, Maria, and her family. She loved the music and singing. But now she was going with her dad.

Jim said, "I'm going to call Tommy and see if he wants to go to Sully's with us." Tommy was like the son Jim never had. He was twenty-nine years old. When he was eight, he had been hit by a drunk driver and had spent many months in a coma. When he came out of it, he started having seizures. Sometimes he would have several a week and could not work or drive with his condition. Jim was used to the seizures and knew what to do, so Jim would take him on side jobs so Tommy could have some extra money in his pocket. It gave him some self-worth. Now he could take his girlfriend out to dinner, and he told everyone he met that he was an apprentice carpenter. He was proud of that.

Jim also took Tommy other places, like when he played golf or went on estimates. Tommy would hold the clipboard and take notes for Jim. Tommy was very good at the computer and was always helping Jim with his. Jim was used to having a hammer in his hand, not punching a keyboard. He knew Tommy loved going down to the island and sitting with the elderly people. He would joke with them and sometimes he would do a dance to make them laugh. You could always find him at the local coffee shop, sitting with the older folks. Sometimes a van from a group home for the mentally challenged would come by. All the riders would yell out the window to Tommy when they saw him.

Jim sometimes asked, "Tommy, why don't you hang around with people your own age?"

Tommy would always reply, "Why? I have more fun talking with these guys than them." Jim would just shrug his shoulders. What could he say? Tommy was the most respectful kid you would ever see—something that you don't see that much anymore. It came from his mom and dad, who had taught him what's really important in life. That's why Jim liked being around Tommy so much. Sometimes in all the hustle and bustle of this world, Jim could get all caught up in it, worrying about everything under the sun. But not around Tommy, he always kept Jim laughing.

14

It was a bright, warm, sunny morning in June. When they heard the horn beep from Charlie's truck, Jim was just finishing dressing, but Libby had been ready since seven o'clock. She had emptied her piggy bank so she could buy Dad and Charlie lunch at Sully's. She wanted to surprise them—especially her dad, because he seemed to be serious about changing his life, and she was so proud of him.

Libby had been to the Pentecostal church several times with Maria, but Jim had never been to one before. In fact, it was several years since he had been in his neighborhood Catholic church. When they pulled up to the New Covenant Church on L Street in South Boston, Jim saw no difference in all the people walking in, except for the fact that they weren't all Irish Catholic. They were white, black, Asian, and from all different walks of life.

When they entered, Jim immediately tried to sit in the back row. In fact, if he could have sat in a closet, he would have. He seemed embarrassed to be there. Charlie whispered, "What's wrong?"

Jim said, "I just don't want anyone to see me here."

"Oh, I understand. You have no problem falling off a bar stool in front of a hundred people, or staggering through the center of town drunk and walking into parking meters, or getting your name in the papers after being arrested for public intoxication, but God forbid anyone sees you in a church on Sunday morning honoring God."

"All right, all right." Jim said he didn't want to draw any attention to himself, and the last thing he needed was for Charlie to yell out, *Hallelujah, hallelujah, praise God, the sinner's made it here.*

Of course, Charlie made a beeline for the front row where he sat every Sunday. Jim grabbed at his coattails, trying to get him to sit down as he walked past every pew. Charlie was having no part of it. The pastor came out and greeted Charlie, who introduced Jim and Libby. Trying to be courteous, Jim managed a smile while thinking of how he was going to get back at Charlie later on. The pastor's name was Paul, and he always had an awesome message. Each week he seemed to be right on target. He constantly reminded everyone not to get caught up in the things of this world, especially themselves, but to give their wills over to Christ and do His will through Him.

The six-piece band came out and set up their instruments. After a couple minutes of tuning up, the lead singer leaned into the microphone and said, "Can we please stand for some worship?" Everybody stood as the lights dimmed a little and the screen on the wall behind them came on. Jim thought, *Oh God, they're going to film me and put it up on that screen.* Then the music started, and Jim was so startled he fell back into his seat. Charlie reached down with one arm and pulled him up. The expression on his face said, *What you are doing, dude?* Libby saw this and had to cover her mouth with both hands to keep from busting out laughing. The band belted out the song "Shine Jesus Shine" in a fast-paced, almost rock-and-roll style.

Jim was shocked; he had never seen this before. He had been expecting some soft hymn or something. He just stood there, not knowing what to do. All the people had their arms up in the air, some had their arms held lower in an open position, some were clapping, but they all were singing. Not wanting to look different, he started to mumble the words. Then he started to sway side to side a little, looking over at Libby, who was sitting next to Maria and all of her family. All of them were singing their hearts out. He started to softly sing the words on the screen.

Something strange was happening to him. Part of him was conscious of everyone around him. Part of him wanted to burst out and sing. Then, all of a sudden, he heard God talking to him: "Put your hands up and honor me." He pretended he didn't hear it and played it off as the stress of the moment. Then he heard it again: "Put your hands up and honor me." Holding his hands tightly together in a death grip, he said in the back of his mind to the voice, *I'll do it next song.* One more time: "Put your hands up and honor me." Jim responded, *I'll do it when the song gets faster.* "Put your hands up and honor me, and I will set you free from yourself."

Jim was having this wrestling match with God in his head, but when he heard "I will set you free from the bondage of yourself," he didn't answer back. He felt his fists start to unclench. The more he tried to force them back, the less clenched they became. He threw both hands up with open palms, and it was a feeling like he had never had before—not even from the finest alcohol. When his arms went up in the air, he felt God removing all of the guilt, shame, and remorse he had ever experienced, and in return, he felt only love, peace, and true forgiveness coming directly from God. It filtered all through his body. Tears were flowing down his face. He was no longer conscious of anyone around him. It was just God and him. He felt like he was six inches off the floor.

Charlie looked over at him. A huge smile covered his face, and you could see him mouth the words, *Praise God.* Charlie looked around. All the people in the first six rows had their eyes fixed on Jim. Many of them also had tears in their eyes. It is an amazing sight to witness someone allowing God to enter his or her life after years and years of self-destruction.

After the service when everyone was standing outside, several people came up to Jim and introduced themselves. They all seemed like seeing Jim praising God had made their whole day. Most people who have suffered with life's trials and tribulations can sense when someone else is going through the same thing. Libby came up to Jim and asked if they could invite Maria's family down to Castle Island. Jim said, "Sure. Tell them we'll meet them in front of Sully's."

So they all headed down. As always, there was a long line. When they got near the front door, all of a sudden, the line separated into two rows, creating a wide opening between them. It was like Moses parting the Red Sea. Out from the opening came a huge man. It was a couple of seconds before they realized who it was. It was Pastor Pete carrying a huge tray of food. Charlie and Jim yelled simultaneously, "Hey, Pete—over here!" as they waved to him.

When Pete saw them, a huge grin came across his face. "Hey, what's up, guys?" When they came together, Pete asked, "Where you guys sitting?"

Jim responded, "We haven't ordered our food yet."

"Oh," Pete said. "I'll grab some tables outside over by the water."

"OK, we'll be a couple of minutes."

Maria's family walked up then, and Libby asked, "Are you guys going to eat?"

Maria's dad, Carlos, said, "We're going for a walk around the island first." Not surprising; this family was inseparable and did everything together.

"OK, we'll be here when you get back."

"OK, see ya in a bit." And they walked off.

When Libby, Charlie, and Jim got their food, they went outside looking for Pete. Expecting him to be with some other people because of the amount of food he had been carrying, they were surprised when they saw him sitting alone. Jim sat down and noticed that Pete had two thirty-two-ounce drinks, three double cheeseburgers, two hot dogs, and a large order of fries. Jim asked, "Pete, you here by yourself?"

Pete said, "Yeah, my wife and daughter went shopping for a couple of hours. I come here to walk every Sunday after service. Doctor wants me to lose some weight."

Charlie said, "Jeez, man, I hate to see what you would eat if you weren't on a diet." They all broke out laughing, even Libby. Pete had the greatest sense of humor. When he picked up the double cheeseburger, it disappeared in his giant hands.

"The man has the biggest mitts I had ever seen," said Jim. "I know when I shook his hand the other day, I thought he crushed my knuckles. They've been sore ever since."

15

When they were all finished eating, a huge yacht pulled in at the pier. Charlie said, "Whoo, that thing must be worth a million bucks."

Jim said, "More like two million. That's Mr. Edward Donlan. He's one of the richest men in the country, the sole owner of Food World. He owns a hundred and twenty-five stores across the country, and it's one of the only companies that's still making money in this recession. He's buying up all the smaller stores that are going out of business."

Libby jumped up and asked, "Dad, can I go look at the boat?"

Jim hesitated for a minute and said, "All right, but just don't go too close to the water."

When Libby got there, the yacht was just docking. There were about twenty people on board, all dressed up in the fanciest clothes and designer sunglasses. Libby moved to the left so she could get a better look at the people coming off the boat. Suddenly, she tripped and stumbled. She felt two hands grabbing her and breaking her fall, and then saw all this loose change rolling around on the ground. This got the attention of Mr. Donlan, the owner of the yacht. When Libby got up, she looked down. There was a man in old, raggedy clothes. The man asked, "Are you OK, honey?"

Libby said, "Yeah, I'm fine."

The man started to gather up his change and Libby knelt down on the ground to help him. He said, "Thanks, honey, I think I got it all."

"What's your name?" Libby asked.

"I'm Sam, Sam Garret."

"Pleased to meet you, Mr. Garret. I'm Libby, Libby Davis." Just then, people started walking down the plank from the boat. They looked like they were in a fashion show, and they all knew it. As they went by, Sam held out a cup asking for spare change. Every one of them pretended not to notice him. The last person was Mr. Donlan.

Sam held up the cup and once again asked, "Any spare change?" Mr. Donlan stopped right in front of him and lowered his glasses.

Libby thought he was going to give him some change, but he looked at the man with disgust and said, "Get a job." Then there was snickering from all of the people with him. Sam just lowered his head in shame.

Libby felt so bad for him that she thought she was going to cry. She reached into her pocket and pulled all the money she had left after buying lunch for her dad. Seven dollars and fifty-two cents. She went to give it to Sam, but he stopped her and said, "Oh no, honey, I can't take any money from you."

"Why not? It's my own money that I saved up."

Sam said again, "No, no, that's your money."

Libby said, "But you need it more than me right now."

Sam looked at Libby and said, "You're an angel," and accepted the money.

Libby asked, "Where do you live?"

"I'm homeless right now. I'm staying at the Pine Street Inn shelter. They're wonderful people over there."

"You don't have a job right now?"

"No, not right now. I had a wonderful job just two years ago for a great company. But one of my coworkers stole some money from them, and they blamed me for it. They fired me, but I couldn't collect any unemployment, and I couldn't use them for a reference. I worked there twenty-two years. I had a beautiful wife, two cars in the garage, and a wonderful four-bedroom home in the suburbs. Then all of a sudden, bam, like that, I couldn't pay the mortgage or the car loans, and then I lost my health insurance. They foreclosed on my house, repossessed my cars, and it became so stressful on my wife that she left and took my two children to live with her parents in California. They wanted me to go, but I was so ashamed of myself for failing them. The next thing I knew, I was on the street. No job, no car, and ruined credit."

"Wow, I'm very sorry that happened to you."

The man said, "Thank you, honey. I never realized how fast things can go bad in this world. We can be so close to losing everything." Libby thought about Mr. Donlan and how mean he was to say what he had. She wondered if he would have said that if he had known the man's story.

Mr. Donlan and his entourage were just coming back from the beach bar with drinks in their hands. One by one, they walked by. This time the man didn't put out the cup for change, still feeling the humiliation from before. As they all boarded the boat, Mr. Donlan walked by, paying no attention to Sam. Libby startled him by screaming out like she was in pain. He stopped. Libby asked, "Can you give me a hand getting up? I think I sprained my ankle when I fell." All the people stopped and looked over at him.

Not wanting to miss a chance to be the center of attention, he said, "Sure, darling," and reached his hand down. Then Libby leaned forward and grabbed firmly onto him as he pulled her up. As soon as she was up, Mr. Donlan realized he couldn't see. Then a vision started to appear of his ancestors in Ireland during the great potato famine. He saw them in a small, one-room house that had no heat, electricity, or running water. There were two adults and five children all in this one room, huddled around a fireplace. They all looked sickly.

Then he saw one of the children, who had died of consumption, being carried down the street in a funeral procession. The casket was made out of planks painted white. When they reached the burial ground, he saw the headstone that read "Catherine Donlan," and next to that were two more headstones that read "Michael" and "Thomas." These were her two brothers who had also died. So Catherine was the third child who had passed away.

In the next vision, the children were trying to find loose coal in the streets that had fallen off the coal wagon. They needed enough coal to cook some vegetables they had gotten from the garbage. Then he saw another family on a boat heading for America. When they got off the boat, he noticed the father signing the papers with the name "Edward Donlan." It was his great-great-grandfather. He could see signs everywhere: Irish Need Not Apply. He could see into the man's eyes; they were eyes of deep sadness, as his whole family was sleeping in New York's Bowery.

He then saw the next generation of husband and wife in the streets begging for spare change. After that, it was his grandfather, also named Edward, working in a factory with his wife. The working conditions were horrible. Their wages were less than what other people were making. He couldn't take it anymore. He pulled away, looking at Libby with disbelief. He turned and ran up the plank, constantly looking back, while all the guests were saying, "What's wrong, Edward, are you OK?"

He looked back one more time before climbing underneath into the galley. Everybody was silent, only to hear Mr. Donlan yelling out orders from below: "Let's get out of here! Damn it, did you hear me? Shove off now!"

On Monday morning, the alarm clock rang out at six o'clock, waking Jim up. As he began to get out of bed, he quickly remembered that he no longer had a job. He had meant to reset the alarm to seven o'clock so he could wake up Libby for school. Lying back down, he started to worry about his financial security. How would he pay all the bills? When was he going to be called back—if ever? All these thoughts he was wrestling with caused him great anxiety, so he got up and went downstairs to make coffee.

It was about six thirty when the phone rang. Jim grabbed it and said hello. It was Carlos, Maria's father. In a much-excited voice, he said that Maria wouldn't be going to school that day. Jim responded with concern. "Is she OK? She's not sick or anything?"

"No, no. I just got off the phone with one of my coworkers, and they told me we hit the lottery last night for twenty-eight million dollars!"

"What?"

Carlos said, "Yeah, man, every week five of us buy a ticket together, and we agreed that we all would split the money if we hit it!"

"Wow," Jim said, "I can't believe it!"

"Neither can I. It's a dream come true!"

"I'll let Libby know...and congratulations, Carlos."

"Thank you, thank you, man!" And they both said good-bye.

Jim hung up the phone and thought for a moment as a smile came across his face. Most people would have been envious, but not Jim. He said to himself, "It couldn't have happened to a nicer family." Jim sat down at the kitchen table to enjoy his morning coffee.

Libby came downstairs, asking, "What's going on, Dad?"

Jim said, "I just got off the phone with Maria's dad. She won't be going to school today..." Then Jim told her the whole story.

Libby said, "Wow, my best friend's a millionaire."

"Yeah, but you're not, so start getting ready for school, kiddo!" Libby, letting out a sigh and looking at the ceiling, turned and walked out of the kitchen.

Jim knew he had to stay busy while he looked for work, so he called Tommy next door and asked him if he would like to give him a hand rebuilding the deck. Jim really didn't need a hand, but he liked having Tommy around, and Tommy liked being around Jim. They filled each other's needs. Tommy was always ready to lend a helping hand, even on days when his medicine made him tired. He never refused. So it was a perfect scenario. Jim said, "Come over whenever you can, no rush." Jim was washing out the coffeepot when there was a knock on the door. It was Tommy. Jim said, "I said there was no rush. Come over when you get a chance!"

Tommy said, "Well, I have a chance now, so here I am."

"Well, I can't argue with that."

16

At the construction site, Charlie was working on a ten-story roof in the hot sun. It was only eight thirty, and the temperature was already eighty-eight degrees. Of course, Lucky had somehow weaseled his way into running the construction elevator. It was the sweetest job on the site. You just stood there and asked the guys what floor they were going to and pressed the numbers. Lucky couldn't settle for that. He had a chair, a newspaper, and a small, battery-operated fan on the wall. When the guys came on and said what floor they were going to, Lucky wouldn't even get up to push the button. He had a three-foot piece of half-inch copper pipe, and he would just lean over and push the buttons with it. He got all kinds of crap from the guys. He loved the attention. He would say as they were getting off, "Have a nice day, girls, don't work too hard," and he would close the door before they could retaliate.

The only thing that was saving Charlie and the other guys on the roof was a strong breeze coming off the ocean that cooled them down. In fact, the wind was so strong that the supervisor told the crane operator to stop working it. It was too hard for him to handle the boom. The materials he was bringing up from the ground to the guys on the upper floors were swinging all over the place.

When Charlie turned around, he saw a tall, rough-looking guy they called "Big Ben" coming off the elevator. They made eye contact, and you could feel the tension in the air. Charlie didn't like working with him because he swore too much. Every other word out of his mouth was a curse word. Now, Charlie was used to hearing guys on a construction site swear, but with this guy, it was constant, all day. It bothered Charlie so much that he had once wanted to quit over it, but hadn't wanted to look like he was ratting Ben out. His boss, though, kept pushing Charlie about why he'd wanted to quit, since he was one of his better workers. Finally and reluctantly, he'd just told the boss what was going on. His boss had said, "Let me talk to him."

Charlie had said, "No, I'll just find another job." Charlie really liked working for this company, so he had finally agreed to let his boss talk to Big Ben. So when Big Ben walked over to him today, Charlie was ready for an all-out brawl.

Ben stopped in front of him and said, "Listen, you stay out of my way, and I'll stay out of your way. I'll try to watch my mouth as long as you don't push that Jesus stuff on me." Charlie had tried to talk to Ben about his faith, but it always seemed to aggravate Ben more than anyone else. He was just an angry, angry man. Charlie replied by nodding his head, and both men walked off in different directions.

It was now about eleven o'clock. Charlie and Ben were working that day as a team, laying sheets of plywood. They even spoke to each other a couple of times. Suddenly, they heard a huge bang, and Charlie looked over at the safety wire. He saw the hook on the crane boom swaying back and forth and slamming into the steel building. The super yelled over to the operator, "Secure that hook now!"

The wind had really picked up. Charlie, still looking, heard Ben say, "Hey, what the hell was that?" Charlie yelled over to Ben about what was going on. Ben was walking up with a four-by-eight sheet of plywood over his head when, out of nowhere, a huge gust of wind swept across the roof. The wind grabbed him, and in a split second, it had taken Ben for a ride, heading right for the edge of the building. Instead of dropping the plywood, his instinct after years of construction work was to try to hold on to it. Ben was heading right toward Charlie, who reached out to grab him—but he was knocked aside. Now Ben was running at full speed to the edge of the building when he hit the safety wire. He just flipped right over it, and in a split second, he was gone. Hearing him scream, Charlie was in shock. The safety wire is to keep you from falling off if you back up to it; it's just a reminder of where the edge of the roof is. It's not going to stop a three-hundred-pound guy going at full speed. Charlie didn't want to look over the edge, knowing it would be a horrible sight. He thought he was going to get sick.

Just then, he heard Ben's voice yelling out, "Hey, get me off of here!"

Charlie quickly ran over to the edge and looked. He couldn't believe his eyes. There he was: Big Ben, swinging side to side on the crane's hook, about three stories up. It had grabbed onto the back of his vest and had kept him from certain death. The super yelled out to the operator, "Get him down!" All the others guys ran underneath Ben just in case he fell from the hook, hoping to break his fall.

Charlie ran over to the elevator, and the door opened. He got on with a couple of other guys, knocking Lucky off his chair and spilling his iced coffee all over the place. Charlie punched the button to the ground floor while Lucky kept asking, "What's going on? What's going on?" with no one answering him. When they got to the ground floor, the door opened, and they all ran out as fast as they could. When they reached Ben, he was just getting lowered down, with all the guys grabbing onto his feet, then legs, and finally his waist, and they got him to the ground. When Charlie reached him, he was sitting down, looking disoriented. Everyone was asking him if he was OK.

Charlie broke through the crowd. Immediately, Ben looked right at him and said, "What time is church Sunday?"

"Nine o'clock. I'll pick you up, bro." Everyone was relieved as they picked Ben up off the ground, wiping the dirt away. It was like Ben knew. What were the odds that when he fell off the building, the hook, which was swinging from side to side like a pendulum, would grab him at that exact moment? He knew right away it was no coincidence. As they were walking away, Charlie just stood there pointing up to the sky and said, "God, we just got another one."

17

Around noon, Libby was having her lunch with some of the other kids. One was her friend Nathan, an African American boy who had the biggest smile you ever saw. Libby admired him because he was the smartest kid in the class, and he always helped the students who struggled with learning disabilities.

All Nathan ever talked about was becoming an astronaut. He would walk to school with Libby and Maria quite often, always carrying a toy spaceship, rocket, or some kind of Star Wars toy. His bedroom looked like the universe, with all the planets and stars hanging down from the ceiling.

By now, all the buzz was about Maria and her family hitting the lottery. Libby felt proud that everybody was coming up to her asking about Maria, knowing that they were best friends. She felt a little like a celebrity herself. The kids were also talking about Mrs. Stanton and how she was in such a happy mood lately, smiling and joking with them all. She seemed to be a different person altogether. Libby knew it had to do with what she had said to her but didn't tell any of the other kids. Libby thought that it was so amazing how people changed when they knew God forgave and loved them. She only wished her dad could feel that and would not always carry the burden of guilt for the accident that had taken her mom's life.

Nathan and Libby were walking home when Nathan saw his mother on a street corner. She was wearing a leopard-print miniskirt with high-heeled boots and a tank top. He crossed over to the other side to avoid her. Libby wondered why she was always on the corner. She thought, *She has the worst luck trying to catch a cab.* It seemed like she knew everyone who drove by, because she waved to all of them. Sometimes men would stop and give her a ride, but she always seemed to be back on the corner a little while later, looking for another.

Nathan's mom didn't live with him; Nathan lived with his grandmother. All the kids in the neighborhood called her Nana. She always had time to talk to all of them and knew all their names. When Nathan and Libby reached his house, Nana was out front, sitting on the steps and waiting for him. Instead of being her usual cheerful self, it looked like she had been crying. Nathan asked, "What's wrong, Nana?"

Nana wiped the tears from her eyes, trying to compose herself, and said, "Oh, it's only my allergies kicking up again." Nana said to Libby, "Hi, honey, that's a beautiful dress you have on today. You look just like a princess." Even in her pain, she tried to make someone else feel special. Libby and Nathan didn't know what had happened, but earlier, child services had come to tell her that they were going to have to place Nathan in a foster home because she was getting too old to raise a ten-year-old boy. Her health had been failing over the last few years, so she would no longer be able to care for him.

Nathan's mom was addicted to crack cocaine and was now starting to prostitute herself. She was in and out of his life. It was a very sad situation and put a huge stress on Nana. She was seventy years old and did not know how much longer she could hang on. This was killing her. Grace had been the perfect daughter growing up. She had sung in the church choir and was very respectful to her parents. She was definitely "daddy's little girl." She followed him everywhere he went. When he went to work, he would give her a big kiss, and then he would wink at her with his left eye. Grace would always try to wink back but ended up always blinking both eyes. Her dad would say, "Almost, honey. You're getting better." She would practice winking all the time. She always had lumps on her forehead from walking into the furniture.

Then, one summer evening while they sat on the front steps, her father winked at her, and she winked back. She had mastered the left-eye wink. Her father jumped up with excitement and yelled, "You did it! You did it, pumpkin."

Grace's father worked in the shipyards for thirty years and ended up contracting mesothelioma from asbestos exposure. The companies knew the dangers of asbestos, but they also knew that the effects wouldn't show up for thirty or forty years. Grace's dad died when she was a teenager, and she was completely devastated. That's when she started hanging with the wrong crowd and eventually picked up drugs that seemed to heal her emotional pain temporarily. Her life went into a downward spiral from there on.

18

The next day Jim was home, waiting for Libby to get out of school. He had been in a funk all day. He couldn't seem to get motivated to do anything. Newly sober, and out of work, he had a lot of time to think. Having nothing to do, he was torturing himself.

The phone rang. Charlie said, "What's up, bro?" Jim told him how he was feeling. Charlie said, "That's the reason I called. I figured you were feeling like that. If you weren't, I'd be worried about ya. But anyway, I want you to meet George. He's a friend of mine who goes to our men's Christians in Recovery meeting. I think he would be a perfect sponsor for you. He's got more peace and serenity than anyone else I know. When you hear the story of the man he used to be and the man he is now, you'll be blown away."

Jim hated the idea of asking another man to be his sponsor. It felt like asking him out on a date. Growing up in his neighborhood, you didn't talk about your feelings or ask someone to help you. It was a sign of weakness that you were taught never to show. He answered, "I can't go, I have Libby."

Charlie had called Jim on his cell phone while Lucky drove them home in the truck. Charlie said loudly, "Oh, you need someone to watch Libby," nodding at Lucky. Lucky waved and mouthed the words, *No, no.* Charlie said, "Lucky's right here, let me ask him." Lucky looked annoyed and waved, *No, no.* They were on West Broadway, the busiest street in Southie, in bumper-to-bumper traffic. Charlie had to pull out all the stops. He reached over and grabbed his CD of "How Awesome Is Our God" and motioned to put it in the player, when Lucky gave in. Lucky said, yeah, he'd be glad to watch Libby.

Jim still didn't want to go. The vision he'd had when Libby held his hand came back to his mind. "OK, I'll go."

Charlie said, "Great, I'll pick you up at six thirty."

Jim said, "All right, see ya."

Lucky said, "Oh, man. Why did you do that? I had a date tonight with the girl who works on the canteen truck."

Charlie said, "It will help you when you get to the pearly gates of heaven. And man, you're going to need it." Charlie laughed. Lucky just threw up his hands and wouldn't look at him the rest of the way home.

19

Jim hung up the phone just as Libby came through the door with her homework in her hand. Jim said, "Wow, looks like a lot of studying tonight."

"No, this is all my research I had to do."

"Research for what?"

"Mrs. Stanton gave us a new assignment. We got to pick any state in the country and do a project on it. I picked Virginia."

"Well, that's not surprising, since Virginia is your favorite name and your favorite doll." This was because her mother had given Virginia to her on her sixth birthday, so she had a very special meaning. "I have to go out tonight with Charlie to a meeting, and Lucky's going to watch you."

In her excitement, Libby blurted, "Oh, good! That means I get to watch anything on TV again!" Then she realized she had just ratted Lucky out. Trying to recover, she added, "I mean...anything *educational*." Jim tried to look at her sternly but had to turn away to hide his smile. Libby had so many of her mother's great qualities. This was a double-edged sword for Jim. He loved to see his wife, Susan, in Libby, but it also brought back memories of his soul mate. Jim had always credited Sue for saving his life. He had been heading down the wrong path when he met her, and she changed him for the better.

It was exactly six thirty when Charlie beeped his horn. Lucky knocked on the door, but not waiting for anyone to answer, he let himself in. Jim kissed Libby good-bye and thanked Lucky for coming over. Lucky, still pouting, said, "Yeah, yeah."

Jim got in the truck and immediately tried to change Charlie's mind about meeting George. He felt like a teenager on a blind date. Charlie said, "Relax, bro. I think you need a guy like George in your life." Jim didn't even try to respond. One thing about Charlie—when he had his mind made up, there was no changing it.

When they got to Saint Monica's Church, they went down to the basement meeting room where there were about twenty men, many of whom Jim recognized. Many of them he had grown up with; some had been to jail, others had been involved in some kind of criminal activity in South Boston, and some he had just assumed were dead. That's just the way it was growing up. If someone wasn't around anymore, they were often dead, in prison, or on the lam.

George opened up the meeting with prayer and then picked the topic of love. Jim said to himself, "This is crazy, sitting in a room full of men in South Boston and talking about love." He thought, *This'll be a quiet meeting.* But as the men started to speak, one by one, Jim was captivated. He had never seen any of this growing up. These men shared their feelings of loneliness, fear, doubt, and all kinds of insecurities. The meeting was an hour and a half long, but it felt like ten minutes. Jim was blown away with the honesty. The men talked about all the violence they had experienced growing up and the foolishness of it all. For the first time in his life, he didn't see talking about feelings as a form of weakness, but a form of strength. He felt hope for the first time in a very long time.

When the meeting was over, Charlie brought Jim over to meet George. They introduced themselves and made small talk. Jim was trying to get up the courage to ask George to be his sponsor but couldn't find the right words. George, noticing this, said, "Hey, Jim, would you like me to be your sponsor?"

Jim let out a big sigh of relief and said, "Yeah, I really need one."

George said, "No problem. Here's my number. Are you around tomorrow?"

Jim said, "Yeah, I'm laid off right now."

"Well, I'm off tomorrow." George was a captain at the South Bay House of Correction. "Why don't we meet for breakfast at Mul's Diner around nine?"

"Sounds good."

George said, "Good, I'll see you then."

On the ride home, Jim thanked Charlie for inviting him, but Charlie cut him off. "No problem, bro. Whatever you do, always be honest with George. He's not going to judge you, especially after you hear his story."

At home, Jim walked into the kitchen and saw Lucky and Libby playing poker. Libby's pile of money was a lot bigger than Lucky's. Jim said, "Lucky, what did I tell you about teaching her to play poker?"

Lucky said, "What do you mean? She wiped me out again. I haven't beaten her since she was five. Even then I had to cheat! I mean, I can't catch a break. I missed my date with the canteen truck lady, and I lost seven fifty to a ten-year-old." Libby was giggling as she raked in the coins.

"Hey, Lucky, do you know what the meaning of insanity is?" Before Lucky could respond, Jim said, "It's doing the same thing over and over again, expecting different results. Let's face it, the kid's got your number."

"Yeah, yeah, now I'll have to work some overtime tomorrow to recoup my losses." Lucky kissed Libby on the cheek and said, "Enjoy the moment, kid, because that's the last time you'll beat me." Jim and Libby cracked up as they walked him to the door.

Jim stopped Lucky and said, "Seriously, man, I really do appreciate it."

Lucky was taken aback a little and replied, "Anything for you, man," and hugged Jim. Lucky had his faults, but deep down, you wouldn't want anyone else in your corner. He was as loyal as they come.

20

It was about eight o'clock, and Jim had to run an errand so he asked Libby if she wanted a ride to school. Whenever he asked her before, she would always decline because she liked walking to school with Maria. They usually laughed all the way there. But today she said yes. Libby had not seen Maria since her family had won the lottery. She figured that they were celebrating a little, and she didn't want to bother them. Jim called Tommy and asked if he wanted to take a ride with him to drop off Libby and maybe go to the driving range to hit some balls.

Jim and Tommy were very competitive at golf. Tommy may have had a disability, but it definitely wasn't on the course. Tommy was a big hitter, and Jim was always trying to outdrive him. There was always a lot of trash talk going on. As hard as Jim tried, he would very seldom beat Tommy, and Tommy would never let him forget it.

On the way, they drove past the Pine Street Inn homeless shelter. Going by it had made Libby sad since she had met Sam at Castle Island. She hoped that she would see him outside so she could wave to him and make him feel good. When they got closer, she noticed a lot of traffic in front of the shelter. She also saw police cars and several tractor-trailers out front. She thought, *I hope they're not closing the shelter down. Where will all those people go?*

Police were directing traffic. As it was moving very slowly, Libby saw the name on all the trucks: Food World. And that mean man on the yacht was there, directing everybody! They were unloading cases and cases of food. There was a ton of boxes marked "computers" or "clothing," and another truck was unloading brand-new TVs and furniture. There were other trucks removing all the old furniture, beds, carpets, and TVs. She noticed a whole construction crew working on the outside of the building, and another working inside. When she looked at Mr. Donlan, she saw that standing next to him was a man with a clipboard, taking inventory. She had to look twice. She hadn't recognized him at first, but it was the homeless man she had met at Castle Island. She felt goose bumps all over—and just then, Mr. Donlan turned and looked directly at Libby, and their eyes locked. Mr. Donlan mouthed the words, *Thank you.* Libby smiled and said, "You're welcome," as Jim drove by.

21

Jim got to Mul's Diner a few minutes before nine. Mul's was one of the only places in the world were you could see politicians, cops, gangsters, and everyone else in between sitting and having breakfast together, joking and laughing. It was an oasis away from the outside world. When they all left Mul's, it was back to business.

Tommy grabbed a seat at the counter with some old-timers. They all knew him from Castle Island. Jim thought, *Boy, that Tommy's a great kid, always bringing a smile to their faces.* Jim wasn't facing the door, but he knew it when George came in. He could hear everybody saying hi to him like he was the mayor of South Boston. The fact was, he was one of the most likable and respected guys in Southie.

George sat down in the booth and asked Jim, "How's your day going?"

Jim said, "Pretty good, but it's only nine o'clock..."

George laughed a little and said, "Yeah, but this is the day the Lord made." George seemed to know exactly what Jim was feeling, remembering that feeling of impending doom in early sobriety, like a dark cloud was always following him. "Tell me what's going on with your life."

"Oh, things are fine."

"OK, now tell me what's really going on." Jim knew right away why Charlie had introduced George to him.

Jim said, "You can't shit a shitter, huh?"

"You got it," said George.

"Well," Jim said, as he looked directly into George's eyes, "I'm a single father raising a ten-year-old girl. I'm laid off and not working." Then he lowered his eyes to the table and said, "And I lost my wife in a car accident."

When he said that, George picked up on the feelings of guilt. "How did it happen?"

"It was my fault."

George assumed Jim had been driving and said, "Tell me about it."

Jim got a little choked up and took a few seconds before speaking. "It was a lousy winter night, and I was hung over from a two-day bender. Susan asked me a couple of times if I could go to the pharmacy for her to get some cold medicine. She felt like she was coming down with the flu. I told her I would go for her, but as the day went on, I felt worse from all the drinking. I kept putting her off, with all the intentions of going as soon as I felt a little better. Well, she got upset with me. When she asked me the last time, I said, 'Just give me a little while and I'll go.' She said, 'Never mind, I'll go myself.' I got up as she closed the door, and my head started to spin. I felt like throwing up. I lay back down and let her go." Jim was now getting very emotional. "It was so selfish of me. I should have gone instead of her; she would've been here today." As he raised his voice, some people turned around to see what was going on. When they saw George in the booth with Jim, they all turned back quickly like they had never heard anything, because they had seen George over the years helping people, and they respected him. In fact, some of them who had turned around, George helped get sober.

George stopped Jim and said, "Jim, look at me." Jim couldn't. "Jim, please, look at me." Jim looked up and George said, "I want to ask you one question, and I want you to answer me honestly, all right?" Jim nodded. "Jim, if you knew what was going to happen to your wife that night, would you have gone to the pharmacy for her?"

Jim was taken aback by the question and said, "Yes, yes, absolutely. I would have gone, even if it meant me dying instead of her."

"OK. So you have to stop blaming yourself. You have a disease of addiction. You're an alcoholic. It is a terminal disease. If you and you alone decide not to treat it as such, it will kill you. Knowing that, you are now responsible for your own recovery. There are a lot of people who are willing to help you, but you have to be willing to accept the help. If you decide to accept the help and do everything I suggest to you, I personally guarantee your life will get better. Things and situations around you may not get better, but you will get better. Jesus said there will be trials and tribulations in your life—not there *might* be, but there will be. But He said He will never leave you or forsake you. He forgives you, and you need to forgive yourself. I know the guilt and shame you feel, and I know that it's not going to leave overnight. But if you let God into your life and you just keep doing the next right thing, you will wake up one day, and it will be gone. That's called a spiritual awakening, and when that happens, there's no drink in the world that can be equal to it.

"Jim, believe me when I tell you this. I got sober thirteen years ago. My life got better, but I was still insane. Doing things not pleasing to God. I felt like a hypocrite, being sober in AA but acting like I was still drinking. It was about seven years ago when I gave myself to the Lord, and believe me that I have peace in me that is beyond—way beyond—any understanding. I have three precious daughters, and my relationship with my wife has done a one-eighty. I know it's God. When I get up every morning at four o'clock to read my Bible and study scripture, I feel like He's sitting there with me. I call it 'having coffee with the king.' Jim, I'm so very, very blessed. I ask Him every day what His will is for me. Not to help me find my will, but what's His will? I ask Him how I can be an instrument for Him and spread His word. The peace I have today, you can also have. It's a free gift from God, and all you have to do is accept and acknowledge Him in all your ways."

Jim knew that Charlie was the one who had introduced him to George, but he just realized that it was no coincidence—that this was the time and the place to have someone like George in his life. He knew that from this point on, his life would change dramatically, and that the fear it was loaded with would be replaced by faith. It felt like a huge load had just come off his shoulders and realized that God was removing the weight. Jim thought that the conversation was over. George just sat there looking at him, like he was trying to figure something out. It made Jim a little uncomfortable. He couldn't take it anymore and asked George if there was something else he wanted to know. George said, "Tell me how your childhood was."

Jim kind of laughed but noticed that George didn't seem to be laughing with him. Jim got serious and said, "It was great. I had great parents who taught me right from wrong. My older brother, Peter, was the best brother you could ask for. I had a great childhood, why do you ask?"

George said, "I don't know, I just got this feeling that something bothered you when you were growing up."

"How can you tell?" Jim replied.

"Well, I get the feeling you're a real sensitive person."

"Why do you say that?"

"Well, I meet a lot of people who struggle with addiction, and most of the time, there was something in their childhood that really affected them."

Jim got real quiet and looked down at the table. He readjusted the salt and pepper shakers. Then he said, "The only thing that I can remember was, I was born with a deformity."

"OK," George said. "Tell me about it."

Jim said, "I had a concave chest. It was really sunk in. It looked like I had a big hole there. I remember when I went to Carson Beach to go swimming, kids would come over and ask me what happened. I got so self-conscious about it, I never took my shirt off. I used to go swimming with it on."

George said, "Yeah, kids can be mean sometimes."

Jim said, "No, they didn't really make fun of me or anything. They just never saw someone who had this before. But just having them come up to me and point at it really made me feel ashamed, and that shame followed me all my life. When someone even tries to give me constructive criticism, especially in front of other people, it immediately brings me back to being that five-year-old boy standing on the beach with people pointing at me. Shame can be an awful thing. Healthy shame is when you know you've done something wrong. It means you have morals and genuinely feel bad for what you've done. With me, it was different. It's not what I did but who I was. I just always felt inferior. Once my regular friends saw my chest, it made no difference to them. So growing up, I was so competitive. I had to be better than everyone at sports, have the nicest-looking girlfriend, have the first job in the neighborhood, and have the best-looking car. I don't why, but I lived my whole life trying to excel in everything I did. I wanted people to take notice of me in a good way."

George said, "Jim, sounds to me like you've chased all those outside things the world has to offer, thinking that they will make you happy. And all it did was take a lot of your hard-earned money. Jesus said, what good is it if a man gains the whole world, but loses his soul?

"I bet you feel uncomfortable getting compliments. Even though you think that's what you want—until someone actually gives you one. I'll bet you do one of two things. You either brush it off or you don't acknowledge it and quickly change the subject. Why do you think that is?"

Jim said, "Because of my shame, I don't feel like I'm worthy of them. I even have a difficult time going to someone's wake. As soon as I get into the funeral parlor, an overwhelming sense of guilt hits me. I look at the person in the casket and tell myself that I'm the one who should be in there because of all the mistakes I've made."

"That's why it's so vitally important you change your view of yourself. Yes, we have to recognize when we make mistakes and fix them as fast as possible, but we have to also recognize when we have stood up and have done the next right thing, no matter how hard it was. Give yourself a break."

Jim had never talked to anyone else about this. Once he started, he couldn't stop. It was like he was getting answers about questions he'd asked himself all his life. He said, "When I was eighteen, I finally decided to have it fixed, so I had reconstructive surgery. It took six months to recover from it. When I decided to have it done, I thought I would feel different. I thought I'd feel normal, like everyone else. My chest looked normal, but my opinion of myself never changed. Some people develop an opinion of themselves after grade school or high school, or even after they start their careers. I developed mine when I was five, and I adopted it based on what I thought everyone else thought of me. It's been that way ever since."

George said, "That's because the emotional damage had already been done. You see, you can fix the outside, but that will never change the inside. You have to change what you believe about yourself. I bet you are very compassionate toward people, especially the ones society thinks are different, right?"

"Yeah, I feel like it's my duty to stick up for them."

George said, "That's because it's so close to your heart. That's why people become addicted to whatever makes them feel better about themselves, whether it's alcohol, drugs, food, exercise, work, sex...the list can go on and on. But the external quick fixes never last. Jim, this is an inside job. It may be painful at times, but you have to deal with all of this before you can get better. Whether it's through a twelve-step program or some outside therapy, it's going to take some work."

Jim said, "Yeah, I never realized how something like that affected me."

"Don't worry, you just took the most important step. You acknowledged it, and you can't fix something if you don't know it's broken."

Jim picked up Libby at school. On the ride home, a car changed lanes in front of them. Libby noticed that its license plate said "Virginia." She jumped up and said, "Dad, look, they're from Virginia."

Jim said, "Hey, why don't I pull them over, and you can ask them questions about Virginia for your report."

Libby said, "No, Dad."

"I think it's a good idea." He changed lanes and sped up to wave them over.

Libby shouted, "No, Dad, no! You're embarrassing me."

Jim said, "No, really, put your window down and wave them over."

"Dad, Dad, no!" As Jim pulled up beside the other car, he honked the horn. Libby was so embarrassed that she slumped way down in the seat, but the seat belt held her up, so all she could do was look the other way at her dad. He hit the button for the window on Libby's side. The man rolled down his window, and Libby said, "Dad, I can't believe you're doing this to me."

Jim yelled out to the man, "Excuse me. Do you know where Washington Street is?"

The man yelled back, "Yeah, you're on it."

Jim said, "Oh. Thanks a lot, sir."

"You're welcome. Have a good day."

As Jim accelerated past, Libby said, "Dad, I'm going to kill you," and tried to reach over and hit him in the arm, but once again, the seat belt pulled her back.

Now Jim could hardly contain himself, and with a big grin, he said, "Be careful, you don't want your seat belt to come off. The law says 'click it or ticket!'" Jim broke out laughing. Libby again tried to reach out at him but stopped herself, not wanting to give Jim the satisfaction. She folded her arms and looked out the window. Jim said, "You got to admit, I really had you going." Libby tried to remain mad, but her lips started to go up a little, and that's all Jim needed to see. "Aaahhh, you're starting to laugh..." And Libby turned all red and broke into laughter.

Trying to justify her feelings, she said, "Dad, that was so mean."

As he started to dance with his upper body, he sang, "That's who I am! Jim, Jim, the mean dancing machine."

Libby looked at him, rolling her eyes. "Here he goes again."

22

When they got in the door, the phone rang. Libby said, "I'll get it!" It was Maria. Libby said, "Hey, I heard you're a millionaire," expecting Maria to get all excited.

Maria said, "Yeah, I know."

"What's wrong?"

"My parents put me in a new private school out of town."

"You mean you won't be going to the Gate of Heaven anymore?"

"No. I start going there next year." Maria, still being a child, really didn't understand why. All she knew was that it was supposed to be a better school, and since her family had money now, she was supposed to go there. It was hard for a ten-year-old to understand. All she knew was her neighborhood and her friends.

Libby said, "Well, that doesn't mean you're not still my best friend. We can still do things after school and on the weekend."

Maria said, "I know," but it still wasn't any consolation to her.

23

At about seven o'clock, Jim was supposed to call George and let him know how he was doing. Jim still found it an uncomfortable thought. When Libby went up to her room to work on her homework and the state of Virginia project, Jim picked up the phone. He was hoping he would just get George's voice mail. After four rings, he definitely thought he wouldn't pick up, but then he heard George's voice on the other end saying hello. Jim was startled for a moment. He stuttered, "Hey, George, it's Jim from the meeting, and we had breakfast..."

"Hey, Jim. What's up, man?" Jim had thought he would have to remind George who he was, but George said, "I was thinking about you all day and prayed for you this morning."

They chatted for about five minutes on nothing special. George gave him a couple of suggestions. Jim asked, "How's work going down at the prison?"

George said, "Oh, man. It's been a hotbed down here. We had three lockdowns this week. Every time it gets hot outside, things heat up around here. You can cut the tension with a knife."

"Really?"

"Yeah. The whites are fighting with the blacks. The blacks are fighting with the Latinos. The Latinos are fighting with the Asians. It's getting real ugly. Every day I leave here, I count my blessings that I have my freedom, because I didn't deserve it. The way I lived my life, I should be in there with them. But because of God's grace and mercy, He spared my life, and that's why I ask Him what He wants me to do every day."

Jim, agreeing with him, said, "I guess we both have been blessed."

"You got that right, brother."

After they said good-bye, Jim realized that he felt better. As awkward as it was for him, he knew that George had to be part of his life.

On Saturday morning, Libby came downstairs to meet Jim at the kitchen table, and he poured her a bowl of cereal. She looked really tired. Jim asked, "Did you sleep all right last night?"

"Yeah, I think so."

Jim started to butter his toast when he sensed Libby staring at him. "What, you want some toast?" Libby shook her head no. Jim noticed that she looked serious about something and asked, "Anything wrong?" Again she shook her head no.

After a brief pause, she said, "Dad, who's George?"

Jim looked up at her, surprised at the question, and said, "Ahh, he's a friend of mine." Thinking she must have overheard their conversation the night before, he asked, "Were you eavesdropping on me?" Libby said no. "Then how do you know who George is?"

Libby paused for a moment and said, "Mommy told me to tell you that you need to keep George as a friend and to listen to him."

Jim, looking startled, asked, "Libby, what do you mean, Mommy told you?"

"Last night, she talked to me when I was sleeping."

"You mean you had a dream about her last night."

"No, it wasn't a dream. It was real. I know she's not with us anymore, but I know she talks to me when I'm sleeping."

"What else did she talk to you about?"

"She said that you have to move on with your life. You don't have to be sad for her. She says heaven is so beautiful. You can't believe how magical it is. She can't explain it in words. Mommy wants you to find someone that you can spend your life with. She said you need a soul mate here on earth. She said life is so precious; you have to enjoy it every day. Compared to eternity, life is a fraction of a second. Dad, Mommy wants you to be happy. It makes her sad seeing you so lonely."

"Libby, I can't—"

Libby cut him off. "Mommy said so, and remember, she was the boss."

Jim giggled as his eyes filled with tears. Choking up, he said, "She was the boss. She always was," as he pulled Libby in. They embraced and just held on to each other.

24

I t was about ten o'clock. Libby and Maria had made plans to go down the park for the day. Libby asked Jim if he could give them a ride when Maria got there. "Sure, honey," Jim responded.

The bell rang, and Jim answered the door. Maria said, "Hi, Mr. Davis. Is Libby here?"

"Yeah, come on in, hon." Jim shouted up to Libby's room, "Libby, Maria's here!"

When she came down, Jim had his keys ready. Libby said, "Hi, Maria, my dad's going to give us a ride down the park."

When they got to the park, Jim said, "OK, I'll pick you guys up right here at three. Stay together, and be careful."

They both said, "OK. See you at three."

As they walked over to the park area, they heard someone calling out to them. They turned around and saw that it was Eric and his friend, PJ, a couple of their classmates. Eric had Down syndrome, and PJ had cerebral palsy and was in a wheelchair. PJ had limited mobility in his legs and arms. He could move them sometimes, but never with control. These guys were the best of friends, and Eric wheeled PJ everywhere they went. "Where you guys going?" Libby asked.

"We're going to the baseball field; we're playing the kids from City Point." These baseball games were what you call neighbor-hood pickup games arranged by the kids, and the umpires were any of the older kids hanging around the ballpark. There were no trophies, just bragging rights. City Point was a more upscale area of South Boston. Libby knew that her friends were on the team, but also that they were only allowed to play in the practice games, never in a real game. Eric and PJ came to every game, rain or shine, and contributed however they could. Eric would sometimes coach first and third base and be in charge of all the equipment. And PJ would keep all the statistics. Even though they never played in the games, they never complained.

Libby said to Maria, "Let's get a snow cone and watch the game."

Maria said, "OK. We'll see you guys over there."

Eric replied, "OK, make sure you cheer really loud for us. We've never beaten those guys from City Point."

"Never until *today*," Maria said.

"That's right," PJ said, waving his right hand up. And the boys left for the field.

Libby said, "Come on, Maria, let's go get the snow cones before the game starts."

When they got to the stands, there were a lot of kids from both neighborhoods talking trash. Libby noticed a boy on Eric's team, a tall, good-looking kid. His name was Smitty. He seemed to be the unofficial captain, giving orders to his teammates, and they all seemed to listen to him.

The game started, and Smitty got onto the mound. When he threw his first pitch, everybody in the stands said "Whoo!" He threw with so much speed that the batter swung a full second after the pitch. Maria and Libby assigned themselves designated cheerleaders. Inning by inning, the score went back and forth. Libby noticed PJ during the game and saw a certain sadness in him. Eric was more active, running around, picking up equipment, and coaching the bases. PJ knew he was limited in what he could do. Of course, Libby's gift let her experience other peoples' feelings, especially when they seemed to be emotionally hurting. She also heard PJ's mom and dad in the stands. They always went to the games to show support for the team and PJ. Even though he couldn't do that much, all the kids made him feel a part of the team.

It was the last inning, and Eric's team was down by three. Smitty threw some balls, keeping his arm warm in case they made a comeback and had to go into extra innings. When the catcher threw the ball back to Smitty, the sun was in his eyes. The ball hit his glove and dropped out, rolling right to where Libby and Maria were sitting. Libby and an older boy both jumped out to catch the ball before it went under the stands. Libby looked like a middle linebacker from the Patriots and knocked the older boy on his butt. Everybody started clapping for her. She picked up the ball, and Smitty walked over to get it from her, still squinting from the sun. Libby reached out her hand to give him the ball. Smitty said thanks and grabbed at it. Libby held on to the ball while Smitty tugged on it gently a couple of times.

Then it happened. Ten-year-old Smitty's sight went black, and slowly a very old man in a wheelchair appeared to him. He was in his late eighties or early nineties. All around this room he was in were dozens of trophies and awards on the wall. A further look around the room revealed several other people, maybe about thirty. Many were children. Then he saw a birthday cake in the center of a table. It read "Happy Ninetieth Birthday, Grampy Smitty." All the people started to sing "Happy Birthday," with all the young kids climbing on the wheelchair, hugging and kissing him. The look on Smitty's face was of disbelief. As Libby let go of the ball, Smitty backed off slowly, staring at her with a confused look. He walked backward to the dugout, never taking his eyes off of Libby.

The first batter got up and singled. The second batter also singled. The third batter struck out. The fourth batter also struck out. The fifth batter was walked. So the bases were loaded, with two outs in the ninth. As soon as the last batter walked, everybody started to shout out Smitty's name. He was next to bat. He had already homered, and had a triple and a double. Smitty, still looking confused, grabbed a bat and helmet. As he put it on, he looked at Libby. He started to walk out to the plate, and the fans cheered. Then suddenly, he stopped. Everybody got quiet and didn't know what was going on. He took off his helmet, walked over to PJ, and said, "You're up."

"What?" PJ said. "Who, me?"

"You haven't batted all year. I think it's time for you to bat."

"But I can't hold the bat."

"That's all right. Eric can swing and push your chair."

Eric yelled out, "Yay! Let's go."

Now, all the kids loved Eric and PJ, but this was the big game, and they had never beaten the City Points before. They said, "Smitty, what are you doing?"

He stopped them immediately and said, "It's PJ's turn." They had so much respect for Smitty that they backed off. Eric got a bat and two helmets and pushed PJ over to the plate. The other team didn't oppose; they figured it was a sure out.

The first pitch came. It was almost on the ground, and Eric swung and missed. All the kids were yelling, "Eric! Stoop way down," figuring he could make the strike zone smaller, but Eric was having no part of it. He stood there challenging the pitcher. Another fastball: strike two. All the kids had their hands on their faces and couldn't look. This was their big chance, and they were blowing it.

PJ's parents were on their feet, cheering the boys on. The pitcher wound up and fired a fastball down the middle. Eric had his eyes fixed on it. As the pitch came in, he lifted his left foot off the ground. As the pitch crossed the plate, he lowered his left foot and swung with all his might. Next was the crack of the ball hitting the bat. At that sound, all the kids on the bench took their hands off their eyes and screamed, "Go, you guys! Go!" Eric dropped the bat and grabbed the handles of PJ's chair, pushing and running down first base. He had hit the ball right over the third baseman and down the left field line. When Eric got down to first base, the first base coach was trying to hold him up to stop, but Eric never looked at him. He rounded first base, heading to second.

Eric had a huge smile on his face. He looked like the cat that just ate the canary. PJ was waving his arms all over the place. As they were going to second, the ball was thrown above the second baseman's head and headed out to shallow right field. But it didn't matter if it was thrown over the second baseman's head or not; Eric had no plans to stop there. As they approached third base, the third base coach was down on one knee with his hands held together like he was praying, yelling "Eric! Stop, stop!" Now, Eric and PJ had no plans to stop at first or second. Do you think he was debating whether to stop at third? No way. He rounded third and headed for home. The first baseman picked up the ball in shallow right and threw a strike down to home plate. The fans threw their hands up. In their minds, they had lost the game.

That's not what Eric or PJ had in mind. The catcher caught the ball twenty feet before those guys crossed home plate. Now, Eric new that PJ had limited motion in his legs. Some days he could move them, some days he couldn't. He yelled down to PJ, "Lift your feet up!" PJ screamed out, and his feet started to lift up—then suddenly they dropped. Eric yelled out, "Come on, PJ, you can do it!" Once again, PJ let out a scream, and his feet came out of the wheelchair, horizontally aimed right at the catcher.

When the collision at home plate happened, you could see the catcher holding the ball and glove in his chest when PJ's feet hit him. It looked like he was tagged out. The catcher went head over heels backward. The dust was all around home plate. Everybody was on his or her feet. When the dust cleared, the catcher stood up, holding his glove in the air. The look on the City Point kids' faces said it all. The catcher lowered his arm to take the ball from his glove—and it wasn't there. He turned toward the backstop, and the ball was rolling up against the fence.

Everybody in the stands went crazy. Half the team went out to Eric, and the other half ran over to PJ. They were both lifted in the air on the kids' shoulders. PJ in his wheelchair must have been six feet in the air, looking down at his teammates as they paraded him around. This was not a position he had ever been in, so high in the air. His parents were in the stands hugging each other and crying tears of joy for their son. PJ's dad pumped his fist up, telling all the other parents, "That's my boy, that's my boy!" All the other parents gave them high fives.

During the celebration, Smitty looked over at Libby. He gave her a smile, and she smiled back. He realized how the world could put us on pedestals for our gifts and talents, but in the end, what people remember is our characters and how well we treat others. "Love thy neighbor like you love thyself." Smitty had the opportunity to see that he was going to live a long and prosperous life with a great family around him, realizing that it is better to be permanently loved than to be temporarily idolized.

There happened to be a reporter from the local South Boston paper in the stands. The next morning, the headlines read, "Dynamic Duo Hits Grand Slam to Beat City Point Team." They had a picture of Eric and PJ being held up in the air, both with their fingers pointing "number one."

25

Sunday morning, Maria called to ask if Libby was home. Jim said, "Yeah, sure, hold on a second." He called Libby down from her bedroom.

When she answered the phone, Maria asked if she could come to church with Libby and Jim because her parents weren't going that morning.

When she asked him, Jim hesitated for a second, not because of Maria, but because he wondered why Maria's family wasn't going to church.

He said, "Sure, tell her we'll pick her up at nine."

After Libby hung up, Jim asked if everything was OK with Maria's mom and dad. Libby said, "Yeah, they're not going to church today. They're going out to buy new cars for them and her brother and sister."

"Well, that's kind of exciting. Why doesn't she want to go?"

"I guess she likes church better than she likes cars."

Jim thought, *Well, you ask a simple question, you get a simple answer*, and that's just what it was. Maria, at ten years old, had not been influenced by the things of this world yet. She still had childlike faith and honesty. She seemed to know what she was brought up to believe. God is more important than anything else.

The phone rang again. Jim answered, and Charlie said, "Hey, bro, what's up?"

"Libby and I are going to church."

"Awesome," Charlie said. "I'm picking up Big Ben, and we'll meet you there."

Jim asked, "Big Ben, from the job site?"

Charlie said, "Yeah. Man, wait till I tell you what happened at work this week; you won't believe it! But I'm running late, so I'll see you at the service."

"OK, see ya." Jim paused after he hung up. He knew that Charlie and Ben never saw eye to eye. He couldn't imagine what had to have happened that would get them into the same car. He just shrugged. He had just moved a few steps away when the phone rang again. "What is this, Grand Central Station?" Libby heard him while she was sipping on her orange juice and spit it back up from laughing. Jim looked at her and started to laugh as Libby giggled, and then he couldn't stop. He tried to pick up the phone a couple of times but kept cracking up.

Libby said, "Dad, get the phone, or they're going to hang up."

Jim picked up the phone and said hello. "Oh, hi, Nana, how are you doing?"

Nathan's grandmother, Nana, whom everyone knew, said, "Jim, I need to ask you a favor. If you can't do it, don't worry about it."

"No, no, Nana. What do you need?"

"Jim, I don't know what happened to my daughter, Grace, but she came home last week and begged me to get some help for her. I called Boston Medical Center and they have a wonderful thirty-day rehab facility there I was able to get her into."

"Nana, that's great news."

She said, "I know. God has answered my prayers. Well, Grace just called, and they have visiting hours today from noon to three, and she wants me to visit her with Nathan. We can walk to church, but the bus lines don't run by the hospital on Sundays. I might be able to walk there one way, but with my arthritis, not both ways. Do think that you could either drop us off or pick us up?"

"Nana, don't be crazy, I'll drive you both ways. Besides, I'd like to see my childhood friend Grace too."

"Oh, Jim, you're a saint."

"No problem, Nana. I'll pick you up at eleven forty-five. Libby and I will be getting out of church around then."

"Oh, bless you, Jim, bless you."

"OK, Nana, I'll see you then."

After they hung up, Jim sat there for a moment reminiscing about when he and Grace were kids. She was the best student in the class and the lead singer in the church choir. She had the most beautiful voice he had ever heard. When she sang, the audience was mesmerized. The one thing he remembered most about Grace was that she always made the new kids in their class feel welcome. She had so many of Nana's qualities in her. It was mind-boggling to him how she'd ended up where she did. He remembered sitting on the steps at Nana's house with Grace, Nana, and a couple of other kids. Someone had asked Nana, "What made you pick the name Grace?"

He remembered Nana getting real emotional. Then she said, "When I was carrying Grace, I went into premature labor. Grace was born almost two months early. The doctors gave her almost no chance to survive. It's not like it is now. They didn't have the knowledge or medical equipment they have today. She was in an incubator for seven weeks. The whole time, I prayed to God to spare my baby. I still had faith in God that He could do what all the doctors said couldn't be done, and He did. He spared her life. It was by the grace of God she survived, and that's why I named her Grace." Jim still remembered this word for word, and he could still see Nana hugging little Grace on those front stairs.

26

Jim and Libby drove over to pick up Maria. When they got there, Maria's family was outside. Jim rolled down the window and said, "Hey, how you guys doing?"

They said, "Great. How about you?"

"Couldn't be better."

Carlos said, "Thanks for taking Maria."

"No problem," said Jim.

"We should be home around eleven thirty."

Jim said, "OK, that's perfect timing. Good luck."

As they pulled away, everybody waved to each other. Jim said, "Well, it's pretty exciting getting a new car, huh, Maria?"

"Yeah, I guess."

Jim sensed that she was upset and just turned the radio on. "Hey, Libby, this your day for the radio. You and Maria can listen to whatever you want." This seemed to get Maria's attention for a minute. They both pushed buttons and turned the radio all the way up. They found Snoop Dogg rapping away. Jim said, "Oh no, not the rap stuff."

Libby said, "Dad, you said whatever we want!" Jim knew how important it was to keep a promise to Libby. He just squinted at them like he was in agony listening to the stuff, which made Libby and Maria crack up and give each other high fives.

When they pulled in to church, they were right behind Charlie and Ben. Charlie's truck was leaning to one side where Ben was sitting. He was about six foot six and close to 350 pounds. When they all got out, Jim said, "Hey, Ben, how you doing?"

"Good, Jimmy, how are you? I'm sorry about your layoff."

Jim said, "Thanks, something should break soon."

"Yeah, it always does, buddy," said Ben as he patted Jim on the back. This was a side of Ben that Jim had never seen. Ben walked a few steps ahead of them, and Jim looked at Charlie with both palms held open, like he was asking Charlie, *What's up with this?* Charlie, with a big grin on his face, just pointed up to the sky and pumped his fist.

On the way in, Jim bumped into someone. When he turned to say "excuse me," he was stunned to see Danielle, Libby's babysitter. Immediately he felt ashamed and started to apologize to her. The way they had left things had really bothered him.

She stopped him and said, "It's really nice to see you here again." Jim looked a little confused. Danielle said, "I was sitting five rows behind you last week but didn't get a chance to say hello." As fast as the guilt had come, it left just as quickly. Danielle said, "I could really use some extra money, so if you need me to watch Libby, just give me a call."

"Absolutely, absolutely."

Then Libby yelled out, "Danielle!" and came running over to give her a big hug. "I miss you," she said.

"Oh, you'll see her again soon. I have a busy week with job interviews."

"Oh, cool," Libby said.

Jim didn't have any interviews lined up. But he still wanted everything to be back to normal. He suddenly realized he hadn't finished apologizing to Danielle, but just doing the next right thing was all anyone close to him ever wanted. The music started to play. This time he was ready for it and didn't fall back in his seat. As people started to sing, he had one eye on Ben. He felt like he wasn't the new guy anymore, and that everyone would be looking at Ben instead of him. Jim was actually getting a kick out of it. When he looked over at Libby and Maria, he saw that Libby was singing her heart out as usual, but Maria was just going through the motions. Her heart was not in it. She missed her family terribly. Libby right away sensed this and put her arm around Maria. Libby was always very sensitive of people around her, but since receiving the gift from God, her sensitivity was heightened tenfold.

During the last song before the sermon, Jim looked over at Ben. He was actually lip-synching and had a little sway going on. His hands weren't up yet, but the seed was planted. *Progress, not perfection*, he thought. *If a big, strong, tough guy like Ben can let down his guard, then so can I.* He knew it was just the beginning of a long journey, one he had never traveled before. But he felt that he didn't have to travel it alone.

The Bible talks about the advantages of companionship. It says, "Iron sharpens iron, so one man sharpens another." It also says that two people are better than one, for they can help each other succeed. If one person falls, the other can reach out and help. But someone who falls alone is in real trouble. A person alone can be attacked and defeated, but two standing back to back can conquer. Three are even better, for a triple-braided cord is not easily broken. Libby, his friends, and God were Jim's triple-braided cord.

27

After the service, Jim and Libby dropped off Maria. Her brother and sister were outside when they pulled up. They came over to say hi and mentioned their new cars. Maria acted as if she didn't hear them and walked into the house. Her brother asked, "What's wrong with her?"

Jim said, "I don't know. She must be tired."

When they pulled up to Nana's house, they didn't have to beep the horn. She and Nathan were anxiously waiting outside. When they got in, Nana started to thank Jim again. Jim said, "Nana, I told you, it's no problem." Nathan and Libby exchanged greetings, and Nana told Libby she looked adorable.

When they got to the hospital, everyone could tell that Nathan felt nervous about seeing his mother. In the past, he had never known what to expect from her. They rang the bell at the rehab facility and let the attendant know they were there to see Grace Wheeler. The attendant said she was only allowed three visitors at once, but that they could count the two children as one.

As they walked into the unit, Libby stopped in her tracks. Jim asked Libby what was wrong. She couldn't tell them about her overwhelming feelings of sadness, discouragement, hopelessness, shame, and remorse. It all seemed to really upset her. Still, she walked forward. She saw people with their heads down, and all of them looked very sickly. Going past several rooms, she thought it seemed like everyone was sleeping in the fetal position under two or three blankets. Libby thought, *That's really odd. It's very warm out today.*

She knew what everyone was in there for. One woman had been an acute care nurse and had started using pills to handle the stress of the job so she could sleep at night. Another woman looked to be in her eighties; Libby knew she hadn't taken her first drink until three years ago. All of her family had moved away, and once she took that first drink, she felt better inside and not so lonely. Then one day, she realized she couldn't stop, even when she was at the point of having to take a morning drink to get out of bed.

She couldn't believe the number of young people in there: teenagers fifteen, sixteen, and seventeen years old who were hooked on drugs. One man had previously been an alcohol and drug counselor. After years of doing that, he figured he didn't have a problem anymore, since he knew all the answers about addiction—until the day he took some painkillers for an operation and didn't stop for two years. He had lost his career, his family, and most of all, his self-respect. Every patient there looked like he or she had been poisoned.

When they got to Grace's room, they found that she was no different. She was shaking and sweating feverishly. When Nana saw her, it was everything she could do not to break down and cry. She stayed strong because she didn't want to upset Nathan. Jim hardly recognized Grace. He remembered the beautiful face she'd once had. Now she looked like a skeleton, with her face all drawn in and bags under her eyes.

When Grace saw Nana and Nathan, whatever strength she had drained right out of her. She immediately broke down and cried, saying, "I'm sorry, Mama, I'm so sorry. Nathan, I'm so sorry, honey."

Nathan and Nana just knelt down and hugged her, saying, "It's OK. You're going to get better in here."

Grace sobbed and shook her head. "No, Mama, I don't deserve to get better. I don't deserve anything good in my life because of the mistakes I made."

Libby really felt for her. She went over to Grace, who looked up at her. Libby took her hand, and as soon as she did, Grace's expression changed. She felt real compassion and love filtering through Libby. Libby said, "Mrs. Wheeler, Jesus forgives you, and He wants you to forgive yourself. He loves you and wants you to get better."

Grace just looked at Libby and said, "Thank you, thank you, honey."

A nurse came in and asked everyone to step outside so they could draw some blood for Grace's lab work. They went to the main room where some of the patients were sitting, but most of them were still in their rooms. Libby grabbed one of Nana's hands and one of Nathan's, signaling to her dad to hold on to Nana's other hand. Jim thought that Libby wanted to comfort them because that was just who she was. Jim took Nana's hand.

Suddenly, music started to play. It was so beautifully arranged that it sounded better than the Boston Pops Orchestra. The nurses all looked at each other because the patients weren't allowed to have radios. They checked all the intercoms, baffled at where the music was coming from. The patients in the room looked up and around to see who was playing it.

Then a beautiful voice sang out, and it seemed like a hundred-person choir joined in.

Everyone needs compassion,
Love that's never failing;
Let mercy fall on me.
Everyone needs forgiveness,
The kindness of a savior;
The hope of all nations.
My God is mighty to save,
He is mighty to save.
So take me as You find me,
All my fears and failures,
And fill my life again.
I give my life to follow
Everything I believe in,
Now I surrender.
Shine Your light on me;
Shine Your light on me.

The staff ran in and out of rooms trying to figure out where the song was coming from. The beautiful harmony continued. Slowly, the patients in the room joined in, holding hands and singing. Nana, Nathan, Jim, and Libby were all singing along in perfect harmony. Soon patients came out of rooms one by one and held hands in a circle. The words of the song really resonated with them. They realized they were forgiven and worthy of a second chance. The more patients that gathered, the louder they sang. Every time another patient joined, an opening in the circle appeared. Even though they didn't know each other, they hugged and held hands as they sang.

More and more patients came out until all but Grace were there. Finally, the nurses were so overwhelmed with emotion that they also joined in. The chorus was so loud that people in the street stopped in front of the hospital. The looks on their faces as they went about their hectic days said it all. They suddenly realized that they were not alone, that God was everywhere. Smiles came across all their faces.

Now the tempo picked up, and the sound was electrifying. The music and the chorus were in perfect sync. There must have been about fifty people singing their hearts out for the Lord. Nana was in her glory. When she looked up, she saw Grace's face peeking around the corner. Grace saw all the people who had been lying in their beds looking very sickly just a few moments ago. It seemed like a metamorphosis. They all had their color back. They looked amazingly strong, and you wouldn't know they were the same people. Grace looked at Nana, and Nathan ran over and held on to Nana's hand. Libby switched positions with Nathan so he could hold his mother's hand. Then it came, a voice above all voices. It was Grace, singing and crying her eyes out. There it was, the old Grace who could sing like nobody else. Her voice sounded like that of an angel of the Lord. She was head and shoulders above everyone else. Even though there were fifty people singing as loud as they could, it seemed as if all you could hear was Grace.

With all the noise, the doctor on the floor came running into the unit. He thought there was some kind of commotion. When he got there, he was surprised to see the same patients he had seen earlier in the morning. He hardly recognized them. It looked like they had been brought back from the living dead. Hope can do that to you. He asked the head nurse, "What happened? Did they break into the medication room?"

"No...they broke into God's medication room."

"Wow, if we could only bottle that."

The head nurse looked back him and said, "You can. And what's even better than that is it's totally free. There's not even a co-pay."

28

It was eight on Monday morning at the Pine Street Inn. Sam was still helping out, dispersing the items that Mr. Donlan had donated, when one of the staff people called out, "Sam, you have a phone call." Sam didn't even acknowledge it because it had not resonated with him. He hadn't gotten a phone call in months. "Sam Garret, you have a phone call on the residents' line." Sam looked up and couldn't understand who would be calling him. Nobody even knew he was there.

When he picked up the phone and said hello, Mr. Donlan was at the other end. "Good morning, Sam, this is Ed Donlan."

"Oh, hi...hi, Mr. Donlan. How are you?"

"I'm doing great, and you?"

"Oh, well, we're all doing great here today, thanks to your generosity."

"Thank you. Listen, Sam, I have one of my drivers in the area. I'm wondering if you have time to meet me this morning? I have something to discuss with you."

"With me? Ahh...ahh, yeah, yeah, sure, Mr. Donlan."

"Please call me Ed, OK? I'm working at home today, so my driver will pick you up at nine thirty. Will that be OK?"

When they hung up, Sam went upstairs to shower, shave, and put on his best clothes, wondering what Mr. Donlan wanted to discuss. It was nine thirty exactly when the driver pulled up in a white limousine. All the residents standing outside thought it was some politician pulling up for a photo shoot to help his public relations. The driver got out, standing there in a black tuxedo and a chauffeur's hat. "I'm here to pick up Mr. Sam Garret."

Sam looked at everyone, feeling a little embarrassed. "I'm Mr. Garret."

"Very well, sir, let me get the door for you." All the residents stared at Sam as he got in. As they drove off, he waved to them. They hesitated and then waved back.

On the Mass Pike heading west out of the city, Sam felt a little sense of self-worth, something that he hadn't felt in very long time. After about forty-five minutes, they took the exit to Weston, which he knew was a very rich town with very exclusive, multimillion-dollar homes. As they drove down winding roads lined with pine trees and beautiful, landscaped homes, Sam enjoyed seeing the exquisitely designed yards with their trees, shrubs, and flower beds, as well as waterfalls pouring into fishponds. The driver made a sharp left turn heading up a steep hill. The road seemed to go nowhere, but then without notice, a spectacular home appeared before them. It was white brick, with two huge, marble pillars in front of the door. There were several round balconies on the second floor, all with bronze railings. There were many sculptures in the front yard. All the homes he had seen up to this point now seemed miniature compared to this one.

The driver pulled up to the front of the house, walked around the car, and opened the door for Sam. A maid answered the door, looked directly at Sam, and said, "Please come in. Mr. Donlan is expecting you." All of a sudden, Sam froze. His nerves were starting to get to him. He couldn't imagine why Mr. Donlan would want to see him. While he was homeless, he had lost all of his self-confidence. He felt less than everyone else, almost to the point that he felt he didn't deserve any respect due to his current situation. The maid said, "Please, Mr. Garret, follow me."

As they walked, he couldn't help staring at the beautiful, circular stairway with all its custom woodwork as he passed by it. He couldn't get over the ceilings—they must have been twenty feet high, and they had huge chandeliers that lit the hallway exquisitely. He knew they must have been custom made. Every room had antique furniture that looked like it was from the nineteenth century. When they got to the other side of the house (which seemed to take forever), they stood in front of a room that had two oak doors that looked ten feet high. The maid knocked. "Mr. Donlan, I have Mr. Garret here to see you."

"OK, send him in." When she opened the door, Sam was amazed at the office. Again, it was beautifully decorated to the hilt. These were things he had only seen in the movies. Mr. Donlan was on the phone but signaled to Sam with his hand: *Come on, sit down.* When he hung up, he said, "Sam, thanks for seeing me on such short notice."

Sam thought, *Why is he thanking me? This is like a dream vacation, getting out of the homeless shelter for one day.* "Well, thanks, Mr. Donlan—"

"Sam, please, call me Ed."

"Oh, yes, Ed. I'm sorry."

"Sam, first, I need to apologize to you for the way I treated you that day at Castle Island. I should have apologized the other day at the shelter, but it was so busy that I wanted to do it face-to-face."

"That's OK, Ed. Apology accepted."

"Good. Now that that is out of the way...I need your help."

"You need help from me?" Sam asked. "What could I possibly help you with?"

"Well, I noticed how well organized you were the other day, helping me distribute the donations at the shelter. I saw how you interacted with people. I think you would be a perfect man for the job."

"What job is that, sir?"

"Sam, I want to start up a charity organization, the Ed Donlan Foundation. I would like you to be in charge of it and run the whole operation."

"Wow, I would love to run such a charity in your name."

"No, Sam, it's not my name. It's my great-grandfather's name. You see, all these years, I thought that I was the one who had started this empire. However, that day when I saw you over on the island, there was that little girl there you were talking to. When I reached down to help her up, something happened to me—I saw my ancestors and what they went through. Well, I realized that I would never have had the opportunity to be as successful as I am without their sacrifices. Here I am, taking all the credit for building this huge business of mine, walking around like some pompous ass and thinking that I had everything to do with it—and not knowing that I had nothing to do with it. It was all their hard work, blood, sweat, and tears that allowed me this fortunate opportunity. I'm not in the best health right now, and I'm winding down my career. Therefore, I would like nothing more than to give back to the community and others. So I would like to formally offer you this full-time job. It comes with a generous salary and all the benefits. So how about it, are you interested?"

"Wow, jeez, sir, I don't know what to say."

Ed said, "How about yes?"

"Yes, yes, sir! I would love to accept the offer."

"Great," said Ed. "Then it's a done deal."

"Thank you, sir, thank you very much."

"I would like to show you one more thing, if you will. Follow me."

As they left Ed's office, Sam noticed a family photo hanging on the wall. "Oh, is this your family, sir?"

"Yes, yes. That's my wife, Olivia. She should be home shortly."

"And is this your son?"

"Yes, that's Edward, Edward Junior. But I'm afraid he doesn't like to be called 'Junior' anymore." Sam felt awkward, feeling some regret from Mr. Donlan. "We haven't talked in almost ten years. He's married and has seven-year-old twin girls, who I've never even met."

"I'm sorry, sir, I shouldn't have asked."

"That's OK. All I ever wanted was the best for him. I hoped that someday he'd work for me and take over my business. But he never had any interest in doing so. He's a free spirit, traveling and mountain climbing all over the world. I patiently—or not so patiently—waited for him to outgrow it. We had some awful arguments over it, which tore his mother apart. So finally, he moved away. Now he works as a nurse in a hospice home for the terminally ill. Funny, I could buy him all the nursing homes he wanted, but I know he would have refused. He would rather be just another worker than an owner. Maybe he had the right idea after all...I'm sure his life is very simple and stress free. Anyway, let's go outside."

As they walked through the sunroom and entered the backyard, Sam was blown away. There must have been five acres of perfectly manicured lawn, and flowers like you've never seen before. Then, there it was: a massive, three-thousand-square-foot house. Ed said, "Sam, this is the guesthouse, and I would like you to stay here."

"My gosh, sir. I can't believe it."

"And over there is your new company van that you can use for the foundation. I will set up a small staff in my office downtown for you to handle the logistics of what you need. Oh, yes, one more thing—my yacht. Well, it is now property of the foundation. You will have to find a crew that can operate it, but not just any crew. I want you to go to the veterans' homeless shelter. I'm sure you can find people there who have some nautical training from when they were in the military. After all, those men and women put their lives on the line for the people of this great country. I figured you could use the boat to take out inner-city schoolchildren, the elderly, the homeless, or whomever else you might need it for. Just as long as you take me out occasionally."

Sam couldn't believe this was the same man he had met on the island. Mr. Donlan seemed to have a new awareness for other people today. Whatever had happened between him and Libby on the island had changed him from a taker to a giver. That only happens when you have God in your life. And Libby was responsible for that.

29

Jim picked up Nathan, Maria, and Libby from school. When Libby got in the car, she could hardly speak straight, saying "Dad, Dad, Dad!"

"What, Libby, what?"

"I got an A-plus on my Virginia report!"

"Great honey, great!" This was not surprising to Jim. Libby was a perfectionist in every way. Everything she ever did, she did 110 percent. Libby told Jim about all the information she had collected on Virginia: what the population was, what they manufactured, their tourist attractions, who the governor was, and all the other statistics. Jim was trying to look at her report without driving off the road.

Then Nathan, who was holding a picture of the solar system that he had drawn, pointed out all the planets to Jim. "This is Mars, this is Neptune, Uranus, Jupiter, the Moon..."

"The moon!" Imitating Jackie Gleason as Ralph Kramden, he said, "How would you like a one-way trip to the moon, Alice?" He thought the kids would all get a kick out of it, but they all looked at him as if he had ten heads. "I guess I'm talking to the wrong generation."

Libby looked at Jim and said, "Whatever."

Jim asked Maria, "What did you do your report on?"

"I did it on my family history."

"Wow, that's great. How did you get all your information?"

"I went to ancestry dot com."

Jim, who was computer illiterate, said, "Huh?"

Libby said, "Forget it, Maria, you're talking to the wrong generation." Everybody laughed.

After Jim dropped off Nathan and they all greeted Nana, Maria's house was next on the stop. When they got to Maria's house, there were three brand-new cars in the driveway. One was a Mercedes-Benz, and the other two were BMWs—one red and one blue.

"Wow," said Jim. He especially loved the Mercedes-Benz.

Maria shrugged, unfazed. "Thanks for the ride, Mr. Davis."

They all said their good-byes, and Maria walked by her family's cars without even looking at them. Her parents, brother, and sister came running out and excitedly asked, "What do you think?" She just stood there looking confused.

Her dad asked, "Maria, what's wrong? Don't you like them?"

Maria looked at her dad and said, "I don't understand. All those cars have only two seats in them. How are we all supposed to go somewhere together?" Everybody looked at each other. None of them had even thought of that. They had all thought only about what each of them would look like in their own cars.

After a moment of silence, Carlos said, "Maria, we can take turns."

Maria said, "I might only be ten years old, but I do know that families are supposed to do things together and not have to take turns being with each other." Maria seemed to be the only one who realized that hitting the lottery could break the family up rather than bring them closer.

Jim and Libby were driving home when Billy Joel came on the radio, singing to a woman named Virginia. Libby jumped up and turned it up. She said, "Dad, listen! That's so weird. Every time we talk about Virginia, the name shows up again somehow."

Jim said, "Yeah, maybe God's trying to tell us something."

"Like me taking a week off of school, and you taking me to Virginia Beach for a vacation?"

"I don't think that's what He's trying to tell us."

"Are you sure, Dad?"

"I'm pretty sure God doesn't want you to miss school."

Libby just snapped her fingers and said, "Shucks, I tried."

30

When Jim got home, he went to the mailbox. The first piece of mail was from the bank he had his mortgage with. He was expecting a letter soon. This was the first time he had ever been late with his payment. He wasn't like a lot of people who are in trouble today because they overfinanced what they couldn't afford. When Jim and Sue bought their house, they were both working and made good money. Then Sue passed away, cutting their income in half. Now he was collecting unemployment, and that cut the income in half again. Now he was getting only 25 percent of what they had been making when they got the home loan.

Feeling the financial pressure, he started to project the worst possible scenario for Libby and him. Then he thought about his sponsor, George, and decided to call him. Dialing felt awkward, but he knew that he was supposed to do it. "Hey, George, it's me, Jim. I just thought I'd give you a call."

"Everything going good?"

"Oh, yeah, everything is great."

"You don't sound so great...something bothering you?"

Jim was astounded that George had picked up on it. He didn't know what to say at first. "Why do you think something's wrong?"

George said, "I can hear it in your voice."

"Well, there is something. I got a late notice from the bank on my mortgage. But I've known them for a long time, and I'm not concerned."

"Well, if you have a good relationship with them, why don't you go down there tomorrow and talk to them? Maybe you can work something out."

This had never occurred to Jim. In his mind, he was already getting foreclosed on. He said, "Yeah, I'm friendly with the loan officer there. We're on a first-name basis."

"Good, that sounds like you're living in the solution and not the problem. Just ask God for help before your meeting."

"Great, thanks for the advice."

Jim still sounded unsure of himself, and George sensed it. "Hey, why don't you come down to the prison tonight, and we can talk about what to say and do at your meeting tomorrow. There's a shortage right now, and a lot of people are on vacation. So I have to cover for someone tonight."

"I don't know if I can get a sitter for Libby on such short notice."

"Bring her with you. It's perfectly safe. I'm working in the watchtower, four-to-eleven shift."

Jim said, "All right, I'll stop and get some dinner for us. How about Chinese food?"

"Oh, my doctor will kill me. But in consideration for him, it will just be between you and me."

"Always thinking of others, aren't you?"

"Hey, that's the kind of guy I am." Both chuckled, and George said, "When you go to the front desk, just have me paged and I'll come down, all right?"

"Great," Jim said, "we'll see you then."

Jim yelled up to Libby, "Libby! Shut the TV off and do your homework right away!"

Libby looked out her bedroom door and said, "Why, what did I do wrong?"

"Nothing, honey, we're going to pick up some Chinese food and go see my friend George at work."

Libby yelled, "Chinese food! Yee-hah! Where are we going to see him?"

Jim said, "He works down South Bay prison."

"Prison...am I going to be put in a jail cell?"

"Only if you don't finish your homework."

"OK, OK, OK!" Libby said as she ducked back into her room.

31

Jim called in an order at their favorite Chinese restaurant. Libby always grabbed a handful of mints from the counter, even though Jim would say, "Libby, only take one."

The hostess, a beautiful Chinese woman, would always tell Libby, "That's OK, take as many as you like." Then Libby would look at Jim with this grin that said, *I'm not at home, and you can't tell me what to do, ha-ha.*

The food wasn't ready yet, so they sat down to wait at the front. A young couple came in with a carriage holding the cutest little baby girl you ever saw. There was something about this child that made you stop what you were doing and take notice. Looking at her, it was impossible to keep a smile off your face. She reminded Jim of Libby when she was that age, probably about a year old. He realized just how fast kids can grow up. He said to himself that he would never let life get so busy that he didn't have time for Libby. He swore right then and there that she would always come first, no matter what.

While the dad was ordering the family's food, the baby girl had her eyes fixed on a Chinese piggy bank. Her hands stretched out from her carriage as she smiled away and made noises to let her mother know what she wanted. Her mom noticed immediately and grabbed the piggy bank off the counter. She handed it to the child, who got so excited that her legs kicked frantically.

Her mom kept tight hold of the bank and said, "Be careful, honey, we don't want to drop it." When the baby girl had her hands on it, she looked right at Jim, smiling from ear to ear. She seemed to be saying, *Look at my piggy bank!*

Jim thought, *It must be great to be a baby, when all you want out of life is to hold on to a Chinese piggy bank.* It saddened him to know that she would outgrow that Jim asked her mom, "What's her name?"

"Amelia."

"Wow," Jim said. It seemed like the perfect name for her. He envisioned Amelia growing up a strong and independent woman. The love that poured out from her mother and father was so comforting to Jim. He thought, *This kid will have a real shot at life.*

Jim and Libby were soon handed their order and said good-bye to Amelia. She turned and gave them a big smile. Jim said again, "She's beautiful."

"Thank you," said the parents. "Have a good night."

When the Davises got to the front desk at South Bay, Jim said they were there to see Captain O'Leary, and the officer paged him while they took a seat. Jim looked around at all the families waiting to see relatives who were locked up—little children waiting to see their fathers, and the wives sitting there, all with a very sad look to them. Jim thought of how lucky he was that he never got caught all those times he used to drink and drive. It could have been him. It was only by pure chance that it wasn't.

Then he heard George. "Jim, come on in." Jim and Libby walked over to greet him. George said, "Well, this must be Libby. I've heard so much about you. Jim, you're right, she is the most beautiful girl in the world." George reached out his hand and Libby put her hand out, turning a little red.

Libby said, "Hi, nice to meet you."

"What, are you going to feed all the inmates?"

Jim had two big bags of Chinese food. "Well, I didn't know what you like, so I got a little bit of everything."

George said, "Well, variety is the spice of life, isn't it?" George directed them in through the door and said, "Follow me."

They walked by several administrative offices. Libby kept looking around for prisoners, but obviously, George wouldn't have her anywhere near the jail cells. The stairway felt like it was five or six stories high. When they got to the top, they walked down a long hallway and took a right turn down another, where George rang a bell at a door. A little window opened. A guard looked through it and said, "Just a second, Captain." The door opened, and the room had all glass windows that looked out on the prison yard. All the prisoners were out there. You could see all the different factions, and each one seemed to have a piece of the yard for itself. Some of the men were playing basketball, many were lifting weights, and some were walking around the perimeter. But none of them were interacting with each other. They all had their own territories.

Jim and George opened up the bags of food. George said to the guard, "Joe, there's plenty of food here if you'd like some."

Jim said, "Sure, help yourself to whatever you want."

Joe said, "Thanks, but I'll wait for you guys to finish. I have to stay at the window."

George said, "I'll take over as soon as I'm done."

"Thanks, Cap'."

It seemed like George got a lot of respect from his fellow workers.

Libby, who loved Chinese food, would normally have torn open the bags by now, but instead she was captivated with staring out the window. When she walked over to the glass, Jim sensed that Libby was getting very strong feelings from the inmates. She reached out and put both hands on the glass. One by one, the prisoners started to take notice of her. At first, they all were laughing and joking, putting on a facade. However, something started to happen. All the laughter stopped. It got real quiet. The whole yard was looking up at her. It was as if she was giving them a message.

Then it started: that beautiful music. Joe, the guard, was hitting buttons on the intercom feverishly, not knowing what was happening. He knew it wasn't the intercom, though. This music sounded like it was coming from outside. Joe said, "Captain, you gotta see this." George and Jim walked over to the window, and the song began.

There is a redeemer,
Jesus, God's own son,
Precious lamb of God, messiah,
Holy one.
Jesus, my redeemer,
Name above all names,
Precious lamb of God, messiah,
For all your sins He was slain.

All the inmates slowly walked toward the watchtower, looking up at Libby.

They didn't just hear the words. They could feel God saying, "I am your redeemer. Repent in your ways and follow me, and I will set you free. You still may be locked up the rest of your lives, but you will be free." The song continued.

Thank you, my Father,
For giving us Your son,
And leaving Your spirit
Until your work is done.

The men were now all below the window, looking up at Libby. They were no longer separated. They were all on their knees and had tears in their eyes. For the first time, they were very remorseful for the choices they had made in their lives.

When I stand in glory,
I will see His face.
Then I'll serve my king forever
In that holy place.
There is a redeemer,
Jesus, God's own son,
Precious lamb of God, messiah,
Holy one.

When the song stopped, George looked out the window and saw all the inmates holding each other with their heads bowed. George said, "I've been here for almost twenty years, and I never saw anything like this before." He looked at Jim for an explanation.

Jim just put his hands up and said, "I guess I should have told you about Libby."

"Do you think?" George replied.

32

The next morning, Jim went down to his bank to speak to Ted Wright, his loan officer. Jim had known Ted since he'd got his first used-car loan at the age of seventeen for a souped-up '69 Chevy Chevelle SS. Ted had also written all of his other car and truck loans as well as the mortgage. When the secretary told Jim she would take him to Ted's office, Jim said, "No, that's not necessary, I know where it is."

Ted greeted Jim as "Mr. Davis."

"Mr. Davis?" said Jim. "That's my father's name."

"Oh, yeah...come on in, Jim, and have a seat. What can I do for you today?"

Jim immediately felt a little awkward. Ted seemed very formal and a little standoffish. Usually, they went on about the Red Sox or some other community event for a bit. But not now. Jim said, "Ted, you obviously know about Susan's death."

"Yes, I'm real sorry about that."

"I know you are, and I appreciate the condolence card you and your wife sent. The problem I'm having is, with Susan's passing and just getting laid off, I'm having some financial problems. I know I have a lot of equity in the house, and I figured if I could refinance, I could cut my mortgage down by thirty percent. I've never missed any mortgage payment. This month was the first time."

When Ted spoke, it was like he was reading off a policy sheet or a manual, not speaking to a good customer. "The problem I see here is, since the new regulations have come out, the guidelines for loans have tightened up. In addition, I'm afraid that your income from unemployment wouldn't meet those requirements—"

Jim interrupted. "Well, that's why I need to refinance, so I can meet those requirements."

"I know, but the bank has to look at your current situation, and that's what they will make their decision on."

Jim said, "So let me get this straight. The bank believes I can afford what I'm paying now, but I'm a risk for not paying back a mortgage of thirty percent less." He just got a blank stare back from Ted. "You know what I think, Ted? I think if I didn't have the equity that I have, you people would be a lot more willing to help. The fact that I do means your interest is protected. If there was no equity in the house and I walked away from the property, knowing you guys would take a hit, you would be serving me coffee and muffins right now trying to make a deal. And while I'm on the subject, let me ask you this. After you guys lost all kinds of money on greedy bad loans, the federal government bails you out with all this TARP money. Two months later, my credit card that I've always had with you decides to raise my interest rate and cut my credit limit. Why's that, Ted? Can you tell me?"

"In the agreement, the bank reserves the right to raise your interest rate anytime without reason."

Jim said, "Really. So if you and I have an agreement—let's say I'm going to remodel your bathroom for ten thousand dollars. And halfway through the job, I come to you and say, Gee, I'm sorry, Ted, but I made some very bad investments last year and I'm losing a ton of money, so I'm going to have to charge you twenty thousand dollars to help recoup my losses. Would you pay it Huh? Ted, would you? No, you wouldn't. And it's a shame that the banking industry guys are the only ones who can do that. I may be a simple carpenter with not much education. But I'll tell you this. When I get home at night, I can look my daughter in the eye and proudly tell her everything I did today. And when I put my head on my pillow, I can sleep with a clear conscience. Can you tell your family everything you did at work every day, and all the ulterior motives you had? And how well do you sleep, Ted? Can you tell me that, Mr. Wright? What does it feel like to get up every day, trying to figure out how to get over on the people who are paying your salary?"

Ted was baffled. There was nothing in their policy manual on how to answer these questions. Jim stood up and walked out.

33

On the way home, the more Jim thought about what had just happened, the angrier he got. As he passed by Nana and Nathan's house, he decided to stop by to tell Nana he would pick up Libby and Nathan after school and to check in and see how Grace was doing. He knew that the kids would get him out of his bad mood. He enjoyed their innocence.

He rang the doorbell but got no answer, so he rang it again. Still no answer. He knocked on the door, which opened a little. He yelled, "Nana, you home? Nana!" Then he heard a faint voice coming from the living room. He walked in and saw Nana sitting in the recliner. She was sweating and very pale. "Nana, are you all right?"

"Yeah, Jim, just the heat is getting to me, I guess." It was warm out, but she had her air conditioner on, and the room was comfortable. He walked over and touched Nana's forehead, and she was extremely hot.

"Jeez, Nana, you're burning up. Let me get you some water."

"Thanks, Jim. There's some in the fridge; make sure you get some for yourself." Even in her discomfort, she still thought of others.

As Jim got the ice water out of the fridge and set it on the counter, he noticed two empty bottles of prescription medicine. Nana had written "heart medicine" on them in big letters because her vision wasn't so good. He looked at the date; they were supposed to have been refilled six weeks ago. Jim grabbed them and the water and went back to the living room. He said, "I just found your heart medicine bottles, and you've been out of them for six weeks. Is that why you're feeling like this?"

"Well, I haven't been able to afford them since they made those cuts on my Medicare benefits. All my money has to go toward housing, food, utilities, and anything Nathan needs, like his after-school programs and such. Sometimes I can't pay for them all. Nathan comes first, and everything else comes second. I just want that boy to have the best life he can have."

Jim was heartbroken. All the worries he was going through seemed minimal. "Nana, I'm going to call an ambulance and have them take you to the emergency room. Then I'm going to the pharmacy and have your prescriptions filled. I'll pick up the kids at school and meet you at the hospital to take you home. I just want them to check you out."

"Oh no, Jim, I don't want to be a bother."

"Nana, it's not open for discussion, you're going."

"All right, but it's no big deal."

"We'll let the doctors decide that."

When the paramedics got there, they took her vital signs. Nana sat up and said, "You boys look tired, can I make you some lunch?" Jim just raised his eyebrows and shook his head. If it were up to Nana, she would have had them sit down and put their feet up while she waited on them.

After the ambulance left, Jim sat down on the sofa. He thought back to when he was a kid in the neighborhood. He remembered always treating the elderly with great respect. Jim was sort of a history buff and had read up on many different cultures. He knew that in most of the world, the elderly were the most respected people in the community. He thought, *How did we lose that?* It seemed they were now the forgotten society, kicked to the curb and forgotten. *When we were kids, the most interesting people you could talk to were the older people. They had the best stories. But now, with this entire Internet, kids can push a button and find out anything they want to know. We've lost that human connection of communicating with each other. You can read about World War II or the Great Depression. But it will never be the same as someone telling you about what they went through. Jesus said we were to take care of the least of these: the elderly, the children, the sick, the poor, and the brokenhearted.* He thought that the current state of things was a terrible injustice. He decided to do something about it.

He picked up his cell phone and called Congressman Stephen Lynch—not his office; he had Stevie's own number. They had known each other since childhood. Stevie was not a career politician. He was a kid from the neighborhood who had become a Massachusetts state representative and eventually was elected as United States Congressman replacing the late Joe Moakley. He knew the people of Southie, and they all knew him. He was in a well-respected position and made decisions that were good for the people of his district, though maybe sometimes not so good for his party. He was not a man to push around, and all the other politicians knew it.

"Stevie, sorry to bother you. This is Jimmy Davis. I'm over here at Nana's house and just called an ambulance for her." Jim explained the whole situation; Stevie also knew Nana. There was silence on the phone for a second. "Stevie, you still there?"

"Yeah, Jim, I'm still here." He said, "Yeah, you know, we've been trying to fix this for a long time, but when you hear about it affecting someone you know, well, it just hits home a little harder.

Jim, I'm going back to my office tomorrow. I'll look at my schedule and prioritize some things and get working on this right away. You tell Nana to hang in there. We're going to fix this."

"Thanks, Stevie. Like always, I knew I could count on you."

"All right, Jim, I'll talk to you real soon."

Jim got the kids at school and went right to the hospital, expecting Nana to be hooked up to IVs and monitors. She was with three nurses, just chatting and exchanging photos of their families. When Nana turned around and saw Jim, she said, "See? I told you it was no big deal." Everybody got a chuckle out of it.

34

After Jim dropped off Nana and Nathan, he realized that it was later than he'd thought. He had planned to make dinner but decided it would be easier to go out. He asked Libby where she would like to go, already knowing the answer: the Sidewalk Café. It was the local sandwich and coffee shop on East Fourth Street. Jim said, "You got it."

On the way over, Libby said, "Dad, I feel sorry for older people."

"Why's that?"

"They just seem lonely."

"So why don't you do something about it?"

"Like what?"

Jim said, "I don't know, maybe start a group or something."

Libby jumped up and said, "Like...Kids for Seniors!"

Jim said, "Wow, you came up with that pretty quick."

"We can go down to the parks on the weekends to spend time with them. I'm going to call Nathan, Maria, and some other kids from school to help me get started. We can have some T-shirts made up that say 'Kids for Seniors,' and we'll have our names on the front of them so they know who we are when we talk to them."

Jim looked at her and said, "Something tells me that you've been thinking about this for a while."

"Yeah, I have. But today, I think it's time to do something."

Jim just looked at her, as proud as a father could be, and said, "Libby, did I ever tell you how proud you make me?"

"Oh, Dad, don't get all mushy on me."

As soon as he got out of the truck, he heard, "Jimbo, over here." It was Charlie and Lucky, sitting at a table outside. Jim thought how great it was to see them. It had been a while. There were also a dozen other people Jim knew from the neighborhood. After he greeted his friends, he told them he would be right back after they ordered.

Inside, Jim ordered a pizza, and Libby ordered her usual—a turkey club sandwich with no bacon, lettuce, tomato, or mayonnaise, and a fruit smoothie. This always got Jim's goat. He would ask why she ordered a turkey club with no bacon, lettuce, tomato or mayonnaise and not just a turkey sandwich with nothing on it. "It would be cheaper," he would say. Libby would just start laughing. It was just a routine that Libby liked to use to get a rise out of Jim.

Outside with Charlie and Lucky, Jim told them what had happened at the bank and how discouraged he was getting. Charlie said, "You just have to ask God for help."

Jim said, "I ask him all the time to help me find a job, and he hasn't answered me yet."

Charlie said, "God always answers prayers, but sometimes the answer might be no, or not right now." It wasn't what Jim needed to hear, but he didn't comment.

Changing the subject, Jim asked how Big Ben was doing. Charlie and Lucky laughed, and Jim asked, "What's so funny?"

"Ben's got a new nickname on the job."

"What's that?"

Charlie said they were calling him Lazarus because he had come back from the dead with his near-fatal accident. This got

Jim out of his bad mood, and he almost choked on his food. "Even better than that," said Charlie, "me, Ben, and a couple of other guys have a Bible study at lunchtime. I think there are more guys that are curious. But for right now, they're just watching us, and they're starting to see some change in these guys. So we'll see what happens."

Meanwhile, Libby was enjoying her meal. She moved her chair out a little because she was squished between all the guys, but when she stood up and moved backward, she bumped the table behind her and knocked over a drink onto a woman's lap. Jim caught this out of the corner of his eye. He immediately jumped up and picked up the knocked-over glass, saying, "Oh, I'm so sorry, let me run in and get some napkins."

Then Libby said, "I'm sorry, I didn't see you there."

The woman said in a beautiful European accent, "That's OK, honey, it was only water. It won't stain."

Jim came running out and wiped up the mess, apologizing again. The woman again said it was no problem at all. When Jim heard her accent, he stopped wiping the table and was mesmerized for a minute. The woman had blond hair and the brightest blue eyes he had ever seen. She had high cheekbones, and her face looked like it should be on a ballerina doll.

Some water ran down the table, and Libby yelled, "Dad!"

Jim snapped out of it and finished wiping. He asked, "Could I buy you another drink?"

"No thanks, I've already showered." This got an immediate chuckle out of Libby, but Jim didn't get the joke right away because he couldn't take his eyes off of the woman.

Jim asked where she was from. The woman said she was from Lithuania, which Jim had heard of; South Boston had once had a big Lithuanian community, and some of his school friends had been Lithuanian. Jim pulled up a chair next to her and said, "My daughter is usually very careful."

"Oh, this is your daughter?"

"Yeah, this is Libby, and my name is Jim."

The woman said, "Nice to meet you, Libby, and you too, Jim. My name is Virginia." Jim and Libby looked right at each other and busted out laughing. Virginia said in her beautiful accent, "What's so funny?" They explained all about Libby's favorite name, her school report, and all the signs they had been seeing about Virginia.

Jim said, "This must be fate," as he continued to chuckle.

Virginia said, "I am a firm believer in fate."

Jim stopped laughing and said very seriously, "So am I."

Virginia said, "Would you guys like to join me?"

Jim jumped up, almost knocking over the whole table, and said yes. As he turned to get their food, he stumbled again. Libby and Virginia looked at each other and chuckled at Jim. He was acting like a schoolboy on his first date.

Back at their table, he got the thumbs-up from Charlie and Lucky, but he gave them a look that said, *Knock it off*. When Charlie and Lucky left the café after Jim introduced everyone, they walked behind Virginia, and Charlie held his hand up at his ear, signaling that Jim should call her. Jim pretended not to see them.

Virginia said to Libby, "You're so beautiful. Where do get your looks from, your mom or dad?" Jim said it was her mom, and he explained what had happened to her. Virginia said, "Oh, I'm so sorry for asking." She looked at Libby and said, "Your mom must have very pretty." Libby responded with a smile.

Virginia then told them how she had also been married, but that her husband had passed away a few years earlier from cancer.

This seemed to create an immediate connection between them. They felt somehow that they had known each other for years. They talked for almost two hours, until it got dark. Libby kept looking at her dad with facial expressions that said, *Ask her out on a date.* Jim was so nervous that he was almost sweating. Virginia picked up on it and decided to help Jim out. She said very casually, "Well, I really enjoyed sitting and talking with you and Libby. Maybe we can all get together sometime and do something."

Libby screeched out, "Yeah!" She covered her mouth, feeling embarrassed.

Jim said nervously, "Yeah, that would be great. Do you want to give me your number?"

Virginia said, "Sure." Jim pulled out a pen from his top pocket. As she gave him her number, he wrote it on a wet napkin, tearing it apart. Again there was a chuckle from Libby and Virginia at Jim's expense. Virginia said, "I've got an idea, why don't we just exchange numbers on our cell phones; it'll be less messy."

Virginia looked at Libby, and Libby shook her head back and forth and put both hands up in the air. Virginia responded by doing the same thing. Each of them tried not to laugh out loud.

Jim said, "Yeah, yeah," like it was his idea. As they stood up, Jim said, "I'll call you real soon."

Virginia said, "I hope so."

After Virginia got in her car and left, Libby said, "Dad, you're such a goofball."

Jim, acting all proud and a little cocky, waved the paper in Libby's face. "Yeah, but I have her number."

35

S am stopped by the veterans' homeless shelter as Mr. Donlan had suggested. He was there to see if there were any vets who had some nautical experience. When he asked around, it seemed like everyone suggested a man named Tommy Walsh. He was told he could find him up on the third floor. The director said that he was in room twenty-three. "He's probably there; he almost never comes out."

Sam knocked at room twenty-three. A voice said, "Come in." When Sam opened the door, he was taken aback by what he saw. Tommy Walsh was sitting on the edge of his bed. Both his legs had been amputated from the knees down. He and his crew had been hit by an improvised explosive device in their Humvee. Tommy was the only one who survived.

Sam said, "Hi, Tom?"

"Yeah, that's me."

"My name is Sam Garret. I'm the director of the Edward Donlan Foundation." Tom looked at him like, *Am I supposed to know what the Ed Donlan Foundation is?* "Tom, the foundation is brand new. One of our programs is taking people out on cruises on a fifty-three-foot Hatteras that we own."

"What kind of people?" Tommy asked.

"Well, inner-city kids, the elderly, the mentally handicapped, the homeless, anyone who would not normally have the opportunity to experience sailing."

Tom said, "Thanks, but no thanks. I've had my fill of being on the water. It was once my career."

"I know, that's what I'm here to talk to you about. Everyone in this place said you're the most experienced guy in here in regard to operating a yacht." Tom looked up at Sam, somewhat confused. "Tom, I need a captain, and I need a crew to run the yacht. I'm only the foundation's director. I wouldn't know an anchor if it fell on my foot. Would you like the job? It comes with a generous salary and full benefits."

Tom looked at him and said in a soft voice, "Jeez, I don't know what to say."

"Listen, Tom, I know you're the man for the job. I just need you to say yes and put together a crew from the guys in the shelter, and I need them ASAP. So what do you say?"

"OK, I'll do it."

"Great. Here's my card. Call me in a few days, and I'll pick you up and show you the yacht."

"Thanks, Sam."

"No, thank you. I'll call Mr. Donlan and let him know we're making progress. He'll be happy to hear it. I'll talk to you soon."

When Sam left, Tommy just sat there trying to process everything. He had had a career in the military and was a platoon leader when it was all taken away from him. He had been in the shelter for a year, feeling helpless. For the first time in a long time, he felt a sense of responsibility. He immediately started to interview guys in the shelter for the new crew.

Sam got in his car and called Ed Donlan to give him the news. Sam expected Ed to be jubilant, but Ed sounded very down on the phone. Sam asked, "Ed, is everything OK?"

Ed said, "Well, not really. I just got a call from my doctor and got some bad news."

"What's wrong?"

Ed said, "I have advanced kidney failure and am in need of a transplant." Sam was stunned. He didn't know what to say. Ed said, "They're going to immediately start testing my family and relatives for a possible donor. I guess all those years of smoking Cuban cigars and entertaining clients with steaks and drinks has caught up to me." Sam tried to reassure him that everything would work out. Ed said, "Yeah, I'm sure it will."

36

A few days later when Maria came home from school, the first thing she noticed was that her favorite picture wasn't on the wall—the one that said, "It's not a house that makes a home, it's the family that makes a home." She looked around and saw her mom and dad packing boxes. "What's going on? Why are you putting all our things in boxes?"

Her parents turned around and said, "Honey, we're buying a new house. We'll be moving soon!"

Maria got very upset and said, "But I don't want to move!"

Her mother said, "Maria, it's a bigger house in a better neighborhood, and you'll have your own room."

"I don't want my own room or a bigger house!" She was hysterical now. She turned and ran out the front door.

A few seconds later, there was a loud screeching in the street. Her parents ran outside. Their worst fear had come true: Maria was lying in the middle of the road, motionless. She had been struck by a passing car. A woman got out of the car, yelling, "My God, I never saw her coming!"

Maria was unresponsive and was bleeding from her head. Her parents were crying out, "Call an ambulance, call an ambulance!" The ambulance was there in a matter of moments and took her to the Boston Medical Center emergency room.

When her family got there, they had to wait what seemed liked days to hear from the doctor. Finally, after several hours, the doctor came out to the waiting room and told her family that Maria had slipped into a coma and they had had to do emergency surgery to relieve the pressure on her brain due to the swelling. Her parents were devastated. It would now be a waiting game to see if she would come out of her coma and how much brain damage she would suffer from the injury. All they could do was wait and pray, which they started to do right away. It was now in God's hands. Now all the money, the cars, and the new house were meaningless to them. All they wanted was to have Maria back, healthy and alive.

It didn't take long for the news to spread. Jim got a call from Tommy next door about what had happened. After that, he called Maria's dad right away and offered to come to the hospital for support. Carlos said, "We appreciate it, Jim, but she's in intensive care right now. We're just waiting here until something changes. We'll let you know as soon as anything does. We just ask that you pray for her."

Jim said, "That goes without saying."

"Thanks, Jim."

Now Jim had to break the news to Libby. He sat there for several minutes thinking of how to do it. But soon Libby walked in. "Dad, what's wrong?"

He couldn't hide it from her. Jim said, "Libby, I have some bad news. Maria has been in a bad accident. She was hit by a car and is in Boston Medical Center right now."

"What happened?"

"She was hit by a car when she ran across the street in front of her home."

"Can we go see her?"

"No, she's in a coma. Her family is there, and they'll let us know as soon as anything changes." Libby was speechless, which didn't happen that often. She had lost her mother, and now she might lose her best friend. The idea was incomprehensible. "Libby, we can't do anything about it except pray for her. But I think it would be a good idea if you, Nathan, and your friends started on your program for seniors. It would help Maria when she gets out. She might not be that strong when she recovers, but she'll want to help. When you get your first group of kids together, I'll take you down to the print shop to get some T-shirts made up. We'll make sure we have one with Maria's name on it, so when she wakes up, you'll be there to give it to her."

Libby's spirits lifted a little, and now she didn't so feel helpless anymore. This was all going to help Maria. In addition, it gave Libby more motivation to start the program. "OK, Dad, I'm going to call the other kids right now and get started." She came over and gave Jim a big hug and kiss, and said, "Thanks, Dad. You always know how to make me feel better."

37

A few weeks later, Jim drove by Ted Wright's house. He was surprised to see a for-sale sign in the front yard. Jim was still very angry with the loan officer, but his curiosity took over. Mr. Wright was out front, packing two cars in his driveway. Jim pulled up and asked, "What's going on, Ted, did you get another promotion?" This was a little shot at him.

Ted turned to him very seriously and said, "No, Jim. I got fired a few weeks ago. It seemed they needed a scapegoat for all those bad mortgages I sent up to corporate for approval. And in the same week, my wife got laid off from her job." Even though Jim was upset with Ted, he felt immediate compassion for him. Ted said, "Jim, I thought about what you said. And I had to take a look at my life. I decided I was going to make a career change soon. But not this soon. I have three kids in college, and their student loans are all leveraged against the house. I can't pull them out of school, so I'll have to sell the house and hopefully pay off the loans and get a small apartment." He added, "Jim, I'm sorry for the way I treated you the other day."

Now Jim felt bad and said, "That's OK, Ted. You were only doing what they told you to do."

Ted said, "Can I ask you a question?"

"Sure," Jim said.

"Jim, how are you coping with your situation? It must be devastating knowing you might lose your house."

After a brief pause, Jim said, "Well, I guess I just put things in perspective."

"What do you mean?"

"Well, Ted, you have a beautiful wife and three kids who I know love you dearly, and you're all together. As you know, I lost Susan a while back. Ted, she was my soul mate. I think God only gives you a soul mate once in your lifetime, or maybe twice if you're lucky. I know that your wife is your soul mate. Ted, I lost my soul mate, and if I had to lose my house, sell everything I own, live in a shelter, and work until I'm a hundred to get Susan back with Libby and me, I would do it a million times over. So, to me, none of the material things, which come and go in this world, compare to the love of your family. So that's how I prioritize it. I still have Libby, and I'm going to be OK as long as we're together. Trust in God. He has a plan for all of us—not to harm us but to help us, and to give us hope and a future. Go home and tell your family how much they mean to you, and all your other problems will seem minimal. And Ted, don't worry, He'll help both of us get through this."

"Thanks, Jim, thank you very much."

As Jim pulled away, he was surprised at the peace he had started to feel despite his own storms he'd been going through. George had told him he had to turn his life and will over to God every day, and that then, and only then, would he begin to feel peace beyond all understanding. George had told him that things in his life might not get better, but that he would get better. He was now starting to understand what that meant. It was impossible to do without the full trust of Jesus Christ in his life.

38

Ed Donlan was in his office at home when his wife Olivia came in. She had a very nervous look on her face. She was holding the phone, grasping it with both hands. She said, "Ed, the doctor is on the line, and he would like to talk to you." This was the phone call they had been waiting for. It was the testing result for any possible kidney donors on Ed's behalf.

He took the phone and said in a positive voice, "Hey, Doc, how you doing? Do you have good news for me?"

The doctor answered, "I'm afraid I don't, Ed. None of your relatives was a match."

The look on Ed's face said it all. He looked like he had just been kicked in the stomach. "Oh, that's too bad. What do we do from here?" Olivia's head just dropped down, and she put her hands over her mouth.

The doctor said, "Well, we would go on a national donors list and hope that it proceeds as fast as possible." Ed knew the reality: the average wait for a kidney transplant was five years, and he knew he didn't have that kind of time. He tried not to look disturbed because he didn't want to upset Olivia. The doctor said, "We could still test any volunteers that come forward in the future."

Ed said, "Sure, hopefully that will be a possibility." He thanked the doctor for calling and said he would talk to him soon.

Olivia was visibly upset. She came over to Ed, and putting both hands on his cheeks, she said, "Edward, we have one more option...we have to call Ed Junior and ask him to be tested."

"Olivia, we haven't talked in ten years. I just can't call him up and ask him for something like this."

"Ed, sometimes God allows affliction for a reason. Maybe this is a chance for you and Junior to put the past behind you."

"I don't know, Olivia. I pushed him away from me a long time ago by trying to force him to follow in my footsteps, and I know how much he resented me for that."

Olivia said, "That was a very long time ago, and I'm sure he has thought long and hard about his part in all of this. Ed, we have to call him. Besides, I haven't talked to the twins since last week."

Ed sat silent for a moment and then said, "All right, you can call him, but don't get your hopes up. I'm not sure how he'll react after all this time."

Olivia said, "Let me worry about that." She kissed him on the forehead and left the room with the phone. Ed just sat there thinking about their past relationship and how he wished he hadn't been so hard on Junior.

Ed waited in his office for what seemed like hours, but it was only about fifteen minutes later when Olivia walked back in. Ed said nervously, "Well, how is he?"

"Why don't you ask him yourself? He wants to talk to you." Ed sat there frozen and expressionless while Olivia handed him the phone. He held it up to his ear and paused for a moment. Olivia waved at him to say something.

Ed said, "Ah, hello?"

Junior said, "Hi, Dad."

"How are you doing?"

Junior said, "Well, I think the question is, how are *you* doing?"

Ed said, "Well, I'm in a bit of a pickle."

"Yeah, Mom told me what's going on. Dad, I'm here for you, and I'll do whatever it takes. I'll call the doctor in the morning and start the procedure to see if I am a match."

"Thanks, thanks, Junior." Ed's voice started to crack. This man never showed any emotion. He said, "Junior, I'm real sorry that all this time has passed and that it took something like this to happen for us to talk."

Junior cut him off and said, "Dad, we both played a role in this. We have plenty of time later to make amends to each other, but right now, we're going to concentrate on getting you better. I'm going to get tested as soon as possible. But Mom wanted to see Judy and the twins, so we're coming up in a few weeks."

Ed let out a sigh and said, "Junior, I would really love that."

"OK, Dad. I'll talk to you real soon."

"Bye, Junior. And take care."

Ed hung up the phone. He looked at Olivia, and she had tears of joy in her eyes. That's all Ed had to see, and he began to weep. Olivia came running over and hugged him as they cried together.

39

Jim and Libby were watching TV when the phone rang. Charlie asked, "Jimbo, how's the job search going?"

Jim replied, "Still the same, nobody's hiring. They're all cutting back."

"Well, hang in there, something will break," Charlie said. "I'm calling to let you know that we're having a prayer service for Maria on Sunday at the New Covenant Church. Pastor Paul is dedicating the whole service to Maria and her family. They'll all be there."

Jim said, "We wouldn't miss it for the world. Libby and I have called Maria's family every day, but there is still no change."

Charlie said, "Well, I've seen the power of prayer work many times in my life when I put all my trust in the Lord."

"That's true," Jim replied.

"I'm also going to invite Pastor Pete to come and join us."

"Are Big Ben and Lucky going?"

"Yeah, I already talked to them."

"OK," Jim replied, "then we'll see you Sunday."

"OK, talk to you later."

Jim hung up the phone and gave Libby the details. Libby said, "Great, I'll bring Maria's T-shirt and show it to her parents. Nathan and I have already signed up twenty-two kids for the Kids for Seniors program. But we all agreed we wouldn't start it until Maria's back home with us."

Jim said, "Twenty-two? I'll have to buy more T-shirts."

"That was the deal, and a deal's a deal." Jim just shook his head, thinking that he should have thought twice about that promise before he'd made it. He knew that once Libby made up her mind, nothing was going to stop her. She got that trait from her mom.

A few minutes later as Jim flipped through TV channels, out of the corner of his eye, he caught Libby standing next to him. When he turned to look at her, she had a piece of paper in her hand. She said, "Dad, you've had Virginia's number for almost a week, and you said you were going to call her. It's time."

Jim just sighed and said, "I'll call her later."

"Dad, can I ask you a question?" Jim thought, *Oh boy, here it comes.* Libby didn't wait for Jim's answer. She said, "If I told you I was going to clean my room on Saturday, but when Saturday morning came, I said, 'I'll clean it later,' what would you say?"

Jim slid further and further down the sofa. He said, "All right, all right. Give me the number. But you have to leave the room. I don't want you to be listening with your big ears." Libby just smiled and handed him the piece of paper. Her smile said it all. Like, *You know I'm right.* Jim didn't say anything; he just rolled his eyes. Libby walked away giggling.

Jim dialed the number, expecting and hoping he wouldn't get an answer. Then Virginia picked up the phone and in her European accent said hello. Jim jumped up from the couch. Virginia again said hello. Jim said, "Ahh, hi, Virginia. This is Jim Davis. I met you last week at the Sidewalk Café."

"Oh, yeah, how are you doing? And how's Libby?" This caught him off guard. He was surprised she remembered Libby's name.

Jim said, "Oh, she's doing fine. In fact, she's the one who made me call you." As soon as he said that, he realized what it sounded like. He added nervously, "No, no, no, that's not what I meant to say."

Virginia laughed and said, "I know, don't worry about it. I'm glad she reminded you."

Jim said, "Well, I'm calling to, well, I was wondering if you wouldn't mind—or if you do mind, that's OK—"

Again Virginia cut him off before he embarrassed himself any further. "Are you asking me if I would like to go out sometime?"

Jim, relieved, sighed and said, "Yeah, yeah."

Virginia said, "Of course I would." She continued, "You know, it's weird. I just got off the phone with a friend of mine. She called to ask me if I would like three tickets to the Red Sox game Saturday night. She and her husband were going to take their five-year-old son, but he came down with strep throat. It's funny—I thought of you and Libby, but I didn't have your number. Isn't that really strange that you called as soon as I hung up with her? Libby must have a sixth sense or something."

Jim replied, "Oh, she does, but that's a whole other story I'll tell you about later."

"Well," Virginia said, "do you guys want to go?"

Jim said, "I know I would, and I don't even have to ask Libby. She's a huge Sox fan."

"Great," Virginia replied. "Do you have a pen and paper? I'll give you my address."

Jim said, "Sure." He stood up to reach for a pen and dropped the phone on the glass coffee table. He yelled out, "Shoot!" Grabbing and fumbling with the phone, he said, "I'm sorry, I'm sorry, I just dropped the phone."

Virginia giggled and said, "OK, let me give you my address before you hurt yourself!" Jim laughed with embarrassment.

They exchanged information and a time for Libby and Jim to pick her up. After they hung up, Jim slapped himself on the forehead and said out loud, "You knucklehead!" He paused for a minute, wondering why he was so nervous around Virginia. He figured it must be because she was so special.

Jim went up to knock on Libby's door to tell her about the game Saturday night. Libby said exuberantly, "Yeah! I want to go to the Red Sox game!" She caught herself and said, "Was there something you wanted to ask me?"

"How did you know that Virginia had tickets to the Sox game?"

"I didn't...I just had a feeling that you should call her right away."

"Do you have any more feelings today that I should know about?"

"No, that was it."

Jim leaned down, kissed her on the cheek, and said, "Good. Because I can only take one premonition a day."

40

Sam pulled up to the homeless shelter to pick up Tommy Walsh and his new crew for the yacht. The guys were there waiting for him. Tommy introduced the crew to Sam, and they all got into the car to go down to Marina Bay where the yacht was docked. To be honest, Sam was quite nervous. After all, they were going to take out a two-million-dollar yacht with a brand-new crew that had never worked together before.

They piled out all their bags at the marina parking lot and got Tommy into his wheelchair. He was still waiting for his new prosthetic legs. As they were all walking down the boardwalk, people stared at Tommy, and Sam overheard someone say, "Oh, isn't that nice, they're going to take the man in the wheelchair on a boat ride."

Sam got upset, turned around, and said, "No, he's taking *us* on a boat ride!" Tommy and the crew looked at Sam and started to laugh. They respected Sam for speaking up for Tommy. A few people overheard the conversation and gathered to witness the boarding. By the time they got to the yacht, there were thirty or forty people leaning over the rail.

At the boat, they all stood there for a moment in disbelief at how massive it was. It was a beautiful summer day, and the man at the marina had just taken off the canvas cover so they could enjoy the sun. The only problem was that it was still very windy.

It could make maneuvering any boat difficult, never mind a fifty-three-foot yacht. As they boarded, Sam was just astonished at it. Down below decks, it looked like the Ritz-Carlton.

The crew brought Tommy aboard and over to the captain's chair and lifted him up. When he got into it, he just looked at the instrument panel, touching the steering wheel very gently.

As the man from Marina Bay got off the yacht, he asked, "Are you sure you guys really want to go out today?"

Sam asked, "Why not?"

"Well, the marine forecast said that the winds are fifteen to twenty knots coming from the northeast, and the outgoing tide is extra strong today because of the full moon. That's why all the boats haven't gone out." This was all Greek to Sam.

Sam and the crew looked at Tommy for an answer. Tommy said in a calm and collected voice, "We're going out. Get ready, boys." And he started the blower to remove any fuel gases from the engine compartment.

The crew all got to their respective positions, which Tommy had already assigned them. He went over everybody's responsibilities and then started both engines. By now, just about everyone in the marina was looking at them, anticipating a disaster. When the engines were warmed up, Tommy barked out orders to his crew. All of them responded, "Aye, aye, Captain!" Sam was quite nervous but also quite impressed with the crew. After all the ropes were untied, Tommy started to pull away from the dock very slowly. People were now standing on their boats to watch along with the people on the boardwalk. When Tommy pulled the yacht out of the slip, he calculated where he had to turn; there was absolutely no room for error. The current was starting to move the yacht sideways, so Tommy increased the power to offset it. He had two Volvo Penta engines; he put one in reverse and the other forward, compensating ever so slightly for the winds.

The yacht started to turn as if on a dime. It was an amazing sight to see this man control the yacht in these conditions. It turned a full ninety degrees without moving forward or backward. When it was facing the exit off the canal, Tommy put both engines in the forward position, and the yacht moved ahead. Sam was so impressed by Tommy and the crew and how they never seemed to panic, how disciplined they were. It was obvious to everyone that all these guys had been in the military just by the way they handled themselves.

When the yacht started to pull away from the marina, there was loud cheering and applause. The crew looked back and saw everyone cheering for them. They waved back in appreciation. Sam looked at Tommy. He seemed to be three inches taller in the chair. The looks on all their faces showed nothing but pride, something these guys hadn't felt in a long time. Even though they were all disciplined military men, they were also human beings who needed self-worth and a sense of purpose, just like the rest of us.

41

Grace was sitting in the hospital lobby with her bags packed. She had completed her twenty-eight-day rehab. She was more scared now than when she had gone in. Now she had to face the real world and had to deal with life on life's terms. Grace was feeling overwhelmed, like the people you see on TV coming out after a tornado has just struck, destroying everything around them. They don't even know where to begin picking up the pieces.

The rehab unit had made an appointment for Grace to start seeing a counselor that afternoon. It was eleven o'clock, and Jim had offered to pick up Nathan and Nana and go to the hospital to get Grace. Grace was moving back home with them. Libby was staying with a friend for a few hours while Jim picked them up.

Libby had asked her dad if they could go shopping for clothes for the Sox game that night with Virginia. Jim had said, "Libby, it's only a baseball game. We don't have to get dressed up."

Libby had said, "Yeah, Dad, but it's the first time we're going out with her, and you have to have new clothes."

"You're growing up to be a woman too soon. Can't you stay the way you are for another thirty or forty years?"

"Sorry, Dad, a girl's gotta do what a girl's gotta do."

Jim had just sighed and said, "Oh boy."

When they got to the entrance of the lobby and saw Grace, they were amazed. She looked like a whole new person. She had put some weight back on, and color had come back to her face. More important, when she saw Nathan and Nana, she wore a huge smile, something they hadn't seen on her in years. All the nurses hugged her and wished her good luck. While she was in there, she had felt real unconditional love from the other patients and the staff. It wasn't the false love she had experienced in the streets.

On the ride home, Grace kept looking out the window and saying how much the neighborhood had changed. She would ask when this store or that store had opened. But these stores had been there for several years. When you're out there running on the streets, you're in your own world and don't notice anything around you.

When they got out of the car, Grace just stared and stared at Nana's rose plants. Nana asked, "What's wrong, Grace?"

Grace seemed to come out of a trance and said, "Oh, nothing, Mom. It's just those roses are so beautiful." You knew she was coming out of her numbness to the world when she started to notice the small things in life that we sometimes don't appreciate. Jim and Libby helped to bring Grace's bags in, and Nana thanked them. Then they went down to the South Bay Center to do some shopping.

Libby was more concerned about making her dad look good than about herself. She had plenty of clothes already. As Libby walked right over to the men's department, it was Jim's chance to get Libby going. He said, "I really don't need anything. I still have my rust corduroy pants and jacket."

Libby said, "Dad, I told you to throw those out!"

Jim said, "Why? They're perfectly good. They just need a few stitches here and there. In fact, I think I have a pair of white bell-bottoms I used to wear at the school dances." Libby stopped in her tracks and gave Jim a look like, *You're not serious.* Jim figured he had teased her enough, so he backed off. He said, "OK, pick out what you want me to wear." A smile of relief came across Libby's face. She picked out some new Levi's jeans, new sneakers, and a new sweatshirt. Walking back to the truck, Jim couldn't resist. He said, "I still think the bell-bottoms would've been fine." Libby, not giving him the satisfaction, just kept walking as if she never heard him.

42

It was about four o'clock, and Libby had already changed her outfit three times. She wanted to look perfect for the ball game. Jim was just lying in the recliner and, as usual, flipping through the channels. Libby asked, "Dad, when are you going to get ready?"

Jim said, "Well, we don't have to leave until six o'clock, so I guess five minutes of six would be OK." He knew this would get Libby riled up.

"Dad, you're supposed to make a good first impression. You didn't do such a good job when you met her."

Jim jumped up, grabbing Libby and tickling her. "Wow, I think you just gave me a shot. Why are you so nervous?"

"I'm not nervous. I just want you and Virginia to like each other." Libby lowered her eyes to the floor and shuffled her right foot back and forth. Jim felt like a train had just hit him. The smile left his face, and he realized what was going on. His heart sank. He realized that Libby wasn't nervous for herself, but that she wanted everything to go perfectly between Virginia and him. She loved her dad so much and just wanted him to be happy.

Jim leaned down in front of Libby, and in the most caring, compassionate voice, he said, "Libby, look at me." Libby looked up at Jim. He said, "I promise you—I know this is just as important to you as it is for me—I'll try to make this a fantastic night for all of us." Libby didn't say a word; her smile said it all. She grabbed him with both arms around his neck and gave him a huge hug.

When Jim started to get ready for the night, a real fear came over him. What was he going to talk to Virginia about? After all, the past few months hadn't been a great time in his life. Newly sober, laid off from work, and the bank threatening to foreclose on his home...he started to feel inadequate. What would she see in him? Then he remembered George.

He dialed the phone, and George picked up right away. "Hey, Jim, what's up?" It made Jim feel good to know that George had programmed his number into his phone.

Jim said, "Ahh, well, I haven't talked to you in a while, but I'm going on a date tonight with a woman I met at the Sidewalk Café last week."

"That's great, where are you taking her?"

"Well, to be honest with you, she's taking Libby and me to the Sox game tonight."

"Oh, it's going to be perfect weather for a ball game."

"Yeah, I know."

George asked, "What's up, you nervous?"

Jim replied, "It's not that I'm nervous, but I was just thinking: what do I have to offer her with this stuff that's been going on with me the last few months?"

"Oh, you're worried that she's not going to be interested in you because of your temporary problems. Well, if you're honest with her and she's not interested in you for those reasons, then it will be good to find that out on your first date. If those things don't matter to her and she's interested in you for who you are rather than what your problems are, then it's a slam dunk. You see, if you're honest with her, it will show her your character.

If she doesn't like you for your situation, then it will show her character."

"How do you see things so clearly, George?"

"Well, I'm not emotionally involved."

"What do you mean?"

George said, "Let's pretend Libby was in your shoes. What advice would you give her?"

"Wow, you're right."

"See, Jim, our problem is that when we make decisions based on our emotions, most of the time, they are wrong. But if you can remove yourself emotionally and look at the problem logically, then most times, you'll make the right choice."

Jim said, "You know, now that I think about it, most of my bad decisions were based on my emotions."

"That's why you need friends in your life to bounce things off of, because they are emotionally removed from the problem," George said. "OK, that'll be seventy-five dollars. I'll send you the bill."

"Well, I'll be glad to pay it; it was worth it."

George laughed and said, "OK, pal, have a great time, and remember, just be yourself."

"All right. Thanks, George, I appreciate it."

"No problem. Call me tomorrow and let me know how it went, and tell Libby I said hello."

43

As soon as Jim hung up, the doorbell rang. Before he could answer it, Lucky and Charlie walked in. Jim said, "Hey, what are you guys doing?"

"Oh, we just stopped by to see how you were doing." Jim hadn't told them anything about his date with Virginia, so he figured they didn't know anything. Charlie said, with a smirk on his face (and Lucky snickering in the background), "What's up, any plans for tonight?"

Jim knew instantly that they knew about the date. "How did you guys know? Only Libby and I knew about it." Then it struck him. Charlie had called last night when Jim was in the shower and Libby had taken the message, but Jim had forgotten to call back. Jim turned to the stairway and yelled up to Libby, "Libby, come down here right now. I want to talk to you." Jim was a little upset.

When Libby came to the top of the stairway, Jim, Charlie, and Lucky just stared at her. Jim's anger left him immediately. Libby looked like a poster girl for the Red Sox. She had her Red Sox baseball cap on, a Red Sox T-shirt that had Big Papi's name and number on it, and a baseball glove in her hand. Jim just melted. He said, "Honey, you look adorable."

"Thanks, Dad, but you need to get ready or we'll be late!"

Jim knew Charlie and Lucky were there just to tease him like a couple of high school boys. Jim said, "OK, you guys, you had your fun, now get out of here."

As Jim pushed them toward the door, Charlie yelled out, "Libby, your dad gets a little clumsy around Virginia. Make sure he stays at least three feet away from her." Libby started laughing.

Jim said, "OK, very funny. Now let's get going."

Lucky said, "Oh yeah, Libby, make sure he has a pen and paper so he doesn't have to use a wet napkin." This cracked Libby up even more.

Jim said, "OK, you kids got your kicks, now go home and watch your cartoons," as he pushed them out. They held each other up while they laughed so hard.

The door closed in Charlie's face as he yelled, "Good night, Romeo." By this time, they were almost on the ground.

44

Jim and Libby were driving down East Fourth Street. Virginia was only over on East Fifth, so they didn't have much time for conversation. She was already standing outside her apartment. Jim was relieved that he didn't have to go up and ring the bell or anything. Virginia looked stunning in her white-and-pink sneakers, Calvin Klein jeans, and a white sweatshirt, and her hair was in a ponytail.

Libby yelled out, "Hi, Virginia!"

As Virginia got into the truck, she said, "Well, look at you! We don't have to guess whose team you're rooting for. You look adorable."

Libby said, "You, too."

Jim said as they drove off, "Well, I tell you, I have to be the luckiest guy in the world."

Virginia and Libby looked at each other and then at Jim. Both of them asked, "Why?"

Jim said, "It's a beautiful Saturday night, and I'm going to the Sox game—with the two best-looking girls in Southie."

They both said, "Ohh." They couldn't believe they had taken the bait. Jim started giggling, and Virginia said, "Oh, your dad's a real charmer, huh?"

Jim responded, "The old man's still got it."

The girls let out a much louder "Ohh!"

As they walked down Yawkey Way, Virginia was amazed at all the vendors outside selling Red Sox memorabilia. The atmosphere was electric. It was a weekend game, and there were a lot of kids there. Virginia took out the tickets and gave them to Jim. She said, "Here, why don't you take them? I don't know which way to go." Jim nodded.

They walked through the gate, but Jim hadn't looked at the tickets to see where the seats were. When they got into Fenway Park, he said, "OK, let's see where we're going." Jim knew the seating pretty well after going there all his life, but he didn't recognize these seat numbers since he'd mostly sat up in the bleachers. He asked an usher about them, and the guy said, "Wow, nice seats. They're directly behind the Red Sox dugout, first row."

Jim yelled, "Yes!" He had never been that close to the dugout in all those years.

As they made their way down the stands, Jim almost ran. Libby said, "Dad, slow down!"

"Oh, I'm sorry." The stairway was jam-packed. Jim grabbed Libby's hand so she wouldn't get pushed aside. When they got down to the seats, Jim looked back to make sure that Virginia wasn't too far behind and saw Libby holding on to Virginia's hand. They were smiling at each other. They reminded him of Libby and her mother, who had always held hands everywhere they went. Jim looked at Virginia, and she looked back at Jim. He saw so much compassion on her face. You could tell she knew exactly how Libby was feeling and how she missed holding on to her mother's hand. When Jim and Virginia locked eyes, Jim knew that she would be a big part of their lives. Sometimes, very rarely, you meet someone, and something inside tells you right away. They smiled and seemed to know what each of them was thinking.

When they sat down, Jim and Libby couldn't believe how close they were to the players. They could have reached out and touched them. Virginia asked, "These good seats?" Libby and Jim looked at each other and couldn't believe it. "What's wrong? Are these seats OK?"

They said, "They're awesome!"

Virginia said, "Oh, I'm so glad. I was worried."

Libby reached out and grabbed Virginia's hand and said, "Are you kidding? These are the best seats my dad and I ever had." Virginia seemed relieved. Jim again looked at Virginia and thought, *Wow, she really is something special.*

45

The crowd roared as the Red Sox players took the field. Libby recognized Big Papi as soon as he came out of the dugout. She couldn't believe it. He was standing right there in front of them. As he was putting on his hat and glove, Libby yelled out, "Big Papi, over here!" Everyone looked at her. He turned and looked right at Libby. When she saw that, she immediately stood up and turned her back to show him her Red Sox Big Papi T-shirt. Everyone sitting nearby clapped and cheered. When she turned around, Big Papi smiled and gave Libby two thumbs up, and it was only one minute into the game. This was an experience that she would never forget. The people around her gave Libby high fives and patted her on the back. Jim and Virginia looked at each other, mouthing *Wow!* They leaned down and hugged her.

Once the crowd settled down and the game went on, Jim felt nervous again. He remembered what George had told him, so he looked over at Virginia and asked, "So, what do you do for work?"

Virginia said, "I'm a nurse."

Jim said, "Wow, that's a good career. Were you a nurse in Lithuania?"

"No, I actually was a director of physical education at a university."

"Really? That sounds like a real important job."

Virginia said, "Well, it was, but the salary wasn't very good." She explained about the economic conditions in her country at that time and that she'd always had to work two or three jobs just to get by. She said that she came to America for a better quality of life. When she first arrived, she made more money being a nanny and cleaning houses than she had working at her college. So she became a nurse's aide and then went through nursing school. She explained how difficult it had been because English was her third language. Her first was Lithuanian, but her second was Russian, because when she was growing up, her country had been under Russian dominion since 1945. Russia had finally pulled completely out of Lithuania by 1993, and it was a free country again, but now it was struggling to establish capitalism. Jim found this fascinating. He was reminded of how lucky we are to have our freedom and the opportunity that America offers.

Libby said she had to go to the bathroom, and Jim started to stand up to take her, but Virginia put her hand on Jim's shoulder and said she would go. Libby smiled at Jim as if to say, *I was hoping she would take me.* Jim told them to be careful and remember where their seats were. He watched them hold hands all the way up the stairs, and they were talking and giggling the whole time. Jim got a little nervous again. He knew Virginia would ask him questions when she got back. He just kept thinking about what George had told him.

When they came back and sat down, Jim asked if anyone wanted refreshments, hoping to buy a little time. They both said no thanks. Jim looked out at the ball field. Then it happened. Virginia said, "OK, I told you what I do. Now it's your turn."

Jim said, "Oh," trying to sound like he hadn't expected the question. He said, "I'm in construction. I'm a carpenter."

"Really? I had a funny feeling that you were."

"Why's that?"

"Well, you just look like someone who would have that type of talent." Jim didn't know what to say except thanks. "Do you work for yourself or for someone else?"

"Well, I'm a union carpenter. So I go wherever the union hall sends me."

"Oh. What are you working on right now?"

"Well, the job I was on slowed down, so it had to lay me off. It's been like that the last few years because of the economy." Jim was trying not to make eye contact and was feeling a little embarrassed.

Virginia said, "Wow, then you're lucky."

Jim looked up at her and asked, "What do you mean?"

"Well, it only means that God doesn't want you there. He has bigger and better plans in mind for you somewhere else. Have you ever heard Jeremiah twenty-nine eleven? God says, 'For I know the plans I have for you. They are plans for good and not for disaster and to give you hope and a future.'"

Jim sat there with his mouth open. He had never met anyone like Virginia. She could see the good in everything. Jim said, "Wow, I never looked at it that way."

"If you don't look at every situation with complete faith, then you are looking at it with fear. I would rather look at them all with faith; it's more peaceful."

Jim was silent. He had never heard wisdom like this. He had only known her for a week but felt so comfortable. He felt he could tell her anything without being judged. Virginia looked at Libby and said, "I should have gone to the bathroom when you did. I have to go now. Libby, do you want to go with me?"

Before Virginia finished her question, Libby jumped up and said, "Sure."

Jim said, "Libby, you just went fifteen minutes ago."

Libby said, "Dad, it's a girl thing," as she rolled her eyes.

Virginia said, "Guys, they never get it."

Jim, putting both hands in the air, said, "Well, excuse me!" as Libby and Virginia went up the stairs laughing.

46

The game was now in the ninth inning, and the Sox were down six to three. They were last at bat. The first two batters had singled, so there were men on first and second. The next two batters struck out. The next batter had walked. So here they were, down six to three, with two outs in the ninth. Next up? Who else: Big Papi.

The crowd went crazy. After three balls and two strikes, it was a full count. The pitch came in. It was a fastball. Papi swung, and the ball was fouled off. The next pitch—another foul ball. It was nerve-racking. The next ball was another high fastball. Papi swung at it like he knew it would be coming special delivery, just for him. Even though the crowd was so loud, you could still hear the crack of the bat. The ball took off to right center field, climbing like a 747 taking off from Logan Airport. The crowd was on its feet in suspense.

A huge gust of wind came gushing in from center field, taking velocity off the ball. It all seemed to be in slow motion. The ball decelerated quickly, and the right fielder ran to the wall. The ball came down, and the player jumped up with both feet on the wall and glove in the air, leaning over the fence. The crowd went silent, and the fielder came back off the wall with his glove closed. The noise went from deafening to complete silence in anticipation of the result of the play. He rolled on his back when he hit the ground, his glove opened up, and everyone saw that there was no ball in it. The crowd went mad. The noise was off the Richter scale. It was a game-winning, walk-off home run. Papi circled the bases, and the rest of the team greeted him at home plate, jumping up and down. Everyone cheered for him to come back out. When he did, the crowd went nuts. He took his hat off to the crowd. Then he turned and looked at Libby, yelling out, "What's your name, kid?"

Jim yelled, "Libby! Her name is Libby." Papi had come prepared with a marker in his hand. He signed his hat to Libby, jumped up on the dugout and handed the hat to Jim. Jim leaned out and grabbed it. Big Papi waved to Libby, and Libby waved back. Giving the hat to Libby, Jim asked, "What does it say?" He was more excited than anyone.

Libby looked down and read, "To Libby, my good luck charm."

Jim said, "Wow, I've been coming to Fenway since I was a kid, and I never got an autograph. What's up with that?"

Libby looked at Jim and said, "When you got it, you got it!"

47

So far, it had been a perfect night. Libby and Virginia talked all the way home, and Jim could hardly get a word in. When they reached the bridge at the Black Falcon pier in South Boston, the traffic was backed up. Black Falcon pier is where people board the big ocean liner ships for cruises to the Caribbean islands. Jim thought there might have been an accident until he noticed all the construction crews working on the bridge. They usually did this type of work during the evenings because traffic was lighter.

Jim looked to see if he recognized anyone from the union hall. Then Libby jumped up and said, "Dad, look—a black Mercedes."

Jim turned and said, "Wow, that's a beauty."

Virginia said to Libby, "What, does your dad like European cars?"

"Only Mercedes-Benzes, and especially black ones." Jim had a fascination with them and had always dreamed of having one.

The police officer waved them on, and Jim followed the Mercedes as they went over the pier, never taking his eyes off of it. There was a ten-wheel dump truck in front of the Mercedes carrying a load of gravel. Jim thought, *Man, if that were my car, I wouldn't be driving so close to that truck.* Jim reached down for a second to turn the radio on. All of a sudden, he heard a huge bang. He looked up and saw that the tailgate on the truck had malfunctioned. Gravel was pouring out. The Mercedes swerved off to the right to avoid being buried by the stone, but the driver panicked and hit the gas instead of the brake. The car crashed through the temporary guardrail. Although it all seemed to happen in slow motion, before Jim knew it, the car was airborne and nose-diving toward the water.

Jim stopped his truck and slammed it into park. He yelled to Virginia to watch Libby and jumped out. When he reached the edge of the bridge, he saw the car in the water as buoyancy brought it back up to the surface. It rotated so that Jim could look directly into the eyes of the driver. It was a woman of about forty. There was sheer terror in her face, and she looked right at Jim as if to say, *Please help us.* Then Jim noticed the passenger. It was a teenage girl, about sixteen years old. He couldn't hear them, but both were screaming, with the most god-awful, desperate looks on their faces.

Jim did not have to think. He pulled his shoes off, looked down, and jumped feet first into the water. When he came back up, the car was completely submerged. All he saw were huge bubbles coming up. Jim swam down, following the bubbles, until he reached the car. By now, Virginia and Libby were out of the truck. When they saw Jim jump in, they ran down toward the embankment. Now there were about ten construction workers looking over the side of the bridge, yelling, "Call nine-one-one!" The rest of the workers ran down the embankment behind Virginia and Libby, who were both calling to Jim.

When Jim reached the car, it was sitting about twenty feet below the surface. He could see that it was quickly filling up with water. Jim hit the driver's side window as hard as he could, but he couldn't do it at full power underwater. Jim knew he had to get something to break the glass. Fortunately, because of all the construction lights on the bridge, he was able to see quite well.

He dove down to the bottom, frantically searching in the mud for a rock. When he found a large stone, he came up and swung at the window as hard as he could several times.

Jim was exhausted and running out of breath. He was torn between trying to save the women and saving himself. Then a sense of calmness rapidly came over his body. He remembered hearing about people who stop struggling and become full of peace just before they drown. Then everything went black. He saw a beautiful vision of him walking Libby down the aisle on her wedding day. Everyone was there: Virginia, Charlie, Lucky, Pastor Pete, Big Ben, George, Tommy, Maria and her family, Grace and Nathan, people from his congregation, and many, many more. He felt an overwhelming sense of pride. Then he heard the music. He saw Libby and him being called out for the father-daughter dance. He recognized the song immediately. It was Rod Stewart's "Forever Young." Everyone was cheering and taking pictures.

The vision disappeared. The calmness and peace left him, and a huge adrenaline flow hit him like a ton of bricks. He looked down at the round rock in his hand, and as clear as day, he remembered someone telling him that the best way to break a window underwater is to push on it with something sharp. The only thing he had on him was his set of keys. He didn't know why he had grabbed them when he left the truck. Maybe it was just a habit. Or maybe not. He reached down and grabbed them out of his pocket. He took the longest key he had, placed it against the window, and pushed with both hands as hard as he could.

Almost instantly, the glass exploded into a thousand pieces. The water rushed into the car like a waterfall. The woman grabbed her daughter and passed her to Jim and started to climb out herself. Jim didn't know if he had any more breath in him. He reached up and pulled his left arm up and down while holding the girl in his right arm. His legs were so heavy because his clothes were weighing him down, but still he kicked as hard as he could. Just when he thought he couldn't hold his breath any longer, he broke the surface, and both of them gasped for air. As he swam over to the embankment, a couple of construction workers swam out to meet him. When they tried to help him, he said, "No, help the woman." They said there was no woman. Jim looked back, assuming she was right behind him. He yelled to the workers, "Take the girl, I'm going back down."

Jim swam as fast as he could, knowing every second was crucial. When he reached the point where the car had gone in, he dove down, only to find that the woman had gotten tangled up in her seat belt. When Jim reached her, she was unconscious. He untangled the belt and pulled her out of the car. He pushed off of its hood, which helped him to catapult up. He was so tired that he knew he wouldn't have made it if he had had to swim all the way.

When they reached the surface, he swam toward shore, yelling, "She's not breathing!" Two other workers swam out and helped him onto shore. Someone yelled that the ambulance was on the way. Then the big construction workers who were standing over the woman, helpless as could be, were pushed aside and almost knocked over. It was Virginia. Jim yelled, "Virginia, you got to help her!"

Virginia immediately started CPR, pushing down the woman's chest and counting, "One, two, three, four, five." She held the woman's nose and gave her mouth-to-mouth resuscitation. The daughter was hysterical, calling to her mom to wake up. They could hear the ambulance siren in the background, but Virginia knew these were crucial moments. After the fourth try, the woman coughed up a huge amount of water and gasped for air.

Virginia immediately turned her on her side to help her breathe and then sat her up, holding her from behind.

Everyone broke out in cheers and applause. The daughter reached over and hugged her mom, with tears coming down her face. "Mom, I thought you were gone." Some workers put their coats around the women. When Jim knew everything was OK, he collapsed, lying flat on his back just trying to catch his breath. When he wiped his face, he noticed that both his hands were bleeding very badly. He must have cut them when the window exploded. The paramedics came running down the hill to attend to all of them.

After all were stable, the ambulance took them to the hospital. Jim told Libby to get the second key hidden in the truck and give it to Virginia. Libby knew just where it was because Jim had a habit of locking his keys in the truck. Virginia said they would meet him at the hospital.

48

At the hospital, Virginia and Libby had to wait in the lobby. Jim had so many pieces of shattered glass in his hands, and removing them was going to be painful. This gave Virginia and Libby time to talk. Libby said that this was the second bad thing that had happened to her in a month, and she explained about Maria and the next day's prayer service for her.

Virginia said, "That sounds like it's going to be beautiful."

Without hesitation, Libby said, "Can you come with us? Besides, Dad won't be able to drive with his hands all bandaged up."

"Then I guess I'll just have to go."

Libby said, "We like to sing, real loud."

Virginia said, "Well, I've been known to belt out a few songs myself." They both laughed.

Libby got serious. "I'm glad you were here tonight to save that woman's life."

Virginia said, "So am I, so am I."

After an hour or so, the female nurse came out to say they could see Jim. They jumped up and followed her to his room. Jim was sitting there with both hands all wrapped up. He asked the nurse when they would be able to leave, and she said he would just have to sign some papers. Virginia asked Jim, "How do you feel?"

"I'm OK, but I have a doctor's note."

"For what?"

"Well, it says that I can't do any cooking, cleaning, or laundry. I must have twenty-four-hour rest on the recliner, and Libby has to do everything for me. Even change the channels when I want." Libby and Virginia had been listening intently until he got to the TV clicker. Then, once again, they knew they were being had.

Virginia said, "We want to see the doctor's note."

Jim said, "Oh, I must have misplaced it."

"Yeah, yeah, yeah...we don't think so!"

The nurse came in and said, "We have the paperwork out here whenever you're ready, Mr. Davis."

Virginia asked, "Jim, can you wait a minute while I use the ladies' room?" Jim said sure, and the nurse directed her to the restroom.

When Libby and Jim were alone, he asked her, "Libby, remember that time at home, when you showed me what my future would be if I didn't change?"

Libby, looking down at the floor, said, "Yeah."

"Did you do the same thing to me when I was under the water?"

"I had to, Dad. You were drowning."

"Well, both times you did it, you were saving my life. This time, I enjoyed the experience much better." Libby smiled. Jim said, "I am so proud of you, and how God has chosen you to help people turn their lives around. You are a very special girl, and I am a very blessed man to have you as my daughter."

Libby got all shy and said, "Oh, Dad, I just want you to be really happy."

"Thanks, honey. I want the both of us to be happy, and I know we will."

49

When Virginia got back, they all headed for the nurses' station so Jim could fill out the paperwork. Jim asked the nurse how the mother and daughter were doing, and she said with a big smile that they were doing great. "In fact, the father is here, and they should be leaving soon."

Jim and Virginia said in tandem, "That's great!"

The nurse stopped, turned to them, and said, "It was remarkable what you people did tonight. Everyone in the hospital is talking about it. You guys are real heroes for doing what you did."

Virginia and Jim didn't say anything, but Libby wasn't going to let this opportunity slip by. She said, "That's right! My two heroes."

At the counter, the secretary asked how Jim would like to pay his portion of the emergency room visit. Jim just said, "You'll have to bill me. I think my checkbook is on the bottom of the Atlantic right now." Everyone chuckled, and the secretary said it wasn't a problem.

Then Jim heard a man's voice behind him. "Excuse me. Are you the people who helped my wife and daughter?"

Jim said, "Yes, yes we are. We hope they're all right."

"Well, they're still a bit shaken up, but the most important thing is, I get to take them home with me. I know that wouldn't have been possible if it wasn't for you two." He was getting emotional. He said, "I just couldn't imagine leaving here without them. I want to thank you guys for your incredible bravery." He looked at the secretary and said, "Excuse me, ma'am. I would like to take care of all the medical expenses they have incurred."

Jim said, "Oh, no, that's not necessary. My insurance will pay for it. At least for now. Hopefully, I'll get called back to work soon."

"What is it that you do?"

Jim said, "I'm a union carpenter."

The man asked, "Which union hall are you out of?"

Jim said, "Boston. But, unfortunately, there isn't too much going on right now."

The man said, "This is amazing. How long have you been in the trade?"

Jim looked puzzled. "Almost twenty years..."

The man said, "I'm sorry, I forgot to ask your name."

"Jim—Jim Davis—and this is my daughter, Libby, and our friend, Virginia."

"Very nice to meet all of you. Let me introduce myself. My name is William Parsons."

Jim's mouth almost hit the floor. "Are you William Parsons, owner of Parsons Development?" Parsons Development was in the beginning stages of a five-to-ten-year project down on the waterfront. They were going to build condos, a shopping mall, restaurants, and a new convention center. All the guys on Jim's job had been talking about it for the past two years. It would be like hitting the lottery to get on that project.

Mr. Parsons said, "Yes, yes I am. Jim, I think I have a perfect job for you."

"Wow, that would be great. I promise you, I won't let you down. I take a lot of pride in my work, and you'll get the best carpenter money can buy."

Mr. Parsons stopped Jim and said, "No, Jim, I don't think you understand." Jim thought, *Wow, I just embarrassed myself in front of one of the biggest developers in the country.* He figured the job must be something more minimal.

Mr. Parsons continued, "Jim, my office and I just met this afternoon in regard to this position. You see, we've had problems in the past between the supervisors in the field and the people who run the front office. What we decided to do was to hire an experienced man who has worked in the field and make him a liaison between the construction field and management."

"Wow," Jim replied. "That sounds like an incredible opportunity."

"Well, we hope it will work, so everyone can be on the same page and these projects come in on time and on budget. The job will pay one hundred and fifty thousand a year, with a company car, an expense account, and obviously, a full benefit package." Jim was speechless, almost in a state of shock. Then Mr. Parsons said, "Well, I realize you'll have to think it over."

Jim said, "No, no, sir, I'd be honored to have the position."

"Great. Welcome aboard Parsons Development. Here's my card. Call me in a few days to go over the logistics, and you can give the office all your information. The preconstruction meetings start next month. I hope that gives you enough time to heal your wounds, and if it doesn't, we'll accommodate you until you're ready."

"Thank you, thank you for everything."

Mr. Parsons said, "Are you kidding me? I should be thanking you. I couldn't imagine going on without my wife and daughter. They mean the world to me."

Jim said, "I know exactly what you mean. Believe me, I do."

50

On the ride home, Virginia said to Jim, "Can I ask you a question? Is this a typical night for you?"

"I promise you," Jim said, "life is never boring around me."

Virginia nodded and said, "I guess not."

Jim asked Virginia, "Boy, where did you learn how to drive a truck?"

"Are you kidding? I grew up on a farm driving tractors, trucks... you name it. We didn't even have indoor plumbing."

"Come on," Jim said.

Libby asked, "Then where did you go to the bathroom?"

"Outside, in an outhouse." Libby asked what that was, and Jim explained. Libby asked what they did in the wintertime. Virginia said, "Well, in the wintertime, we just went a lot faster." Jim and Libby looked at each other, then at Virginia, and they all laughed. It felt good to laugh after everything that had happened that night.

At the Davises', Virginia asked if she could talk to Jim for a minute. He gave Libby the keys and told her he'd be right in, and she said good night. Virginia said, "Good night, sweetheart, and congratulations on your Red Sox hat!"

"Thanks! I'm going to put it on top of my dresser so I can see it even when I'm in bed. Hey...are you going to pick us up for church in the morning?"

"Did I promise you I would?" Libby said yes. "Then I guess I'm picking you up for church in the morning." Libby gave Virginia a hug. After they watched Libby enter the house, Jim turned to Virginia. She asked, "OK, well, do you remember when we met at the Sidewalk Café?"

"Yeah."

"Do you remember how I told you I'm a big believer in fate?"

"I certainly do remember that."

"You know, I've been thinking a lot about what happened tonight. I believe that it was not a coincidence that we happened to be behind that car tonight. I also think it's not a coincidence that we've met. I mean, just think about the series of events leading up to tonight. Both of us have gone through similar tragedies, losing our spouses. We had a chance meeting at the Sidewalk Café. I get a call from my friend that they have some Red Sox tickets they want to give me because their son came down ill. Ten minutes later, you call and ask me out. Then we end up right behind that car. You had the physical strength and courage that not many people have, or they just wouldn't have done what you did in that situation. I am a nurse with CPR training."

Jim was listening intently, nodding in agreement. He said, "Wow, I never connected the dots like that, but yeah, now that you describe it, it couldn't be anything else but fate. I feel like God is sitting here with us right now. You know, you're right. If He has arranged all of this, and we trust in Him with our lives, than it's our duty to Him to keep His plan in place. He has put us together, and we should make sure it stays that way."

Virginia replied, "I couldn't agree more." They leaned over and gave each other soft kisses on the cheek. Then they heard clapping. They looked up at Libby's room and caught her looking out her window.

She yelled down, "Sorry! I was just opening the window to let some air in."

Jim shouted, "Yeah, wait till I get up there. I'm going to tickle those big ears of yours!" He looked at Virginia and said, "So, I guess I'll see you in the morning."

"Yup. Libby said to be here at nine."

"Oh, I'm sure she did. Little Miss Director. Good night, Virginia."

"Good night, Jim."

51

Sunday morning came too quickly for Jim. He was emotionally and physically exhausted from the night before. He could hear drawers opening and closing in Libby's room, so he knew she was getting ready for church. He dragged himself out of bed. When he went to lift himself up, he felt an excruciating pain in his hands. The Novocain they had given him had completely worn off.

Libby heard him groan and came running to his room. "Dad, are you OK?"

"Yeah, just a little sore from last night."

"Don't worry. I already made you breakfast and coffee."

"You did? Well, let me look."

In the kitchen, he saw blueberry pancakes, scrambled eggs, bacon, toast, and orange juice all laid out. "Wow, I didn't know you knew how to do all this."

"I just didn't want to let you know because it always tastes better when someone makes it for me."

"You're ten going on twenty."

"Are you OK to use silverware? If not, I can help you."

"No, that's OK, honey; I can do it. This looks so good. Thanks for making it."

"Don't get used to it, Dad. Like I told you, it's always better when you make it."

The doorbell rang, and Libby said she would get it. She ran to the door and found Charlie and Lucky there. She yelled to Jim who it was, and he lowered his head, saying, "Oh, great. Here comes the peanut gallery."

Libby told them how she got Big Papi's autograph and that he gave her his hat. They both said, "Whoa," and gave her high fives. Charlie and Lucky were only there to get the scoop on Jim's date last night. They figured they wouldn't get a chance to ask him at church, and the suspense was killing them. They asked Libby, "Where's the old man?" When they saw him, they were stunned that his hands were all wrapped up. "What happened, bro?"

Jim explained everything in chronological order. Charlie and Lucky didn't say a word until Jim mentioned Mr. Parsons and his job offer. Both friends jumped up and said, "William Parsons, from Parsons Development?"

Jim said yes. He toyed with them a little, asking, "Oh, have you heard of him?"

Charlie said, "Are you kidding me, dude? That's all everyone has been talking about for the last two years."

"Oh, really? I had no idea." Jim went on to tell them about his new position and salary.

Lucky said, "Well, when are you going to start with them?"

Jim said, "Oh, I don't know. I still haven't decided to take the job yet." Libby was standing behind them with her hand over her mouth to keep from laughing. She knew her dad was playing them like fiddles.

Charlie and Lucky were going crazy, yelling at Jim, "You don't know if you're going to take the position? Did you hit your head last night?"

"Well, I guess it's a good opportunity. Yeah, yeah, I guess I'll take the job."

Lucky and Charlie knew their bread was buttered now. Certainly, their best friend could get them on that job too. Charlie said, "You're going to take care of us, right?"

"What do you mean?" Jim was really playing them. He could have won an Academy Award. Libby had to look away. She knew her dad was the master at playing people so well that they didn't even know it.

Charlie said, "Seriously, that job is the gold mine of all gold mines. It's the next big dig."

"Well, I guess I probably could get you on." Lucky and Charlie slapped each other on the back. Then Jim lowered the boom. "But weren't you the guys who were here last night, telling Libby to make sure I didn't get within three feet of Virginia because I was so clumsy? Libby, didn't you hear them say that?" Libby took her hands down from her mouth and put on her serious face, nodding her head up and down while Charlie and Lucky turned to look at her. Then Jim said, "Oh, yeah, there was something about writing on a wet napkin, right, Libby?" Again Libby nodded. Now Charlie and Lucky looked like they had just lost their winning million-dollar lottery ticket. "There was something else. I just can't remember what it was. Hmmm, it's right on the tip of my tongue." Now Charlie and Lucky were leaning over the table toward Jim, hanging on his every word. "I don't know...I think you guys called me—"

"Romeo!" they blurted out. Libby couldn't take it anymore. She busted out laughing. When Charlie and Lucky saw her, they knew they were getting played. "Oh, man, that just wasn't right."

"Don't worry, guys, you know Uncle Jim is going to take care of you."

"Oh, thanks, Uncle Jim. You always do."

Libby interrupted. "Dad, we have to get ready."

Charlie asked, "How are you getting there? Do you need a ride?"

"No, Virginia's picking us up."

They both said, "Oh, *Virginia's* picking you up." They were ready to start their routine, but Jim just gave them the look. *I can make you guys or break you guys.* They got it. Charlie cleared his throat and said, "Oh, OK, then we'll see you there." Charlie pushed Lucky in front of him toward the door before he said something wrong.

Jim said, "See ya, fellows." They closed the door as Libby and Jim giggled. Holding on to each other, they walked up the stairs.

52

Libby was looking out the window, watching for Virginia, when she saw the blue Subaru. "Dad, hurry up, Virginia's here!"

"I'll be down in a second!"

At the door, Virginia was holding a bag. When Jim got downstairs, he asked, "What's this? Did you bring me a present?"

"I sure did. I have bandages, gauze pads, iodine, and bacitracin."

"What's all that for?"

"You have to change your dressings twice a day to prevent infections, especially in the first few days."

"Do we have to do it right now?"

"Yes, come on, it'll only take a few minutes." Jim sighed and said it was all right. Virginia had him sit down. As soon as she started to unravel the bandages, Libby got queasy. She ran off to the kitchen, saying she couldn't watch or she'd get sick. While Virginia worked on his hands, Jim couldn't help staring at her. He thought, *She's not doing this just to be nice. She's doing it because that's who she is.* When she was done, she called out, "OK, Libby, I'm all done." With a smirk on her face, she said, "Your dad survived."

"OK," Libby said, "let's go, we're going to be late, and there's going to be a lot of people there. My whole class is coming."

The parking lot of the church was almost full. Libby had been right. Virginia found a spot right next to a large passenger van.

As they got out of the car, Jim heard someone calling his name. It was Carlos, Maria's dad. He asked Jim what had happened to his hands. "Oh, I got in a little accident. No big deal. I'll tell you about it later." Libby got out and immediately introduced Virginia to everyone. Then Jim said, "I didn't realize this was your van, Carlos."

Carlos said, "Yeah, my wife and I got rid of our cars and bought this twelve-passenger van. We figured that Maria would like it for our family outings. There's plenty of room for everybody."

Jim said, "Carlos, I know you're going through a lot, but are you OK?"

"Jim, I don't know what happened. One day, we were a close family, doing everything together. Then the next thing you know, we came into all this money, and everything changed. We didn't have time for church. We were not praying as often. We weren't doing things as a family anymore. The outside things became more important. The only one who seemed to recognize it was Maria. This is entirely my fault. I'm supposed to be the leader of my household, and I've fallen short. I failed them, and I failed God."

"Carlos, listen to me. We all fall short sometimes. Nobody's perfect. Sometimes we think having all these other things that we chase will bring us happiness, but as you know, it doesn't. Give yourself a break. You weren't doing them for your own selfish reasons. You did them to please your family. You just wanted them to have the best. The most important one we are supposed to please is God. So just go in there and ask for His forgiveness, His grace, and His mercy. We are all going to be praying with you for Maria's recovery. Jesus said, 'When there are two or more gathered in my name, I will be there.' Well, look around. There're a whole lot more here than two. So come on, let's not keep Him waiting."

"Thanks, Jim, you're a good man."

As they crossed the parking lot, they saw Charlie, Lucky, Pastor Pete, and Big Ben. Jim said hi to all of them, but he couldn't believe Ben was the same angry man that he had worked with all those years. He really had an inner peace about him that he had never seen before. It was wonderful to see such a transformation in a man who had been tormented with that deep anger all of his life.

There was a group of kids standing on the church steps: PJ, Eric, Smitty, and a dozen other kids from school. They were talking to Mrs. Stanton, who looked obviously excited. The kids looked to her as a mother figure. Nathan, who was there with his mom, Grace, called out to Libby. Jim was so glad to see Grace. He went up and gave her a big hug. She looked so radiant and full of life. He excitedly pulled Virginia over to introduce them. Jim told Virginia that he had had his first crush on Grace when he was in the sixth grade. Virginia said, "Uh-oh, I guess I'll have to sit between you two."

Jim asked Grace if Nana was there. Grace's expression changed and said, "Mama's not feeling too well. I'm trying to get her to the doctor, but you know her, Jim. She's as stubborn as they come."

"Well, make sure you stay on her, and if you need any help, just give me a call."

"Thanks, Jim, I will."

Then Jim noticed Carlos's brother, Victor, who was a Boston police detective. He was working, but he would never have missed this prayer service. They exchanged greetings, and everyone headed into the church.

The front rows were reserved for Maria's family. There were aunts, uncles, nieces, nephews, and cousins there. In just a few moments, the church was full, and there was still a line of cars pulling in and people walking up. Pastor Paul had anticipated this and had had some speakers mounted on the outside doors so anyone outside could listen to the service. That's just the way Southie was. It was a tight-knit community, and when anyone was in need, it always stepped up and supported people.

The worship team came out and started to sing. The atmosphere was so vibrant. Most of the time, at any service, some people loved to sing along, and some people just liked to listen. But today, everyone, inside and outside, was singing and praising God. You could feel the Holy Spirit in the house.

By now, there were at least a hundred people outside. Curiosity was causing a traffic jam on L Street.

53

When the worship music ended, Pastor Paul came to the podium. The mood went from exuberant to somber. Everyone was wondering what sermon the pastor would preach, considering the situation. Pastor Paul asked the congregation to make sure cell phones were off or on vibrate, and then he opened up in prayer. He said, "We are here to lift up Maria and her family. We are all here today, asking the same question. How could God let this happen to a sweet, ten-year-old girl? Well, this has been the question since the beginning of time. I do assure you, I believe that everything happens for a reason.

"Most of the time, we can't see or comprehend this reason. That's where the question of trust comes into play. Do we really trust Him? Or do we only trust Him when things are going perfectly in our lives? When we accepted Him as our savior, this is what we did: we asked Him to come into our hearts and into our lives. We told Him that we would trust in Him and follow His ways. Does this mean that when we're going through a storm in our lives, the situation will get better? No, the situation may not get better, but we will get better so that we can handle these situations. God does not give us any more than we can handle. He says, lean not on your own understanding, but trust in Him and acknowledge Him in all your ways. The book of Hebrews says that since Jesus was a human being and walked among us, He himself went through suffering and testing. He's been where we are, and is both eager and able to help us. So today, we must ask Him for His help.

"We understand the meaning of faith. We know that faith is being sure of what we hope for and certain of what we cannot see. We are certain that he will not leave us or forsake us. We have to be strong in our faith. Psalms 27:14 said, 'Wait on the Lord: be of good courage, and He shall strengthen our hearts.' I want you all to look at the pews that you are sitting on. Before you sat down, did you say to yourselves, 'I better be careful, this bench might collapse when I sit on it'? No, you didn't, because of the hundreds of times you have already sat in them. You're sure that they are strong enough to hold you. In fact, I'm betting by now that it doesn't even cross your mind. Why? Because you have faith and are certain they will not collapse. This is the way we have to trust in our Lord, Jesus Christ.

"Consider Job, and consider all the trials and tribulations he went through. And yet, despite Job's confusion and pain, he was able to conclude his complaint with a statement of faith in God: 'I know my redeemer lives, and He will stand upon the earth at last. And after my body has decayed, yet in my body I will see God! I will see Him for myself. Yes, I will see Him with my own eyes. I am overwhelmed at the thought.'"

Pastor Paul continued, "Listen, everyone. God is on our side, even if we can't see Him right now. So be brave like David. When he was up against his enemies, he said in Psalms 23:4, 'Even though I walk through the valley of the shadow of death, I shall fear no evil. Your rod and staff will protect me.'"

The somber mood the congregation had been in changed and got back to excitement and confidence. It had to be reminded that the Lord has everything under control. That's the job of a great pastor: to move the congregation from fear to faith, and that's just what he did. Pastor Paul said, "Now we invite Carlos and his family up here to receive prayer from anyone who would like to pray for them."

A line automatically formed in the aisle. And yes, even people who had come to services here for years but had never publicly prayed came up. This took almost an hour, because when the people inside finished, the people outside came in to pray. The worship team sang some beautiful hymns that seemed to fit the occasion. Its final song was "Amazing Grace," and it was an amazing service. If you could compare the way the people were now to what they were like coming in, you could tell that they were filled with the Holy Spirit. At the New Covenant Church on L Street in South Boston, there was an anointing like nobody had ever experienced.

When everyone was done praying, Pastor Paul closed in prayer. When he finished, it was so quiet, they could hear a cell phone ringing on vibrate. Everyone looked around to see whose it was. Then Carlos's wife said, "Carlos, it's your phone. Hurry, pick it up—it might be the hospital." Carlos's hands were shaking. Nobody moved, except to close their hands together to symbolize prayer, or to make the sign of the cross.

Carlos held the phone up to his ear. "Hello, hello. Yes, this is him." Then Carlos made the sign of the cross and said, "OK, OK, we'll be right there." Everyone held his or her breath with anticipation. Then he yelled, "That was the hospital. Maria's come out of her coma." The whole congregation erupted. They were clapping and cheering, inside and out. Many were so overwhelmed that they just dropped to their knees and thanked God for His intervention. Even Pastor Paul was speechless, holding one hand over his mouth and wiping away his tears with the other.

54

Carlos and his family quickly gathered their things together and made their way down the aisle, with everyone patting them on the back. Jim, Virginia, Libby, Charlie, Lucky, Ben, and Pete followed behind them. Carlos turned to Jim and asked, "Will you guys come with us?"

Jim said, "Sure, Carlos, we'll all come."

As they all packed into the passenger van, Libby noticed Nathan and his mom looking on. Libby said, "Hold on, I want to see if Nathan wants to come."

Jim yelled out the window, "Gracie, come on! You and Nathan come with us!"

Nathan jumped, excited, and said, "Mom, can we go?" Grace's face held an expression of confusion. It had been a long time since anyone had invited her to go somewhere. She was very moved by this. Nathan pulled on his mother's hand to say it was all right. They ran over to the van and got in, and Nathan jumped next to Libby. They could hardly hold in their excitement. They could not wait to see their best friend.

Carlos was fumbling with the keys. Everyone was telling him to hurry, which made him more nervous. When he finally got the keys in the ignition and started the van, everyone let out a sigh of relief. They all looked back to see if anyone was behind them. Then Carlos put the van in gear and hit the gas. Instead of going in reverse, it jerked forward, knocking over a big, yellow trash barrel. Carlos was shaking. Charlie looked at the odometer, and it read only six miles. Charlie said, "Carlos, is this the first day you've driven this?"

Carlos stuttered, "Yeah, Charlie, we just picked it up last night."

Charlie said, "Carlos, move over, let me drive." Carlos offered no argument there. They switched seats.

Just out of the parking lot, they heard a loud police siren. They all thought they were being pulled over. Then Carlos said, "Look, it's my brother, Victor." He had put his police light on the roof of his car and waved for them to follow. With sirens blowing, they pulled out onto L Street and turned onto East Broadway toward the hospital. All the cars pulled over to let them pass.

At the hospital, two security guards came flying out the door when they heard all the commotion. Carlos and his wife were the first ones they met. The smaller security guard was a dead ringer for Deputy Barney Fife. His hat and uniform were two sizes too big for him. The other was a much larger man, with his hat and uniform two sizes too small. The smaller man stood in front of Carlos with his hand up and his chest all pumped out. He said to Carlos, who was about the same height, "Excuse me, sir. There's no parking in front of the hospital." Both guards then put their hands on their waists as if to say, *You're not getting by us.*

Then the expressions on their faces changed from stern to *Oh, shoot.* There they were: Pastor Pete and Big Ben, running toward them. The guards' hands came off their hips and went onto their hats. As they quickly tried to move aside, they ran into each other. Then they ran off, falling into a beautiful flower bed filled with perennials and azaleas.

The entourage followed Carlos down the hall and then piled into the elevators. Lucky happened to be standing next to the sign announcing the maximum weight limit. He looked at the sign and then looked at everyone in the elevator. He realized they probably had twice the weight limit in there. Now, Lucky was not a real religious man, but you could see him mouthing a prayer not to let the elevator plummet to the ground. When the doors opened up, Lucky couldn't get out of there quick enough.

They all ran down the hall until they reached Maria's room. Carlos and his wife made the turn first, and they stopped in their tracks. It was the most beautiful sight they had ever seen. Maria was sitting up and talking to the doctors. She looked at her parents and tried to get out of the bed to hug them, so the nurse had to grab her. Mom and Dad walked over slowly, tears in their eyes. Maria's mom spoke in Spanish. Not everyone there understood the words, but they all knew what she said. She was thanking God for answering all their prayers. Everyone else stopped at the door to give the family some privacy. After a few moments of hugging and kissing Maria, they asked the doctors if she was OK. The doctor said, "To tell you the truth, she's perfectly normal. There's no brain injury that could cause her any speech impediment or neurological problems. To be honest with you, I'm flabbergasted. Normally with this kind of injury, the outcome is very severe."

Maria noticed Libby and Nathan at the door, and her eyes lit up. They came running in. Libby said, "We knew you would be OK." Then she said, "I have something to show you." She reached into a small bag and pulled out a green T-shirt that read, "Kids for Seniors," and then pointed out Maria's name. Jim looked at Libby and wondered why she had brought the T-shirt, since they hadn't planned on seeing Maria. Then he said to himself, *Wow, she knew all the time that we'd see her today.*

Libby told Maria all about the program that she had started. She said that all the kids wanted her to be president of the club and that they did not want to start until she was back with them. Maria was so excited. She started coming up with ideas for the club. The doctor stopped her and said, "Listen, little girl, we have to take things slowly. You're still recovering." Libby, Maria, and Nathan giggled.

One by one, everyone came into the room. Libby introduced Virginia to Maria. Then the nurse said, "I'm sorry, but only the immediate family is supposed to be in here."

The doctor interrupted and said, "It looks like they all love her like they're immediate family." Then he instructed the nurse to give them fifteen minutes and told Maria she had to get some rest.

The nurse looked at the doctor and then at Maria and said, "He's a real softy."

Carlos turned to Jim and gave him a hug. Then Carlos said, "Man, I tell you, God is good."

Jim, looking over at Virginia, said, "Well, that's why they call Him a 'God of second chances!'"

Carlos agreed, nodding and saying, "Amen, amen."

55

When they got home, Virginia told Jim that she had to change his bandages before she went home. Jim made an attempt to get out of it, but it was too late. Virginia was already pulling her supplies out of the bag. Libby said she was going upstairs to change and that she'd be right down. Virginia started working on Jim's hand. With every piece of bandage she took off, Jim let out a screech. Virginia kept saying, "I'm sorry, I'm sorry." Then she reached for his other hand, and he let out another screech. Virginia jumped back and said, "I didn't take anything off." Jim couldn't hold it in anymore, letting out a big, I-got-you grin. Virginia knew she'd been sucked in one more time. She punched Jim in the shoulder.

Jim said, "Whoa, that hurt."

"You haven't seen hurt yet. I'll show you hurt!" Jim backed away, laughing. They heard the front doorbell ring. Virginia said, "Saved by the bell again, huh?"

Jim hobbled over to the door, trying to regain his composure, but it took him a few seconds. When he opened it, he was surprised to see Smitty standing there. "Hi, Mr. Davis."

"Hey, Smitty, how you doing? Heard you guys whipped those kids from City Point, huh?"

"Yeah, it was long overdue. Is Libby home?"

"Oh, yeah, come on in." Jim introduced Smitty to Virginia and called up to Libby. Libby ran down the stairs and was surprised to see Smitty there.

After quickly straightening her dress and fixing her hair, she said, "Hi, Smitty, what are you doing here?"

"Well, I just wanted to see if I could talk to you for a minute."

"Sure, let's go into the kitchen. Do you want a Coke or something?"

"Sure, that'll be great." They exited the living room.

Jim turned and looked at Virginia, putting both hands up in the air as if to say, *I don't know what's going on.* Jim sat back down on the sofa. Before Virginia could say anything, he said, "He probably just wants to know how Maria is."

Virginia, grinning and shaking her head, said, "I don't think so."

"What do you mean?" Jim inquired.

"Listen, I was a ten-year-old girl once. I saw how they were looking at each other."

"What! Are you crazy? She's not interested in boys."

Now, instead of Virginia's head going from side to side, it was going up and down. "Oh yes, she is."

"Come on, don't be crazy."

Virginia said, "I'm telling you, a girl knows these things. Unlike you guys."

"Yeah, well, we'll just have to find out." Jim got up and headed for the kitchen door.

Virginia grabbed his shirttail. Trying to keep her voice down, she said, "Don't you dare." Jim, paying no attention to her, continued on his mission. Virginia followed close behind him, whispering, "Jim! Don't, don't." But by now, he had his ear against the door for anything to prove her wrong. Virginia knew she couldn't move him from the door, so she resorted to painful measures. She grabbed him by the hand and tried to pull him away. Now there were no more fake screeches. This one was for real. But before any sound came out of his mouth, Virginia whipped her hand over it. With one hand on his shirt and the other over his mouth, she dragged him back to the sofa, where he groaned in pain. She said, "I'm sorry, but you made me do it."

Just then the kitchen door opened, and Libby and Smitty came out. Jim and Virginia, trying to look like they had forgotten they were even there, said, "Oh, hi, guys."

Libby looked at Jim nervously, as if to say, *Dad, don't embarrass me.* Then she said, "Dad, Smitty wants to know if I could go to the CYO dance with him next Saturday night."

Jim, sitting there with his mouth open, didn't say anything for a few seconds—which felt like an eternity for Libby. Then Virginia kicked him under the coffee table, and he snapped out of his trance. Virginia interjected, "Wow, I remember my CYO dances. I went to my first one when I was your age." This was really to send a message to Jim that it was no big deal.

Jim said, "Ah...ah...well, ah..." Then Jim noticed Libby staring him down with that don't-embarrass-me-Dad look again. "Well, where is it going to be?"

"Right here at Gate of Heaven."

"Yeah, I guess that would be OK."

"OK, thanks, Dad," said Libby as she shuffled Smitty toward the door before Jim could change his mind. When Smitty had gone, she turned to Virginia and said, "Oh my God. I can't believe he asked me to the dance!"

Jim was still stunned and didn't know what to say, but Virginia said, "Why can't you believe it? You're the prettiest girl in the class." Jim looked at Virginia and then at Libby like it was all just a bad dream.

Libby ran to Virginia and said, "I'm going to have to buy a new dress. Can you help me pick it out?"

Jim snapped out of his coma and said, "I'll take you and help you find a dress."

Simultaneously, Libby and Virginia objected with their hands out, saying "No, no." Jim just put his hands on his head and lowered his eyes to the floor. Libby said, "Sorry, Dad, you know I really love you, but I've seen your style, and it's not pretty."

Virginia broke out laughing, leaning down and hugging Libby. She said, "Don't worry, I won't let him near your wardrobe." Jim looked at them as they chuckled, leaning his head to one side with a pretty funky look on his face.

Libby kissed Jim, said good night to them, and went up to her room. When she reached the fourth step, she stopped and turned around. "Dad?"

Jim turned and looked at her. "Yeah, honey?"

"Thanks." There was nothing but love in her eyes.

For Jim, it was like time just stopped, and her look said it all. He suddenly felt an overwhelming sense of gratitude and realized how very blessed he was to have her for a daughter. "You're welcome, honey, you're welcome."

After Libby went upstairs, Virginia said, "Come on, I have to finish your bandages."

Jim said, "Oh, come on, you're killing me."

Virginia said, "This pain is nothing like the pain you're going to experience raising a teenage daughter. So you better toughen up, you big sissy!"

56

The next morning, Jim decided to get up early and went down to the Sidewalk Café to grab a cup of coffee. He wanted to surprise Libby with her favorite pastry, a cheese Danish. As he walked down East Fourth Street, he heard a horn beep. When he looked over, there in a car pulling up was Stevie Lynch. "Jim, I was going to call you today. We're putting a Medicare reform bill to the house floor next week."

Jim said, "Stevie, that's great. How's it looking? Do you think it will go through?"

"It looks real good, Jim. We've gotten a lot of help from both sides of the aisle on this one, and that doesn't happen too often. You know how Massachusetts politics can be. I think we got a lot of people on board because we were able to put a face on the bill. We're naming it 'the Nana Green bill,' which has gotten everyone curious. Once we tell them the story of Nana—well, it seems to get my constituents' attention."

"Wow. Wait until Nana hears about this one. She'll be the local celebrity."

"If anyone deserves to be a celebrity, Jimmy, it's Nana."

"You got that right."

"Keep your fingers crossed on this one, Jim."

"You got it. And Steve, thanks again."

"All right, Jimmie. Hey, no problem. Do know how many kids she's saved over the years?"

"Yeah, too many to count." Jim tapped on the roof of the car and told Steve to take care.

When Jim got to the café, he bumped into a guy named Brendan Curran. Jim had seen him get his one-year medallion at a meeting at Saint Monica's church a few nights before but hadn't had a chance to congratulate him. Jim told him he should be proud of himself for the achievement. As they were talking, Jim noticed that Brendan's whole personality was different. He joked with him, saying, "Look at you. You can't wipe the smile off your face if you tried."

Brendan laughed and said, "You know, Jim, I finally accepted that I needed help with my depression." Jim nodded in agreement; Brendan had often talked about it. He said, "For years, I thought I could beat it by myself. I tried going to the gym, eating right, playing golf, buying all kinds of things. They would help for a little while, but then it always came back. So I started to take some antidepressants my doctor gave me, and after a couple of months, I'd feel great. People around me always knew when I was on or off my meds. They said the first thing they would notice is that I didn't laugh anymore, and then I didn't smile anymore, and from there, I got worse. When it got bad enough, I would go back on them, and the whole cycle would start all over again. It was a merry-go-round I couldn't get off of."

Jim asked, "If you knew what was going to happen, why didn't you just stay on them?"

Brendan said, "I know, that's the crazy thing about it. Because the problem was between my ears, and I thought I could beat it. After this last time, it got to the point it owned me. I would have a roofing job that I could make a couple of grand from in one day, but I couldn't get any motivation to get out of bed and do it. Sometimes I would stay there for a couple of days."

Jim said, "Wow, that must be awful."

Brendan said, "Jim, I've had three back surgeries since I fell off that roof five years ago. I'm still in pain every day, but I tell you, I would take physical pain over depression any day of the week."

"So what was it that brought you out of it?"

Brendan said, "After this last bout, I lost all my passion to live. I just wanted to die. I was even to the point of how I was going to do it. My wife called the ambulance, and they took me to the hospital."

Jim said, "Brendan, you have a wife and kids that love you. How could you do that to them?"

"People don't realize it. They say suicide is selfish, and now I know it is. But when I was contemplating it, I truly believed that it was in their best interest. I thought that they would be sad for a while, but after I was gone, I wouldn't be a burden to them anymore and they'd be better off without me. I've had diabetes for twenty years and I don't fool around with it now. I try to eat right, exercise, test my blood sugar, and always take my insulin on time." Brendan continued, "When I first got it, I didn't take it serious. I would eat what I wanted and take the insulin when I remembered."

Jim asked him, "What happens when you do that?"

"I start feeling tired and sluggish. A couple of times, I had to be hospitalized. Well, I have to respect the disease of depression as much as the disease of diabetes. I can't mess around with it or I'll pay the price. So I've been on meds for over a year, and my whole life is different. I have passion in my life again, just like when we were kids hanging down Carson Beach. All I remember about those times is that we were always joking and laughing. I look back now on those last few darkest days and think, how could I ever think about doing that to them? Jim, I used to pray all the time for God to help me. I would get real angry at Him. I would scream at the top of my lungs, 'Why aren't You helping me?' Little did I know, He was. He let it go to the very edge of the cliff so I could see how close to death I was before I would give up control and listen to the doctors. I tried to do it my way, and I failed. I don't believe I would've ever gotten better unless I experienced what I did. It's ironic. I've been going to AA for years and couldn't get sober. All the while, they were giving me the same suggestion: you have to surrender to win. I guess a disease is a disease."

Jim said, "Man, Brendan, I never realized you were that bad."

"That's what people with depression do. They try to make it look like everything is OK, but inside they're dying. I heard depression described like this: when things in their lives are difficult, normal people feel sad. When things in their lives are going great, people who suffer with depression still feel sad."

Jim said, "Wow, you've really opened my eyes about this."

Brendan said, "Now I'm not ashamed of it. If I ever see people struggling with depression, I don't hesitate to reach out to them and throw them a lifeline. God said we should be our brother's keeper."

Jim replied, "Amen to that, brother. Amen."

When Jim turned to go into the café, he saw Paula, one of the employees, coming out to bring bowls of food and water to a beautiful, young chocolate Lab sitting at the front door. He asked her, "Is he yours?"

Paula looked up and said, "Hey, Jim. No, he's not. He's a stray. He's been out here for over a week. He must be lost or something. I feel bad for him. I've been taking care of him every day. I'd love to take him home with me, but my landlord doesn't allow pets. Hey, Jim, why don't you take him home for Libby? I know she'd just love him."

"Nah, I don't think so. Dogs are a lot of work. You have to walk them twice a day, feed them, and bring them to the vet all the time. It's just too much of a responsibility." Meanwhile, the dog hadn't taken his eyes off of Jim. Jim couldn't look at him anymore. He knew how much of a softy he was when it came to underdogs (literally). He said to Paula, "I'm sure somebody will take him home." He waited for Paula to agree, but she never acknowledged him.

Looking directly at the young Lab, Paula said, "It's OK, puppy. I'm sure someone will take you home and take care of you." Jim knew Paula was working on him.

Jim was right behind Paula as she went back inside. He ordered his coffee and two cheese Danishes. Out of the corner of his eye, he could see Paula staring at him. He tried not to look at her. He grabbed his order as fast as possible and turned toward the door, his back intentionally to Paula. When he stepped outside, the dog was waiting for him. Jim walked over to pat him on the head. "See ya, fella." As he turned to walk away, he saw Paula in the window holding up a leash. Jim shook his head, mouthing *No, no, I can't*. He turned to the Lab and tried to make his case. "I can't take you. I don't have the time to look after you. Besides, you'd be better off in the suburbs instead of the city." The young Lab just kept looking at him with those huge brown eyes that seemed to be saying, *I wouldn't be any problem*. Jim stopped talking. He was out of excuses.

Looking back at Paula, who now had all the other waitstaff glaring at him, he threw his hands up to say, *OK, I give up*. Paula came running out with the leash, and giving Jim a big hug, she said, "I knew you'd take him. Libby's just going to love him to death."

"I hope so, or I'm coming to your house with Fido here." Paula clipped the leash onto the dog's collar. Jim took the leash, and the dog immediately bolted. Jim tried to hold on to him and his coffee while he was being hauled down the street.

Paula, giggling, waved good-bye and shouted, "Tell Libby to take good care of him!"

On the way home, Jim was trying to figure out what had just happened. Twenty minutes earlier, he had left his house for a cup of coffee; now he was walking home—or rather, being dragged home by—a rambunctious chocolate Lab who was not even close to being full-grown. As Jim got closer to home, the thought of Libby's reaction on seeing the pup superseded his fear of the responsibility of owning a dog. The little kid inside of him tried to find the best way to surprise her.

At the front door, it took Jim a couple of minutes to settle the Lab down. He put the key in as quietly as possible. But as soon as he opened the door, the dog tried to push his way through it. Jim said, "Shush," and held on to him. He could hardly believe how strong the pup was for one so young. Jim hoped that Libby was still sleeping. He walked gingerly over to the swinging door of the kitchen. Jim led the dog over to the kitchen table and tied him to one of the chairs. Right away, he started to bark.

Jim quickly calmed the dog down and looked around for some food to keep him quiet. He grabbed the biggest bowl he could find and a box of Cheerios. He filled the bowl to the brim, and it worked. The dog buried his face in it like he hadn't eaten in a week. Jim slowly walked out of the kitchen and into the living room. He sat down on the sofa and tried to look as casual as possible, like nothing was going on. About ten minutes later, Libby came down the stairs yawning and rubbing her eyes. Jim said, "Good morning, honey."

"Morning, Dad." Libby pushed on the swinging door to the kitchen.

Jim had expected her to yell out in excitement. It was nowhere near excitement. It was more like sheer terror. Libby screamed as she pushed open the door and came running toward Jim. This was not what Jim had planned. The dog was right on Libby's tail, crashing through the door and dragging the kitchen chair behind him. It was knocking over everything in its path. First went the coat rack, and then the small antique table with the goldfish bowl sitting on top of it. The fish were flapping all over the floor. Then he turned directly toward Jim and Libby, jumping onto the glass coffee table. Libby was still screaming at the top of her lungs as Jim tried to grab the dog. Libby made a run for it around the sofa and bolted up the stairs to her room.

The Lab broke free from Jim's grasp. He followed Libby around the sofa, knocking over two beautiful blue orchid flowers in a ceramic vase. He then turned toward the stairs, dragging the chair that smashed everything in its way like a wrecking ball. The chair had now lost two of its legs. When he got to the stairs, he never missed a beat. As he ran up, the chair smashed against the irreplaceable original wooden railing spindles. The dog was following Libby's screams.

Libby tried to close her bedroom door, but the Lab was right behind her. She ran and jumped into her bed, pulling the sheets over her head. Jim, still stunned, had started toward the stairs when Libby stopped screaming. Jim panicked and ran up the stairs, hitting every third step while calling her name. He came into her room expecting to see Libby hurt, but then he saw the dog licking Libby's face. She was hugging him and wiping off dog saliva. He pulled the Lab off the bed, and like the rest of the house, her room was trashed. Libby asked, "Dad, where did he come from?"

Jim sat on the edge of her bed and asked, "Why were you screaming and running away from him?"

"Dad, I was half-asleep. All I saw was this big brown animal running at me and dragging a chair behind him. What was I supposed to think?"

Jim realized his surprise should have been handled a little more subtly. Again, Libby asked where the dog had come from. He told her the story of how Paula at the Sidewalk had convinced him to take the Lab home because he might be lost.

She jumped up, asking, "Can we keep him?"

Jim said, "We'll put up some signs around Southie, and if no one claims him, we'll keep him—under one condition."

"What's that, Dad?"

"Well, he'll be your responsibility. You have to feed him, clean up after him, and walk him twice a day."

Libby couldn't agree quickly enough. "What are we going to name him?"

Jim looked around at all the damage and thought for a moment. "What about Brutus?"

"Yeah," she said, "that's perfect." She reached over to pat Brutus on the head, which started another licking session.

Jim just mumbled to himself, "What have I got myself into?" But when he saw the joy in Libby's face, he thought, *No matter how much trouble the Lab will be, it'll be worth it.* He hadn't seen Libby this excited in a long time.

57

Carlos and his family were driving to the hospital to pick up Maria. She had made a remarkable and speedy recovery. The doctors were allowing her to go home a few days early. Her mom, dad, brother, and sister were all in the new family van. By now, Carlos had improved his driving skills with the new vehicle.

When they got there and reached Maria's room, she was already packed up and ready to go. The nurse came in and removed the last IV, leaning over to kiss Maria on the forehead. Technically, this was against hospital policy, but the nurse knew Maria was a walking miracle. Her profession was very challenging. She saw sickness and death every day, so when she saw a patient beat the odds, especially a young child, it could keep her going for another day. One by one, the nurses, the cleaning staff, and even the maintenance man came in to wish Maria good luck and say their good-byes. Then the caring physician came in to ask her a few final questions. When he finished, he turned and looked at Carlos and his wife. He pulled them aside to talk with them in private.

In the hallway, out of hearing distance from everyone, the look on his face became serious. Maria's parents got very nervous, and Carlos asked him if Maria's diagnosis for a full recovery had changed. After looking away for a long pause, the doctor turned to them and said, "When I first came into the emergency room and saw Maria, her injuries, and her vital signs, I had very little hope that she would survive. Even if she did, I was certain that there would be some severe neurological and brain damage. When I opened her skull to relieve the swelling, something very strange happened to me—something I had never experienced in thirty-nine years of practice. Usually, this procedure is very nerve-racking. There is absolutely no room for error. But as I started it, without any notice, I suddenly felt a calmness come over me. It seemed as if my hands were being controlled by someone else. It felt like I was the only one in the room. I didn't hear or see anyone from the surgical team, but I felt I wasn't alone. I felt the presence of someone or something in that room with me. Every move you make on this type of procedure has to be performed with absolute precision. I figured this had something to do with a lack of sleep or the stress due to the crazy week and long hours spent on emergency surgeries. My hands continued to move without me making any kind of conscious decision to move them. I never even looked up at her vital signs. I just knew that everything was going to be OK.

"As I was completing the surgery, I started hearing the voices of everyone else in the room, the monitoring machines, all the energy and controlled chaos that normally goes on. You know, we are taught in medical school that everything that happens in the human body can be proved with scientific evidence. I have to tell you, there is no medical scientific evidence that can be found for what happened to me on that particular day while performing the emergency surgery. As much as I tried to find an answer, there is just no explanation for it."

Carlos put his hands on the doctor's shoulders and said, "Well, there is an explanation." The doctor looked into Carlos's eyes as if to say, *Tell me. Tell me what I experienced.* Carlos said, "Doc, on that day in the emergency room, your hands and your mind were being directed by the greatest physician of all time: the ultimate physician, Jesus Christ, king of kings and lord of lords." The doctor's eyes filled with tears, and he was overcome with emotion. For he now fully realized what he had witnessed that day: a divine intervention. And he knew now he would be a better physician because of it. He now knew that when medical science says that someone will not recover, it's not the final verdict, for he had seen supernatural evidence that could trump any medical prognosis.

As Maria and her family were waiting at the elevator, she looked at them and felt like they were all together again. The thought of moving to a new town saddened her, not so much because of losing her friends, but the possibility of losing her family.

Outside the hospital, she had expected to see the three two-seaters there to take all five of them home. She asked her dad where all the cars were, and he pointed at the new white van and said, "There's the new family car. It can fit all of us, our friends, and anyone else who wants to join us." Maria was ecstatic. She looked at her dad and then her mom.

Her mom said, "Don't worry, princess. We never have to be separated again."

As they crossed over the Fourth Street bridge into Southie and drove up West Broadway, they saw signs in the storefronts saying, "Welcome Home, Maria." Maria was smiling, looking from one side of the street to the other. Southie may be a very small part of Boston, but it is a close community. Everyone knows everyone.

There were at least a hundred people outside the family's house. Jim, Libby, Virginia, Lucky, Charlie, Nathan and his mom, Maria's classmates, and many people from the congregation clapped and cheered. Some were holding balloons and welcome-home signs. Maria and her family thanked each and every one of them for coming.

As Maria and her family walked into the house, she expected to see most of the furniture moved and things packed in boxes. Instead, everything was in its place: furniture, paintings, knick-knacks, china, Bible scriptures, and the most important thing of all, the frame on the wall that she could see as soon as she entered that said, "It's not a house that makes a home, it's the family that makes a home."

Carlos gently touched the frame and said to Maria, "Honey, we're all sorry we lost sight of this. We realize now that there's nothing wrong with having money. Jesus said He came to give us life, and life more abundantly. But we allowed the money to come first instead of Him. It seemed like you were the only one who still knew the right thing to do, and we promise you, we'll never make that mistake again. If we ever think of moving again, we will pray on it and ask God for His wisdom and guidance to help us make the right decision."

Maria replied, "All I ever wanted was for us to be a family."

"We know, honey, we know. Maybe it took almost losing you for us to realize that. Again, we promise you we will never forget."

Then Maria's mom, Anita, yelled out, "Family hug, family hug—and come on, get in close!" They all hugged each other longer and tighter than they ever had before.

58

Ed Donlan was nervously pacing back and forth in his office. His health was rapidly declining, and he couldn't make the trip to the airport to meet Ed Junior and his family. Sam had driven Olivia to pick them up. Ed had never been so nervous in his life, and he had met many prominent people in his lifetime: CEOs of large corporations that he had signed multimillion-dollar contracts with, heads of state, all kinds of celebrities. President Clinton had even once invited him to the White House to accept an award for running the fastest-growing company in the country. But even after all these monumental accomplishments, he didn't know what to say or how to act with his son. Would Junior be cold and standoffish? Would his daughter-in-law accept him? Did she know how much pain he had caused her husband? Would the twins even recognize him? Had they ever even seen a photo of him? The round trip to the airport was supposed to take about two hours, but it had already been almost three. Had they changed their minds at the airport?

Then he heard a car coming up the gravel driveway. He was paralyzed with fear. Then the door opened, and Sam walked in carrying the luggage, followed by Olivia. Then Ed Junior and his wife entered, holding hands with each of the twins. Nobody saw Ed at first. He was standing halfway out of his office. Then Olivia caught sight of him out of the corner of her eye. "Oh, Ed, you're up!"

Junior turned and looked at him. He was taken aback a little by his father's looks. He was so much older and frailer looking than he remembered. The kidney failure was really taking a toll on him. Junior walked over very slowly and said, "Hey, Dad, how are you?"

These were words Ed hadn't heard from his son in over ten years. Trying to sound as strong as possible, he said, "Oh, I'm hanging in there."

After a long pause, Junior turned to his wife and said, "Dad, I want you to meet my wife, Megan."

She walked toward Ed with her hand out and said, "Hi, Mr. Donlan. It's so nice to finally meet you." Then she said something he never expected to hear. "Wow, it's amazing. The girls have your eyes." She turned to the girls and said, "Cindy, Ashley, come and meet your grandfather."

They ran over, and each of them grabbed onto his hands. "What do you want us to call you? Grandpa or Papa?"

"What would you like to call me?"

Cindy said, "I like Grandpa."

And Ashley said, "I like Papa."

He placed his hands on both their heads and said, "Well, you can call me Grandpa, and Ashley here can call me Papa."

Cindy said, "Wow, that's a good idea. We never thought of that!" Junior looked at his dad. This was not a familiar concept to him from when he was growing up. He never would have had a choice. Junior had been told what to call his grandfather.

When they were all hugging each other, Olivia looked at Sam. The scene was bittersweet for him. He felt a lot of joy for them, but she could still see sadness on his face. He so terribly missed his own family. She could see how remorseful he was. Olivia walked over to him, gave him a hug, and said, "Sam, I know what you're thinking about right now. Even though you work for Ed, we still consider you part of this family. If it wasn't for Ed meeting you, he never would have had this amazing transformation. He's so much more compassionate and caring, and we all thank you."

Sam nodded, saying, "Thank you, Mrs. Donlan, thank you," but Sam was still riddled with the feeling that he had failed with his own family.

59

Jim and Libby were just arriving home from doing a few errands. As they pulled into the driveway, Virginia pulled up behind them. Jim said, "Oh, look who's here." Libby turned around, and when she saw Virginia, she got so excited that she hardly could take off her seat belt. They got out of their cars, and Libby ran over and gave Virginia a big hug. Jim leaned over Libby and gave Virginia a kiss on the cheek.

Virginia said, "I've been trying to call you, but all I got was your voice mail."

Jim looked down for his phone and realized he didn't have it in his belt clip. He said, "Oh, man, where's my phone?" He looked in his truck.

Libby said, "Dad, you were talking to Charlie this morning before we left. Did you leave it on the back porch?"

Jim looked over and saw it on the railing. As he moved to go get it, Virginia leaned over and whispered to Libby, "It's always the mind that goes first." Libby busted out laughing, which made Jim turn around and ask what was so funny.

Libby said, "Oh, nothing."

Jim said, "I think I'm the butt of your jokes again."

Virginia said, "No, we wouldn't do that to you, would we, Libby?" Libby tried to respond with a no but couldn't get the smile off her face.

Jim just said, "Yeah, yeah." He said to Virginia, "I thought you had to work today."

"I was scheduled to, but another nurse needed the night off, so we switched shifts. I'm going to the South Shore Mall for a few things and wondered if Libby wanted to go with me. I thought she might want to find a dress for her school dance." Libby jumped at the opportunity.

Jim said, "Sure, do you want me to come and help?"

"No, no. I'm sure you have other things to do." She winked at him as if to say, *I got this.*

Jim realized that this would be an opportunity for Libby and Virginia to bond a little. He replied, "Yeah, I got a ton of things I can do." Jim handed Libby some money and said, "OK, have a good time, and call me when you're heading back."

Virginia said, "You're sure you won't forget your phone..." as the girls turned toward her car, giggling.

As they left, Libby rolled down the window and said, "Love you, Dad."

"Love you too, honey; put your seat belt on."

"OK, Dad."

Jim's cell phone rang, but he couldn't see who was calling because the sun was so bright. He just assumed it would be Charlie or one of the guys. "Yeah, what's up?"

"Oh, hello. Is Jim Davis there?"

"You're speaking to him."

"Oh, hi, Jim. This is William Parsons, from Parsons Development."

Jim said, "Oh, I'm so sorry, Mr. Parsons; I thought you were one of my friends calling."

"It's quite all right, Jim. Listen, I know it's very short notice, but we're having kind of an emergency preconstruction meeting in the office on Friday. With this economy, the board of directors and the banks are getting real strict on some policies and how they're going to run things in the future. So we have to see what the new guidelines are and the changes they want to implement. Will you be able to make it?"

"Oh, absolutely."

"Great. So we'll see you at nine o'clock on Friday."

"Yes, sir, I'll be there."

When Jim hung up the phone, he wondered, *Why would they want me in a meeting with the banks and the board of directors?* He started to wonder if he was qualified for the job. After all, he was just a blue-collar carpenter. Would he be able to sit next to these guys, who probably were college educated with PhDs and master's degrees in finance? The more he dwelled on this, the more self-doubt crept in. After all he'd been through, being newly sober and thinking of his past fears and failures, he wondered if he should even take the job. He didn't like how he was feeling. Knowing he should call George, his sponsor, Jim decided not to deal with it. He would just finish working on the deck and try not to think about it, hoping somehow that what he was feeling would all go away.

60

Jim took all the necessary tools out to complete the finishing touches on the deck. He had to install the custom spindles on the railings. This finish work took much more concentration than the rough framing. He found himself continuously making mistakes. After a half dozen wrong cuts, he knew his mind was still on the construction meeting, so he decided to leave it for another day. As he wrapped up the extension cords, he heard a horn beeping in the driveway and figured Libby must have forgotten to grab something at the house. When he looked up, to his surprise, there was George, getting out of his car. "Hey, Jim, what's up?" Jim thought, *OK, God, I didn't go see George, so you brought him here. I get it.*

"Oh, just working on my deck." They met each other halfway and shook hands. Jim said, "What are you doing over here?"

"Well, I had to drop one of my daughters off at the soccer field, and something just told me to swing by and see how you were doing. I haven't heard from you in a while."

They moved back toward the deck. Jim looked down at his work boots, smiled, and said, "Ah, yeah, I'm doing great."

George asked, "How's Libby?"

"Great. As a matter of fact, she's with Virginia right now at the South Shore Mall, looking for a dress for her first school dance."

"Oh, she's getting to that age. You better put your seat belt on, buddy."

"Yeah, I know."

"It sounds like you and Virginia are hitting it off, huh?"

"Yeah, she's been great to have around, especially with Libby."

George looked at the unfinished deck. He said, "Hey, I've got a couple of hours to kill, need some help?"

"Oh, no, I'm all set. I was just finishing up."

"Looks to me like you're just getting started. I can see something's bothering you, what's up?"

"No, I'm OK. I didn't want to bother you."

George said, in a much firmer voice, "Jim, you have a lot on your plate to deal with right now. Tell me what's going on. Who knows, maybe I can help," he added with a little sarcasm. "Listen, you're only human. You need to know when to ask for help." After a long pause, George said, "Wow, you really did a great job on the deck."

Jim, relieved, figured they had dropped the previous topic. He immediately said, "Yeah, it came out good, huh?"

"It sure did. Did you do it all by yourself?"

Jim said, "Are you kidding me? Charlie, Lucky, and Big Ben gave me a hand with the rough frame, and Tommy next door helped me dig the footings out and pour the concrete."

George just nodded and asked, "Who taught you how to do carpentry?"

"Oh, I worked for this old-timer for my first six years in the trade. Let me tell ya, that guy was old school. He knew how to do everything. If there were something I couldn't figure out, he'd show me how. He was incredible."

George said, "Well, there's nothing like experience, huh?"

"Yeah, you can't learn this stuff out of a book."

"Well," George said, "let me ask you a question."

"Sure." Jim was expecting George to ask how he knew how to build the stairs or to have the perfect distance between spindles, or how he'd even thought up their design. He eagerly waited to answer.

"Why is it that when you built this deck, you had no problem asking all those guys for help? You also had the knowledge and talent to do it and to order all the supplies because someone with a lot more experience at one point showed you how."

Jim realized that George had thrown the bait out, and he took it. Knowing he was being reeled in, he said, "OK, OK."

George said, "Hold on, one more question. What else did you need to build the deck besides the materials and the labor?" Jim knew what the answer was, but was now too embarrassed to say it, so George volunteered. "It's the tools, right? And I bet you have that whole shed over there full of them, and it took you a lot of years to acquire them, huh? You also know what tools you need for what job, right? Then why is it when it comes to something about you that you haven't dealt with before, you think you can do it all by yourself? Huh? Can you answer that?"

"You're right, but it's just hard for me."

George said, "I know, I know, Jim. I grew up in Southie too. We didn't go into the local bar and talk to our buddies about our feelings. What do you think would have happened to us? They would have thrown us out. Listen, those days are over. You better learn how to use the tools the program teaches you, like the tools you wear around your belt, to learn how to survive, OK?"

"OK, I'll try."

"Good," George said. "Now, what's bothering you?"

"Well, Mr. Parsons called from the development company where I got that job offer I told you about."

"Yeah, I remember, it's a great opportunity for you."

"Yeah, I know, but they're calling for a preconstruction meeting on Friday with the banks and board of directors."

"All right," George said, "so what's the problem? Let me guess, you're starting to think you're not going to be able to do the job, right?"

Jim said, "It's not so much that, it's—well, I don't know why they want me there. I mean, I'm supposed to monitor the job site. What do I know about banking and finance?"

George interrupted him. "Look, there's no question why Mr. Parsons offered you the job. For crying out loud, you saved his family. We know that, but that doesn't mean he created this job just for you, like you told me when he offered the position. This has been an ongoing problem for him, and for whatever reason, God put you two guys together. I'm sure he doesn't need you there for setting the multimillion-dollar budget. I'm sure he just wants you to learn what their challenges are on the office end. In most business meetings, seventy-five percent of the people there have nothing to do with the topic they're discussing. They just want to create a team effort atmosphere. Now, out of respect for the company, make sure you're well dressed, but don't go out and buy a new Armani suit or Italian leather shoes to feel like you belong.

"Remember, you're there for your experience on the job site, and they are there for the financial end of it. Just because you wouldn't know the first thing about what they do, believe me, those people probably don't know which end of a hammer to use—and why should they? They're not there for that. So just go in there, be yourself, and don't try to be anyone else. Just be yourself, OK?"

"Yeah, thanks, George. I don't know how, but somehow, you always make things very clear for me."

George, putting both hands up, said, "It's experience, right? We might never have been in the exact same situation like this, but, believe it or not, we've both shared the same fears, doubts, and insecurities. And someday, you'll be on this deck, talking to someone else about how to handle these situations. That's how it works, my friend. One other thing. If you're going to build the project on the waterfront at the same speed you build this deck, you'll be looking for another job. So what do you say, let's get this thing done, OK?"

Jim said, "You got it, let's go." As they worked, Jim realized that he got more done in the first twenty minutes than he had in the last two hours. It was because he was now focused 100 percent on the deck, and the deck only.

61

Jim and George were installing the last spindle when they heard Libby and Virginia arrive. Brutus met them before Virginia even stopped the car. Libby got out with bags full of clothes, which made no difference to Brutus. Excited to see her, he was jumping all over them, almost knocking Libby to the ground a few times. Libby kept yelling at Brutus to stop, which only got him more excited. Libby called out to Jim, "Dad, call Brutus over!"

Jim called Brutus, who came over reluctantly, and Jim tied him up to the deck. Brutus wasn't too happy about that. Jim said to Libby, "I thought you were going to the mall to get a dress, not a whole new wardrobe."

Libby replied, "We tried to, but we couldn't make up our minds."

Jim looked at George and said, "Wow, imagine that, how unique. Women who can't make up their minds." George looked at Jim as if to say, *Careful, you're walking on dangerous ground.* Jim said, "Libby, you remember George?"

Libby looked at George and was a little embarrassed. She said, "Oh, I'm sorry, I didn't recognize you without your prison clothes." Virginia looked at Jim and back at George. Libby asked, "How are things down the jail?"

George said, "Better. Real better now." Libby just smiled.

Jim interrupted and said, "Virginia, this is my friend George. He works down the South Bay prison."

Virginia seemed relieved. "Oh! Oh, it's so nice to meet you."

George said, "Well, finally, it's very nice to meet you. I've heard so many nice things about you."

"Thank you."

George said, "OK, Jim, you can do the clean up without me. I have to pick up my daughter down the field."

"Thanks, George, thanks for your help."

"Anytime. I'll see you guys later."

Libby said, "Dad, I want you to tell me which dress you like."

Jim started to look in the bags, but Libby said, "No, you have to see them on me."

"OK, let me clean up the yard, and I'll be in." Libby and Virginia ran into the house, giggling like a couple of schoolgirls. Jim looked at Brutus and said, "Brutus, the men in this house are starting to get outnumbered." Brutus barked a couple of times as if he understood. He lay down on the grass with his head on his paws and a sad look on his face. Jim said, "I know, Brutus, I feel the same way."

About thirty minutes later, Jim had cleaned up the yard, and he and Brutus went into the house through the kitchen. Jim opened the refrigerator, grabbed a Diet Coke, and walked into the living room, calling Brutus to follow. Sensing he was not behind, Jim turned and looked at him. "What's the matter?" Brutus looked at his water bowl and then at Jim. Jim said, "Oh, sorry, Brutus." Jim filled the bowl and Brutus followed him into the living room. Jim turned the air conditioner on high, put the water bowl on the floor, and sat on the sofa, letting out a big "Ooohhh, that feels good."

Libby, hearing this, called out, "Dad, are you ready?"

"OK, let me see you." Libby walked out in a real pretty violet dress with a matching ribbon in her hair. To Jim's mind, the only problem was that it was a little too short and revealing.

After a few seconds of hearing nothing, Virginia said, "Well, what do you think?"

Jim said, in his smart-aleck way, "Well, I'm just wondering. How can you go into your room looking ten and come out looking twenty? Did I fall asleep for ten years or something?"

"Dad, really, what do you think?"

"I think it's too short for you."

Libby and Virginia just looked at each other as if to say, *We knew he would say that.* "OK, wait there, we'll try another one." A few minutes later, they came out again. Now she was wearing a lovely pink dress, again with a matching ribbon and handbag. "Well, do you like this one?"

After looking at it, Jim had wished he'd never complained about the previous one. He thought the top of this one was a little low cut. He said, "You can't wear that one; the top is to low and it will show too much."

Virginia said, "Jim, she's ten years old, what does she have to show? OK, we have one more."

A few minutes later, Libby came out, expecting Jim's opinion of this dress to be even worse than of the previous two. When Jim looked up, he smiled. It was a wonderful yellow dress with white laces up and down the arms. Not too low and not too high. It was perfect. He yelled out, "Bingo! That's the winner. What do you think, Brutus?" Brutus got excited and ran around in circles, barking up a storm. Jim said, "See, even Brutus agrees."

"Really, Dad?"

"Yeah, it looks perfect, like it was made just for you." Libby gave Virginia a big hug, and this time, she seemed to hold on longer than usual.

Virginia looked down at Jim, and he could see she was starting to get a little emotional and was about to cry. Then she said to Libby, "OK, let's hang it in your closet," and they turned to go up to her bedroom. Right then, Jim seemed to have a revelation about Virginia. He had always looked at her as if it was only about Virginia and him, but now he saw how Virginia and Libby filled each other's needs. Libby was the daughter Virginia had never had, and Virginia was the mother figure that Libby had lost.

The phone rang. It was Big Ben. "Hey, Ben, how you doing?"

"I'm doing awesome, Jim. How about you?"

"Right now, things couldn't be better."

"Oh, that's great. Hey, Jim, I was wondering if you had anything scheduled on Saturday mornings for the next six weeks."

Jim said, "Well, I'm not sure. Why, what's up?"

"Myself and a couple of the guys from the congregation who are in the trades are going to put on a carpentry clinic in the church basement. On nice days, we'll do it in the parking lot. We're just going to show some high school kids who might be interested in the basics of construction. We'll show them how to use nail guns and all the other tools we work with. You know, some kids just are not interested in college, so we're trying to give them an alternative."

Jim wondered if this was the same Ben he knew. The Ben he knew was angry, self-centered, and just generally miserable all the time. Jim said, "Wow, Ben, I've got to be honest with you." Now, Ben was the last guy you wanted to have upset at you. "No disrespect to you, but I never would have expected you to be doing this for some kids you don't even know. Again, no disrespect."

Ben said, "Well, the old me would have agreed with you, but since that near-fatal accident, something has happened to me. I know I should never have survived that fall off the roof. I never really understood the way some people live through bad situations and say they have a new lease on life, but now, I know what they mean. I figure the only reason I survived is that God has a plan for me to accomplish something for Him. So I owe it to Him to try to do His will. I know every day is a gift for me, so if I can help some kid get into the trade so he can go anywhere in this world and find work, well, that's what I want to do. Jim, my life has been spared, and I'm going to make the best of what's left of it by trying to make a difference in this sometimes very hard and cruel world we live in. You remember what scripture says: to whom much has been given, much is required, and I've been given the ultimate gift—a second chance."

Jim said, "You know, Ben, you're exactly right. You and I are walking miracles. With the places we've been and the things we've done, we shouldn't even be talking to each other right now. Listen, put me down, and I'll see if I can round up a couple more guys to help."

"Thanks, Jim."

"No, thank you, Ben. Sometimes I worry about everything that's wrong with my life, and not things that I should be grateful for. I need to hear guys like you to set me straight."

"Well, Jim, that's what we're here for, to lift each other up."

"Thanks, Ben, and God bless."

"You too, Jim. I'll see ya."

62

When Jim hung up, he noticed that he had voice mail. He didn't recognize the number, so he listened to it. It was a message that he wished he had never heard. The call was from a Mr. Kane about Brutus. Apparently, he and his wife had been taking a walk around Castle Island, and they'd spotted the poster for a missing brown Lab that Jim and Libby had put up. This was Jim's worst fear. Libby had already suffered a devastating loss with her mom's passing, and now he had to tell her that Brutus's owners had called, looking for him.

Before he called them back, he had to tell Libby. So he went to the bottom of the stairway and called up to her. Libby came out of the room with the same exuberant look on her face she had had a few minutes ago. Virginia followed her, holding up her dress on a hanger. Jim said, "Libby, I have some bad news." The expression on her face went from one of excitement to one of fear. "Libby, honey, I just listened to a phone message from Brutus's owners. They saw the poster of him we put down the island, and we have to call them back."

Libby said, "But, Dad!"

Jim said, "Libby, that was the agreement we had, and besides, if he were your dog, wouldn't you want him back?"

Libby frowned and said, "Yeah, I guess so."

Jim dialed Mr. Kane's number. He picked up immediately, obviously eager for a return call. The Kanes were still down the island. Jim gave them his address, and Mr. Kane said they would be there in just a couple of minutes. As much as Jim and Virginia tried to console Libby, the more emotional she became. She just sat there, hugging and patting Brutus.

When the doorbell rang, everybody just looked at each other. Finally, Jim got up and answered the door. He was a little surprised, expecting a much younger couple. Mr. and Mrs. Kane were probably in their mid-sixties. As soon as Mr. Kane saw Brutus, he called out to him, "Hey, Champ!" Brutus looked up and ran over to Mr. Kane, almost knocking him over.

Mrs. Kane leaned down and said, "My gosh, look how much you've grown, Champ." She looked at Jim. "Thank you so much for finding and taking care of him."

Jim said, "Well, I just found him. But my daughter, Libby, is the one who's been taking care of him."

Mrs. Kane said, "Thank you, Libby, it looks like you have really taken good care of Champ, and he's twice as big now than when we lost him!"

Jim asked, "How did you lose him?"

She said, "Well, we were walking around the island, and we decided to change the leash to a longer one because we were up on the grass hill, and there would be more room for him to run around. As soon as we unleashed him, he saw another dog that didn't have a leash, and he just took off after it. We searched for hours but couldn't find him. We came back every day for a week, and still no sign of Champ. We thought we would never see him again." While Mrs. Kane told the story, she looked at Libby the whole time. She knew Libby was crushed to lose him.

Just then, Brutus jumped onto Mr. Kane, almost knocking him to the ground. Jim had to reach out and break his fall. Meanwhile, Mrs. Kane was still looking at Libby. She looked at her husband, who was just regaining his composure, and said, "Tom, look how big Champ is, and he's nowhere near full-grown. How are we going to take care of him with your bad back and my sore hip?"

Mr. Kane started to say something like, "Oh, he'll be no problem," when Mrs. Kane interrupted him.

"Tom." When he looked at her, he got the gist of her expression as she looked at Libby and then back at him. When you've been married for that long, you understand looks better than words sometimes.

"Oh, yeah. You're right, Mary. He may be too much for us to handle now."

Mrs. Kane said, "Libby, I was just wondering, since you have done such a good job taking care of Champ—well, do think you can help us by keeping him? I'm afraid he's going to be too much for us to handle."

Libby couldn't believe her ears. She said, "Are you serious?"

"Of course we are. We'd rather give him to you than someone we don't know."

Libby jumped and said, "Yeah, Dad, can we?"

Responding to the excitement, Brutus now ran over to Libby, jumping up and licking her face. Mrs. Kane said, "But there is only one condition." Libby looked up at her. "You have to let us come and visit Champ every so often."

Libby said, "Sure, you can come by anytime." Jim and Virginia thanked the Kanes for their kindness and compassion and promised them they would take very good care of him.

When they left, Jim turned to Libby. "Libby, did you learn anything from this?"

She looked confused. "Learn what, Dad?"

Jim said, "When you do the right thing, like posting pictures of Brutus, God will always reward you."

63

It was now Friday morning at five thirty. Jim hadn't got much sleep before the nine o'clock construction meeting. Even though George's talk had been helpful, he was still very nervous. When you've made many mistakes in your life, each one of them knocks down your self-confidence a little. Jim was up making coffee and going over the suggestions George had given him. He went over his selection of clothes, getting very frustrated, and then he remembered what George had told him. *Just be yourself. Just be yourself.* So he picked out a nice pair of pants and a collared dress shirt, showered, and got dressed.

Jim had called Danielle to sit with Libby while he was at the meeting. The doorbell rang, but when he answered, Danielle looked at Jim as if he were somebody new. She said, "Wow, Mr. Davis, you look so professional."

"Really, do you think so?" It made him feel a little better about himself. After he got his things together, he had to ask Danielle again how he looked, just for reassurance.

She said, "You look terrific."

"Thanks, I'm on my way."

"OK, good luck."

Jim got into his truck and headed down to the waterfront. He wished it would be a long drive, but unfortunately, it was only about fifteen minutes. As he was driving down Summer Street, his cell phone rang. George said, "I'm calling you to wish you luck." Jim was taken aback a little that George had remembered the time and date of his appointment. They talked for a few minutes. By the end of the call, his confidence level had risen.

In the office parking lot, all he saw were luxury cars: a Lexus, a BMW, a Mercedes...and so on. He decided to park his old pickup truck at the other end of the lot. Jim entered the lobby with its beautiful glass doors and Italian marble floors. He looked up Parsons Development on the directory, and of course, it was on the top floor in the penthouse suite. As he rode up in the elevator, a sudden thought came to his mind and he said a quick prayer. *God, please get me through this meeting without me embarrassing myself.*

When the doors opened, he felt like he was in the Hilton: he saw oriental carpets, paintings that looked like they might be by Rembrandt, porcelain sculptures, and a grand chandelier on the ceiling. He stepped out of the elevator. To his left, there it was: a huge, oval, oak table with at least twenty leather chairs around it. He could see that the window faced the waterfront where the first phase of the project was to start. Everyone was extremely well dressed in the finest suits. Now he really felt out of his element.

When he entered the room, no one took notice of him. He thought they probably thought he was someone from the maintenance staff. After he had been standing there for a couple of minutes, Mr. Parsons called the meeting to order, and everyone took their seats. Jim waited a few seconds, not wanting to sit where he wasn't supposed to. When the others were all seated, Mr. Parsons noticed Jim. He got up out of his chair, saying, "Jim, I'm so glad you could make it." Everyone turned and looked at each other as if to say, *Who is this guy?* After shaking Jim's hand, Parsons took his place at the head of the table. "Gentlemen, I think most of us know each other here, but I would like to introduce Jim Davis. Jim will be our liaison with the construction crew." Jim just nodded his head to them, and some gave him a polite nod back, but most just looked at him like, *Who is this person, and what does he think he's going to tell us that we don't already know?*

"All right," Mr. Parsons said, "let's get this meeting started. Obviously, our first and most important order of business is the set of problems we've had coming in on time and on budget on the last three projects. In these economic times, we just can't afford that. I realize that every job has some unforeseen additional costs, but we always allow for that in our budgets. We've really made an effort on this project, but we're more concerned about the time line. Does anyone want to make any suggestions on this matter?" One by one, the meeting attendees all had their own plans to remediate the problem. The longer the meeting went on, the crazier the ideas became. Then all the egos kicked in and tempers started to flare up. Jim just sat there, amazed that these men, college educated in finance, really didn't know a thing about what goes on on the ground during a construction job. Frustrated, Mr. Parsons interrupted and said, "Jim, what are your thoughts on the situation?"

Jim was caught off guard, but he sat up in his chair and after a few seconds, said, "Well, the way I see it is, if you had an incentive program for everyone who worked on the project, they would likely be more motivated to finish on time—or, even better, before the deadline."

Mr. Parsons asked, "What kind of incentive program are you talking about, Jim?"

All eyes shifted to Jim. "Let's just say that phase one gets finished before the allotted time—for example, in two years. Let's say that's ten percent sooner than you've budgeted, and say the cost savings are a million dollars. Then, that million would be awarded back to the subcontractor, who in turn pays out to construction workers on the job proportionately to how many hours they worked."

Then the chief financial officer lowered his glasses and asked Jim, "Tell me why we would want to give away even one dollar of additional profit."

Jim responded, "You wouldn't be giving it away. You would recoup that money, and probably much more, by selling or leasing your properties much sooner. And, you could pay down the investors and save a lot of interest on the construction loans. Not only that, your company would get a reputation for finishing under budget and under time, which is almost unheard of in this industry. Then your company would be sought after by potential investors and large real estate development companies.

"If all the workers knew there would be a bonus in their paychecks if the project were finished earlier, well, I don't think that anyone would put up with someone not giving one hundred percent, because that would be taking money out of their pockets. And you know what they say, the cream always rises to the top. You would be getting the best of the best workers out there. Also, remember, this is a ten-year project, and in these times, people need to make sure they keep working so they can keep their homes and their kids in college."

By now, Mr. Parsons was looking around the room at all these men on the board as if to say, *Why am I paying you all this money to oversee these projects, and none of you never thought of this?* All the men were looking at each other and nodding in agreement. Mr. Parsons said, "Well, I personally think this is a revolutionary idea."

Jim said, "Well, all I know is what happens down on the construction site. I couldn't even begin to tell you what happens behind the scenes in the office."

"Well, Jim, that's exactly why we hired you. We are going to seriously take this under advisement and see how we can make this work. Thanks Jim, thanks for your input."

After the meeting adjourned, no one could get to Jim fast enough to introduce themselves, shaking his hand and patting him on the back. As Jim left the meeting room, under his breath, he murmured, "Thank you God, thank you." Then he remembered what he had heard Charlie say a million times: *Ask God for help, and He will do exceedingly and abundantly more than you ask for.* When he walked out of the lobby and into the parking lot, he didn't worry about anyone seeing him get into his old truck. He just remembered what George had told him. *Don't try to be anyone else. Just be yourself.*

64

Back in Southie, Jim couldn't wait to see someone he knew to break the good news. He often saw local homeless people on the benches along West Broadway. There, he noticed Henry. Henry had been around there a long time, as long as Jim could remember. His older brother, Peter, had always looked after Henry, and Jim was also friendly with him. Whenever he passed by, he'd give Henry spare change. Today was different. For some reason, he knew he had to turn around and go see Henry. Jim pulled up next to Henry's bench and called out to him.

Henry looked up at Jim. "Hey, Jimmie, I didn't even see you pull up." Jim got out and walked right up, taking a good long look into Henry's eyes. What he saw saddened him. Henry asked, "Jimmie, you OK?"

Jim said, "What? Oh, yeah, yeah. I'm good, Henry. How are you doing?" Jim must have talked to Henry a thousand times, but something was different now. He had realized that but for the grace of God, he could have been standing in Henry's shoes. He said, "Henry, when was the last time you ate something?"

Henry looked puzzled. He said, "I don't know, maybe yesterday or the day before."

"Henry, I'm going to give you twenty bucks, and I want you to go down the diner and have a big meal for yourself."

Henry looked like he'd just hit the lottery. "Wow, Jimmie, nobody ever gave me twenty bucks before."

"Well, now someone has." As Jim walked back to his truck, he stopped and looked at Henry. "We all deserve a free meal once in a while, don't we?" Jim was trying to say to Henry that we are all vulnerable, but for God's grace and mercy, though He's always there to give us spiritual nourishment.

As Jim was about to drive off, Henry said, "Thank you, Jimmie. You are a kind man." Jim almost hit the brakes. It had been a very long time since someone had said that to him. He didn't know what he was feeling. For just a couple of minutes, he had gotten out of himself and thought of someone else. This is very unusual territory for an alcoholic, even though most of them are kind. Jim's kindness had always been covered up by self-centeredness.

Jim wanted to look in the mirror to see whether Henry would choose the diner or the package store. Then a voice in his head said, *Keep driving. It doesn't matter where he goes. It's not for you to judge.*

65

Jim heard his cell phone ringing. He saw that it was Libby, probably calling to find out how his first meeting had gone. He grabbed the phone in excitement and said, "Hey, honey!" Jim started to give a word-by-word, detailed description of the meeting.

Libby interrupted Jim and said, "Dad, the printing company just called, and they said the extra Kids for Seniors T-shirts we ordered are ready for pickup. Can you get them, Dad? Can you?"

Again Jim realized the world didn't revolve around him. He said, "When are you starting the program?"

"Tomorrow, Dad, tomorrow!"

"OK, OK, settle down. I'm actually driving right by the printer's now. I'll stop and pick them up."

"Thanks, Dad, you're the best."

"Yeah, yeah, I want that in writing."

Libby said, "OK, Dad, you got it."

When Jim got home with the T-shirts, Libby had already called all the kids. By the driveway, there must have been fifteen or twenty bikes on the sidewalk. Kids were running in and out of the house. Once they saw Jim, they all came running out and attacked him while he grabbed the boxes out of the trunk. The kids each took some and ran into the house. It was chaotic, and

Danielle was right in the middle of it. At that moment, she looked ten years old, which brought a smile to Jim's face.

In the house, the boxes were being torn open and thrown all over the place. All the kids were looking for their own shirts because they all had names on them. This served two purposes. One was to make it easier to start a conversation with seniors by introducing themselves visually. The other was to make it easier for the seniors to remember all their names. The living room was upside down with clutter. Just then, Virginia walked in and asked, "What's going on?" Libby and the others ran over, showing off their shirts. After she greeted all the kids, she came right over to Jim and said, "Well, tell me! How did the meeting go? I couldn't sit home anymore; it was driving me crazy. I had to come over and find out. Please tell me it went good."

"I'm so exhausted. I didn't sleep at all last night, thinking about it. I must have prayed all night."

"So, tell me, how did it go?" Jim couldn't take his eyes off her. Her expression showed how concerned she was. Jim told her the whole story, word for word. Her expression went from sincere concern to sheer excitement. She put her hands over her mouth, and her eyes teared up. She lunged at him from across the sofa. She couldn't let go, saying, "Thank you, Jesus, thank you."

Something started happening to Jim. He felt something he had not felt in a very long time and was getting very emotional. When a person has years and years of inner pain and tragedy, he or she learns how to shut down all emotion. Jim quickly stood up and told Virginia he had to go to the bathroom. When he reached it, he locked the door behind him. With his back against the door, he slowly slid down to the floor, thinking, *What's happening to me?* He tried to control his emotions, but he was quickly losing the battle.

And then it happened. The floodgates opened, and he cried uncontrollably. The more he tried to stop, the more the tears came. It had been a long time since he had cried. When people have one heartache after another, their hearts become hardened, and they won't allow themselves to feel their feelings. It's a form of self-protection to never allow themselves to be vulnerable again. The longer they do this, their hearts become like stone. Jim couldn't stop feeling how blessed he had been to meet Virginia. It's very unusual to meet your soul mate even once in your lifetime. It's rarer to lose one and have God replace him or her with another.

66

It was now two o'clock. Jim and Virginia were heading down the island to pick up Libby. As they were driving down Day Boulevard, Virginia noticed that Jim was very quiet. She asked him if anything was wrong. Jim said no, not really. "What do you mean, not really?"

"Well, I'm just nervous."

"About what?" Virginia asked.

"I hope that everything went OK for Libby today. You know how she puts her heart and soul into everything she does."

"Yeah, I know. You'll just have to explain to her that these things take time to develop. It's going to take word of mouth to get around before people start hearing about it."

Jim said, "Yeah, I guess you're right." But his expression showed that he was still worried.

As they turned into Sully's parking lot, they could hardly believe their eyes. Jim stopped the car and actually leaned forward over the steering wheel. Then he looked at Virginia and asked, "Are you seeing what I'm seeing?" Virginia had her hands over her mouth, looking at Jim and nodding her head up and down as if to say, *Yes, yes I do.* The kids weren't all bunched up together, standing in a corner. They were spread out from one end of Sully's lot to the other. It was a sea of green shirts. They all were with different groups of seniors. Some were playing checkers, some chess, some were just sitting and engaging in conversation, and one group was playing four square (and it looked like the seniors were winning). Everyone had smiles on their faces.

There was a big commotion going on at one of the picnic tables where they were playing chess. One man, who had to be in his eighties, was on top of the table doing a victory dance. He was saying to a boy, "Ha-ha, the old man took you to school today!" Everyone nearby laughed and clapped.

The boy yelled up, "I want a rematch!"

The man stopped his dancing, pointed down at the youngster, and said, "You got it, kiddo." Then the boy and a few other kids helped him get down off the table while the man kept saying, "Oh, am I'm going to feel this in the morning."

The boy who had lost the chess game said, "Are you saying you're not going to be here next week for our rematch?"

The man just said, "In your dreams, kid, in your dreams."

One man had a group of kids on the hill next to Fort Independence. He wore a hat that said "World War II Veteran" on it, and underneath, it said, "Sixty-First Airborne." He was telling the kids about how the fort was built to protect the harbor in times of war. One kid asked him what "Sixty-First Airborne" meant. He explained that they were men who jumped out of planes with parachutes, sometimes landing in enemy territory. Oftentimes, they were being shot at while still in the air. He told them that he had fought against the German troops in Europe and about all the challenges his division had endured over there. Since they were only kids, he spared them the gory details.

All the kids had read about World War II, but none of them had ever actually talked to anyone one who was in it. One girl asked, "If you knew it was going to be so dangerous, why did you go over there?"

The man had only one answer. "I went there because I loved my country, and still do. It was my duty to go, so we could have our freedom."

The kids were so affected by that statement that all they could say was "Wow." This was the whole point of why Libby had started the club. You have all the information you want about anything today at your fingertips, with computers, iPods, and smartphones, but nothing is better than someone telling you a story. You will remember it for a lifetime.

All the parents were pulling in to pick up the kids as scheduled, and everyone was saying good-bye. The seniors looked like they had a new spring in their steps. All of them were asking, "Are you coming back next Saturday?" Some of them had to be reassured several times before everyone went their separate ways. It's amazing what a little human contact can do for some people. It picks them up and gives them life. This was something that many of them hadn't had in many years.

67

Ed Donlan and Junior had been in the hospital for several days for testing and preparation for the kidney transplant. Ed had been very excited when he first arrived, since Junior was a perfect match. The realization that the transplant could save his life was setting in. The only problem was that the more time Ed spent in the hospital, the more of a chance he had to reflect on his life, and it seemed he could only focus on the negatives. Even though he was very successful, he could only think of the failures in his personal life. He was getting very depressed. All the tests were complete, and the operation was scheduled for eight the next morning, but he wondered if he really deserved a second chance. Why him? There were many people who led quiet and humble lives. Why would God give him a chance and not them?

Then there was a knock at the door, and Junior came in. They had talked every day since the testing had started. This time, they both realized that it could be the last time they ever got a chance to talk alone again. After all, with Ed's failing health, the odds were against him for a successful surgery. Ed said, "Come on in, son."

Junior walked over to the side of Ed's bed, never taking his eyes off his father. Ed made some small talk, but Junior interrupted. "Dad, Dad. I want to talk to you about something." Ed began to feel sick to his stomach. He thought that Junior wanted to talk about their past relationship. Ed had gone over all his regrets a thousand times in his head while in the hospital. Ed started to apologize, but Junior said, "Dad, we already went over all that stuff. That's all in the past. What I want to talk to you about is the future." Ed had been so worried that the surgery might not work that he hadn't been thinking much about the future. "Dad, I was wondering if you would consider hiring me. I don't want any favoritism. I'll start at the bottom and work my way up."

Ed couldn't believe what he was hearing. Ed said, "Junior, you never wanted anything to do with my company. Why now?"

"Well, I've been thinking about it. You see, I've been feeling burned out on the job, and it has started to affect me at home. I think I need a change. We could move up here and be closer to you and Mom."

Ed said, "I thought you never would want to work for me."

"No, Dad, I just didn't want my choices made *for* me."

"I guess you and I have that stubborn streak in us," said Ed, and both chuckled in agreement. Ed paused a second and said, "Junior, it would be a dream come true for me to teach you everything I know about the business, and someday hand it all over to you."

"That's great, Dad, but remember, I want to work for it."

"OK...hey, Junior, isn't this ironic? All my life I tried to tell you how to live your life, and instead you chose to live your own—not mine, which was drinking, smoking cigars, eating the best steaks in the world, and being constantly on the road, away from my family. You chose to eat healthy, exercise, be at home with your family, and enjoy life. And in the end, your choices are going to save my life when you donate your kidney to me."

Junior said, "Well, Dad, you can do something for me after we get well."

"What's that?"

"You still have a full head of hair, and I'm getting a little thin up there. So I already scheduled a hair transplant for us when we get better."

Ed said, "Junior, that's the least I can do for you."

"Dad, can you do one more thing for me?"

"Sure, what is it?"

"From now on, can you call me Ed?" Ed teared up. It had been ten years since his son had wanted to be called by his name. All Ed could do was nod yes. "Thanks, Dad, I'll see you tomorrow." He leaned over and kissed his father on the forehead.

When Ed Jr. left, Ed thought about all the times in his business career when he had been grateful for closing a big business deal, but nothing could ever come close to the gratitude he was feeling now.

68

By the time Libby got home, it was almost three o'clock. She should have been exhausted. But the dance started at seven o'clock, and that only left four hours for a girl to get ready for her first date—and not just any date, but one with the cutest and most popular kid in her school. Virginia and Libby wasted no time getting to work. Jim and Brutus had other plans: a nice snooze on the sofa. Jim had settled down with a big pillow and the TV clicker. Life couldn't have been better.

It seemed like he had been napping only ten minutes when he heard Libby calling him. When he looked up at the clock, it was already six fifteen. Libby called down again, "Dad, are you up? Smitty's going to be here soon!"

Jim yelled, "Yeah, yeah, I'm up." Jim looked at Brutus, and he had the same cranky face as Jim. Jim said, "I know, Brutus, I know how you feel. Don't worry, though. Someday when I retire, we'll be able to do this with no one bothering us." Brutus just stared at Jim as if to say, *Yeah, that's not helping us now.* Jim just smiled.

Smitty's dad was picking Libby up at six forty-five. Jim respected Smitty's dad. He was a hardworking guy, a lineman for NSTAR Electric. They hadn't run in the same circles growing up, but the families knew each other. Smitty's father and mother had come to Susan's wake and funeral, and Jim never forgot it.

Jim went up to take a shower, while Libby kept saying, "Hurry up, Dad. I don't want you coming out of the shower with a towel on when Smitty gets here. I'll be so embarrassed."

Jim said, "We don't want that to happen, now do we?"

Jim finished getting ready and was downstairs when Virginia made the announcement that the party girl was about to make her entrance. Jim looked up the stairs and saw Libby coming out of her room. Now, he had already seen and approved her dress, but he had never seen her with a little makeup on, and Virginia had given her some beautiful amber jewelry. This particular amber could only be found on the Baltic Sea coast. Jim was speechless. He usually handled situations where he had to show some emotion with some kind of joke, but today, there was no joke to be found. He just kept gazing at Libby and finally said, "Honey, you are so beautiful. You look like an angel straight from heaven."

Libby really wasn't ready for that. She paused for a minute and said, "Thank you, Dad." You could tell it meant so much to her.

It was exactly six forty-five when the doorbell rang. As Jim went to answer it, Libby said, "Dad, wait," and she ran back up to her room. Virginia went into the living room, trying to look as casual as possible. Jim waited until Libby made it upstairs and then opened the door.

Smitty said, "Hi, Mr. Davis, I'm here to pick Libby up for the dance."

Jim looked out toward the sidewalk and saw Smitty's dad in the car. He stepped out onto the front porch and decided to go out and talk to him. "How's it going?"

"I'm good."

Jim said, "I'm not sure I'm ready for this."

"I hear ya. Let's just hope what goes on at these dances isn't the same as at the ones we went to."

Jim said, "Oh, I don't want to even think about it. Thanks for driving them."

Smitty's dad said, "No problem. I'll pick them up at ten, so Libby should be home around ten fifteen."

Smitty was still waiting outside the front door for Jim. When Jim came back, they went inside, and Jim called up to Libby. A minute later, Libby came out and down the stairs. Smitty didn't quite know what to say. He had never seen her this way either. He said, "Wow, you look so different—I mean, in a good way." Jim and Virginia just looked at each other and smiled.

Libby thanked Virginia and then hugged Jim while giving him another look that said *Dad, don't say anything to embarrass me.* Jim caught on real quick and gave her a kiss, saying, "You guys have a good time." Libby looked relieved. Jim and Virginia walked them to the door and watched them go down the walkway together. They waved to Smitty's dad and Jim again said, "Thanks!" As Jim turned back to Virginia, he saw that she was crying. He hugged her and said, "Hey, I'm the one who should be crying."

Virginia chuckled and said, "I thought tough Irish guys from Southie never cried."

Jim said, "No, that's not true. You should have seen me and Brutus crying when you woke us up from our nap, right, Brutus?" Brutus jumped up and down, barking in agreement. Jim said, "See, I told you."

"Oh, he would agree with you no matter what you asked him."

Jim said, "That's why they call dogs 'man's best friend.'"

69

A t the school, the parking lot was full. Smitty's dad said he would be back at ten to pick them up and wished them a good time. Since it was summertime, most of the kids didn't know who was going with whom to the dance. It seemed that half of them had dates, but the other half were there hoping to meet someone. So the word hadn't got out about who was going with Smitty. When they walked in together, everyone took notice. Libby felt like everyone was staring at her and wondering what she was doing with him. As all the kids greeted them, Libby felt a strong presence in the room that seemed to be directed right at her. She sensed that someone or something was trying to guide her in a certain direction.

As the night went on, Smitty introduced Libby to all his friends. He picked up that something was going on with Libby and asked her if she was OK. She told him what she was feeling, and he knew that if Libby felt something, it was real. He had had firsthand experience with that. She felt that there was someone in that room she was supposed to help, but for the first time since she had had the gift, she couldn't connect her feeling with a person. This really frustrated her.

This was a typical CYO dance, with one large group of boys and girls in the middle of the hall, a group of boys on one side, and a group of girls on the other. Then the large group of kids in the middle moved toward the DJ to request songs. Smitty told Libby that he had to go to the men's room and would be right back. Again he asked her if everything was all right, and she assured him that it was. Then she saw a girl standing just inside the hall doorway, and she felt immediately drawn to her.

Even if Libby had not felt anything in particular about the girl, she would have made a point to talk to her anyway. Libby's parents had always taught her to be kind to people, especially the ones who seemed to be all alone. She was supposed to go out of her way to include them in whatever she and her friends were doing. This is what Jim and Peter's parents had taught them, and they had been very well respected in the community.

As Libby made her way through the crowd, the girl who was standing at the door had turned to leave. Libby wanted to shout out, "Wait!" but she knew the music was too loud for the girl to hear her. The more effort she made to get to the door, the more her friends tried to stop her and ask about Smitty. Libby politely blew them off and kept going. But when she got there, she thought she had lost the girl and was going to give up. Then she saw her on the other side of the street.

Libby looked both ways and darted across the road. When she caught up with the girl, she asked, "Where are you going? The dance just started."

The girl turned and looked at Libby. "Are you talking to me?"

"Yeah."

The girl said, "But I don't even know you."

Libby said, "I know, but something told me I was supposed to talk to you."

"About what?"

Libby let out a sigh and said, "I don't know." The both of them just looked at each other for a few seconds and then started to laugh. Libby said, "Let's start over. My name is Libby, what's yours?"

"Hi, Libby, I'm Sara."

"Hi, Sara. I don't think I've seen you around before. Are you from Southie?"

"No, I just moved from Norwood."

Libby said, "Wow, all the way from Norway? How far away is that from America?"

Sara chuckled and said, "No, I'm from Norwood, Mass."

"Oh, I'm sorry." Then she looked at Sara and asked, "How far is that from Southie?"

"It's only about thirty minutes from here." Sara laughed. "But it seems like I'm from another country..."

"Why did you move here?"

The smile quickly left Sara's face. She looked over at the school and said, "My mom had to take a job in the city."

"Oh, what about your dad? Does he work in the city?" Sara had known that question was coming. Libby felt a huge feeling of sadness from her. After a few seconds, Libby said, "I'm sorry, my dad says I always ask too many questions."

Sara smiled and said, "I wish I could hear my dad tell *me* that." Again Libby felt she had said the wrong thing. Sara said, "You see, I lost my dad two years ago. He was killed in the Afghanistan war."

"I'm so sorry, Sara. I know exactly how you feel." Sara just politely nodded her head like she had so many times before. Libby said, "No, Sara, I do. I lost my mom in a car accident almost the same time ago."

Sara looked up from the ground right into Libby's eyes, almost in disbelief. She said, "You did? Then you really do know I feel." This was the first time Sara had ever met another kid who had gone through the same thing. They felt an immediate bond with each other. Then it struck Libby that the strong presence in the dance hall that she had never felt before was God pulling her to Sara. Not just for Sara, but to help Libby herself. Libby knew that God puts blessings in our lives, and today, that blessing for Libby was Sara.

The two of them walked back to the dance together. When they got in, Libby introduced Sara to Smitty and all of her friends. Then Smitty introduced his best friend, Mike, to Sara. The two of them really hit it off, and they danced with each other all night. The transition in Sara was amazing. She went from feeling very sad and all alone to feeling accepted and a part of something, something all the money in the world can't buy. She felt the very essence of love. That very emotion can change the course of someone's life, and probably just had.

70

The next morning, Virginia came over early to prepare breakfast before everyone went to church. Jim was on the sofa doing his channel surfing. Libby and Virginia were in the kitchen starting breakfast. The phone rang, interrupting Jim's concentration on what channel to pick. He leaned over and looked at the caller ID. He was surprised to see Grace's name. He figured she needed a ride to church, which brought a smile to his face. He answered, "What's up, Gracie?"

"Jim, oh my God, I'm so glad I reached you." So Jim knew this wasn't a social call.

"What's the matter, Grace?"

"Jim, Mama just left in an ambulance to Boston City Hospital."

"Why, what happened?"

Grace said, "I don't know. Nathan and I were up getting ready for church. I noticed Mama wasn't up, which was really unusual for her. So I went to her room, and I couldn't wake her up, and she was hardly breathing. So I called an ambulance. They think she had a heart attack. I need to get to the hospital with Nathan. Jim, do you think you can give us a ride?"

"Sure, Grace, absolutely. We'll be there in ten minutes."

"Thanks, Jim, we'll be waiting for you."

Jim called out to Libby and Virginia and told them what was going on. They all stopped what they were doing and took

Virginia's car because they all could fit in it. When they got to Grace's, she and Nathan were already standing out front. They all crammed in. The ride to the hospital was only ten minutes, but it seemed to take forever.

At the emergency department, they said that Grace could go back there, but no one else. Grace pleaded with the secretary to please let them come in with her. She felt for Grace and said, "OK, go ahead." They thanked her and ran to the ER. Grace told them who she was, and the nurse said they could go in but that she had to call the doctor first. At that same moment, the doctor walked up behind her. He asked if they were here for Mrs. Green.

Grace said, "Yes, she's my mother." He looked directly into her eyes, and they all just knew the news was not going to be good.

He said, "Your mother has suffered a massive heart attack, and she has slipped into a coma. We don't expect her to come out of it. If you want to go see her, I would go in right away. I don't know how she's still alive right now." The doctor took them to the intensive care unit. When Grace saw her mom, she almost collapsed. She had all kinds of tubes and machines hooked up to her. She could hardly see Nana's face. The doctor said, "I'll leave you alone."

Grace walked over and held Nana's hand and said, "Mama, we're here. Nathan and I are here. Can you hear me? Mama, I just want to tell you that I'm so proud to be your daughter. I know I've made some mistakes, but I promise you, I'm going to make you proud of me. All I have to do is live my life like you did, and I know I can make it." She paused. "Jim, I don't know if she can hear me."

Jim looked down at Libby. His face said it all. *Libby, can you help Grace?* Libby took Nana's other hand, and they all held hands to make a chain. Libby asked him or her to close their eyes. They all could feel Nana's life force, but it was very weak. Libby said, "Nana's worried about leaving you and Nathan."

"Please, Libby, can you tell her we're going to be OK?" Libby squeezed Nana's hand tighter. Suddenly, there was a vision of a wonderful church with a full congregation singing and worshipping. They saw Grace up on the podium leading the worship team. Standing next to her was a handsome pastor. Then they noticed that they both had identical wedding bands on, and they realized that they were married and that this was a church they had started up together.

That vision started to fade, and another one began to appear. It looked like some kind of institution or college. There were hundreds of people gathered there. As the scene became clearer, they noticed a sign for Massachusetts Institute of Technology—MIT—a prestigious learning institute in Cambridge. It was a graduation ceremony, and they were handing out diplomas. Then they heard the name, "Nathan Green." There he was, Nathan, a tall, handsome young man. As he walked up to the podium, the master of ceremonies said, "And Nathan has been accepted into the NASA space program." A loud cheer came from the audience as Nathan accepted his diploma.

They could feel Nana's life force slipping away. She now knew that they were going to be OK and that she could go home to the Lord. They could see Nana walking toward a light, although they couldn't make out who was in the center of it. There was just a large silhouette. As she walked closer to it, the figure resolved. It was Grace's dad. The group could feel Grace's breath almost come out of her. Nana stopped and waved back at them, and Grace said, "Good-bye, Mama. We love you." Grace's dad embraced her, and then he looked up and into Grace's eyes. As he turned, he winked his left eye at her, just like he did when she was a little girl. Tears were streaming down her face, and she smiled and blew him a kiss. He reached out and grabbed it. She now knew what that wink meant to her. It said that everything would be OK, and that he and Nana would watch over them until they met again. Then they both walked into the light, and everything faded away.

When they all opened their eyes and looked at each other, they knew they had just experienced something special. Grace leaned over and hugged Libby and said, "Thank you, Libby. You really are an angel." Then the monitoring machine flatlined, and Nana was home. Jim just then got a text message on his phone. He looked down at it. It was Congressman Stephen Lynch. It read: *Jim, the Nana Green bill just passed a few minutes ago.* Jim smiled and thought that even in Nana's passing, she had left something that would help countless people in the future.

71

I t was such a beautiful day that Olivia Donlan decided to tend
to her rose garden next to the guesthouse. She got all the necessary tools out of the barn. She was feeling an overwhelming
sense of gratitude. Ed was getting the transplant that she thought
would never come. She was seeing a whole new side of him. Her
son and his family were there for the first time in ten years. She
felt that all the pain she had gone through over the years had all
been worth it.

As she made her way through the garden, she passed by the
window in the living room of the guesthouse. She was not prepared for what she saw. Sam was sitting on the sofa with his back
to the window. He had dozens of pictures of his family and him
spread out across the coffee table. Olivia felt that she shouldn't be
looking in at all. Then Sam picked up a photo of his wife and him
on their wedding day. That was all it took. He lowered his head,
clutching the photo against his chest, and cried uncontrollably.

Olivia backed away and leaned against the house with her
hands over her mouth. She didn't know what to do. She didn't
want to approach Sam. He would think that she was invading his
privacy. Who could she talk to? Both her husband and son were in
the hospital having very serious surgery. How could she go from
feeling invincible to totally helpless in just a few seconds? She

walked back to the barn. There is a fine line between minding your own business and extending your help to someone.

When she got to the barn, she became silent, closed her eyes, and said, "Dear Lord, I'm so very grateful for what You're doing in my family's life, but right now, there is a man in that house who seems so heartbroken and so helpless. I know he's carrying a lot of guilt and shame, and he doesn't believe he deserves anything good in his life. Please, I'm asking You, please, shed Your wonderful grace and mercy on him. Please let him know that if he trusts in You, he will have the faith that You will protect him. I'm asking this in Your precious name. Amen."

72

It didn't take long for the word to get out about Nana's passing. There were already dozens of flowers and candles on her front steps. Jim got a phone call from Grace. Again she thanked him for supporting her. She sounded a little emotional, which was to be expected. Jim asked her if she was OK. She said she was feeling a little overwhelmed. Jim said it was natural to feel that way with all the preparations that had to be done for the wake, the funeral, the headstone, and so on. Grace said, "Jim, it's not those things at all. It's the fact that just a few months ago, I would have been useless to anyone. Now I am responsible for all these things that need to be done. I'm just feeling very grateful that God has given me a second chance, and in a strange way, I'm glad I went through the things I did—or maybe I wouldn't appreciate all the little things in life. I feel so free from that horrible addiction. All I can think about is that song, 'Amazing Grace,' and how my chains are really gone."

"Grace, I know exactly how you feel. When we say that we're glad we went through what we went through, normal people don't understand us. I suppose it's the same for us when someone has gone through months of chemotherapy and has beaten cancer. We can sympathize with them, but in reality, we really don't know what it feels like. Grace, if you need any help with the arrangements, please call me. We would be glad to help."

"Thanks, Jim, I don't know what I would do if you guys weren't around."

"Well, you never have to worry about that. We will always be there for you and Nathan."

"Thanks, Jim. I'll talk to you later."

"Bye, Grace. Keep the faith."

"I will. I certainly will."

While Jim was on the phone with Grace, he had heard the mail being dropped off. When he opened the front door, Brutus began to bark. Jim said, "Sorry, Brutus, I'm just getting the mail." Jim saw that the mailbox was full. He really wanted to leave the mail there because he figured it was all bills. But since he had been sober, he was finding himself dealing with things head on instead of procrastinating. Nobody had told him to do that; it just seemed natural all of a sudden.

He grabbed the mail with both hands. Going through all the letters, he found that they were just what he'd expected: the mortgage, the gas and electric bills, and Libby's school tuition, all with late notices stamped on them. Jim said, "Here, God, Your bills are here. I know that You'll take care of them." Probably because he had just gotten off the phone with Grace, he was grateful for what he had and realized that those bills weren't going to take that away from him. As he went to put them down, another envelope fell out of the local paper. Jim picked it up. It read "Parsons Development."

Jim figured that the office wanted some more tax forms filled out. As he slipped the paper out of the envelope, the first thing he noticed was the phrase, "Pay to the order of Jim Davis." What he saw next floored him. The check was for ten thousand dollars. He couldn't believe his eyes. He opened the letter that accompanied the check. It read:

Dear Jim,

After considering your recommendation, the board of directors has overwhelmingly agreed to take your ideas and make them company policy. Once the accounting department ran all the numbers, we were quite impressed with the results. Please accept this check as a bonus above your future salary. We look forward to working with you in the future.

Best regards,

William Parsons

Jim smiled and said, "Wow, God, You don't waste any time paying Your bills, do You?"

73

It was a few weeks after Ed and Junior's transplant operation. Things had gone remarkably well. Today was the day the transplant doctor would tell them the results of their final test, and if they would be able to go home or not. Sam had driven Olivia and Megan to the hospital in their limousine. The Donlans had packed clothes for Ed and Junior to change into if the physician approved it. Sam was scheduled to take a van full of veterans on their weekly errands later, so he had brought it to the Donlan residence first, instructing everyone to wait in the backyard with his assistant and relax until he returned.

Olivia prayed with her head bowed as he looked over all the lab results. The doctor looked up, took his glasses off, and said, "Congratulations, guys, everything looks normal. I see no reason why you can't go home today." A celebration erupted. Not wanting to spoil the mood, he said, "I still feel an obligation to tell you that this is only the beginning of a very long recovery." As he went down the list of possible side effects or even rejection of the kidney, it still didn't dampen the mood.

Junior said, "We're not worried about it." The doctor started to reiterate his point when Junior interrupted him and said, "Doc, God didn't take us this far to leave us now."

The doctor looked up and said, "Well, we can't dispute that, can we?" Everyone chuckled and began to exchange hugs.

On the drive home, Ed and Junior were very quiet, just gazing out the window. They really appeared to be taken with the moment. Ed commented on things he had never noticed before, paying attention to the beauty of the landscape. Olivia heard Ed saying several times, "It's beautiful." Sam pulled into the driveway and, seeing the veterans' van, became extremely anxious. In all the celebration, he had totally forgotten to mention to Ed that he had the veterans at his home waiting for him to drive them on their errands. It was too late now. But Ed didn't really seem to take notice of the vehicle. He just assumed it was the pool-cleaning company. But what Sam saw next freaked him out. The guys weren't sitting by the van in the backyard. They were all in the pool, with the assistant begging and pleading with them to get out. They paid no attention to him until they saw the limo maneuver up to the fence. Sam just dropped his head and then looked at his assistant, who had both hands up as if to say, *They're not listening to me.*

Sam figured this was his last day of employment. As he got out of the limo, Ed clearly couldn't take his eyes off of the veterans. Sam thought, *This is the last thing he needs to see on his return from the hospital.* Sam started to apologize. Ed just walked right past him. Olivia said, "Ed, come in the house, you're not supposed to get upset. Your blood pressure will soar." Ed stopped and looked at all the men standing there soaking wet. Most of them were new to the shelter and were still wearing old, ripped, and stained clothing.

Olivia tried to take Ed by the hand, but he pulled away. She looked back at everyone in the driveway as if to say, *He's going to explode,* when Ed blurted out, "What? There's a party at my own house, and I wasn't invited?" Then he began to laugh hysterically. Ed asked his staff to fire up the grill, saying, "These men look hungry." Relief combined with disbelief fell upon everyone.

They all enjoyed their lunch. No one had ever seen Ed like this. He was mingling and seemed genuinely happy and interested in what his guests were talking about. The one thing that everybody really noticed about Ed was that he wasn't ordering his staff around; he was asking them. They were eyeing each other like, *What's up with this?* Marguerite, the head of Ed's staff, came over to Olivia and whispered in her ear, "Mrs. Donlan, I thought you said Mr. Donlan was getting a kidney transplant."

With a confused look on her face, Olivia answered, "He did, Marguerite."

Marguerite said, "Well, if didn't know any better, I'd bet a month's salary those doctors messed up and gave him a heart transplant." They snickered under their breaths.

Olivia looked over at Ed and said, "Marguerite, I think I'm falling in love again."

74

Driving down West Broadway, Jim saw the usual homeless people hanging around. He decided to look for Henry, whom he hadn't seen since the day he'd given him some money. Had Jim made the right decision? He wondered whether Henry had used the money for booze or something to eat. Had Jim helped him or enabled him?

When he got out of his truck, most of the guys recognized him. He asked if anyone had seen Henry around. Just then, he heard Henry's voice. "Jimmie! Hey, Jimmie." Jim turned and saw Henry getting off the bus and carrying a big box full of food, which he handed over to the eagerly awaiting crowd. They all seemed to be expecting him.

Jim couldn't take his eyes off of Henry. He thought his mind was playing tricks on him. He said, "Henry, is that you?"

"Yeah, it's me, Jimmie." Henry came over to Jim with his head held high. Even his walk looked different. Henry had always hunched over with his head down, looking at the sidewalk. Jim had never known whether he walked that way because he was so ashamed of himself or because he was always looking for loose change on the ground.

"Henry, what have you done with yourself? You look like a different person. I wouldn't have recognized you if you didn't call out to me."

Henry stood there full of pride, with a grin on his face a mile wide that said, *Can you believe it?* "Jim, remember when you gave me that money a few weeks ago?"

Jim said, "Yeah, sure I do."

"Well, I'm ashamed to say it, but I headed over the package store to buy some booze."

Jim, nodding, said, "I understand, Henry. I'm not going to judge you."

Henry said, "No, Jim, listen. When I got there, I stood in front of the store, and something hit me. The guys and I were just talking about how hungry we were, so I thought this seemed selfish of me.' I said to myself, 'Jim was nice enough to give me this money, and it doesn't seem right that I should spend it on liquor.' I looked over at the diner and said to myself, 'It would be better to buy all the guys some breakfast.'

"Well, that particular day, the manager waited on me. He asked me what I was going to do with all that food, since I was there by myself. I told him it was for all my friends and how we were just saying how hungry we were before you gave me this money. He said he was so impressed by that and gave us all the remaining breakfast food that had not sold! He told me I can come there every day at eleven o'clock and take whatever breakfast is left over. After coming there for a couple of days, he asked me if I wanted a job. I said sure. I figured he was giving me a chance, so I shouldn't take it for granted. So I gave up the booze and got into the Gavin House." The Gavin House is a halfway house in Southie that is well known for one of the highest success rates in the country. Their attitude is, if you don't want to change your life, there are plenty of people who would love to take your bed. Henry continued, "All my friends depend on me every day, and they are really grateful toward me. Jimmy, I can't remember the last time anyone has depended on me. I was always the person who depended on someone else, and helping people makes me feel good."

Jim was speechless for a moment. Then he said, "They should be grateful to have a friend like you, Henry."

Henry smiled. "Thanks, Jimmie."

Jim got back in his truck and thought, *Wow, I can't believe how doing something so small for people can change their lives.* Jim remembered some scripture his parents always referred to: *Jesus said we are to help the widowers, the homeless, and the orphans.* He grinned and said, "Thanks for the lesson, God. Today is a great day to be alive."

75

Nana's wake was coming up on Friday and would be held from four to eight o'clock. Jim heard there were people flying in from all over the country. Nana had affected so many kids growing up and had helped lead them down the right path—not so much through what she told them, but through just loving them.

Jim was coming out of the Mt. Washington Bank on West Broadway when he ran into Mattie, Peter's childhood best friend. The conversation began around Nana's wake, but then Mattie said that Peter had gotten married a few years ago and that Mattie had been his best man. Mattie told Jim that he had just spoken to Peter the day before and said he was coming to the wake with his wife and new baby son. Jim didn't even know Peter had a son, but he played it off to Mattie that he'd heard. When they parted, Jim stood there in the lobby not knowing exactly what to feel. Was he still angry with Peter? Was Peter still angry with him? Should he just ignore him at the wake, or should he be cordial out of respect for Nana and her family?

His life had started to turn around for the better. He didn't need this right now. Maybe if he had a chance to ponder the situation, he would be able to handle it. At that moment, Virginia called his cell phone. All Jim said was "Hello."

Virginia asked, "What's wrong?" How do women know? They have a sixth sense about this stuff. Guys could talk to each other all day and wouldn't pick up on it.

He said, "Nothing."

"What's the matter?" Jim paused. "Jim, are you there?"

"Yeah, I'm here. I just ran into my older brother's best friend, and he told me that Peter's coming into town for Nana's wake." Jim had briefly told Virginia about the circumstances between them but had never gone into specifics. Not sure what to say next, he quickly said, "I'll give you a call when I get home."

Virginia compassionately said, "OK, I'll talk to you later."

76

When Jim got home, Libby, Maria, and Libby's new friend, Sara, were in the living room. Libby introduced Jim to Sara. Jim said, "Hello, Sara. Nice to meet you."

Sara seemed to hesitate for a moment before responding, "Hi, Mr. Davis." Sara appeared to be considering the struggles Jim had been dealing with, the same ones her mom had had to handle after losing Sara's dad. Libby had told him her story after the CYO dance.

Jim excused himself and went out to the back deck. He had promised Virginia he'd call when he got home, but everything in his mind was trying to justify why he didn't need to. This was something he really didn't feel like dealing with right now. Then he kept hearing George's voice in his head saying, *How would you like it if she didn't call you back?* If you remove self-justification from a recovering alcoholic, he's left with having to be honest in all his affairs. Reluctantly, he pulled out his phone and dialed Virginia's number. "Hey, I just got home."

"Oh good, do you mind if I drop by? I was just about to call again. I picked up a little something for Libby."

"Yeah, no problem, I'll be here."

"OK, thanks, see you in a bit."

Jim knew that Virginia wanted to talk to him about seeing his brother Peter. Jim had already started to defend himself in his mind against his own wrongdoing. After all, Peter had started it.

When Virginia arrived, Libby invited her in and introduced Sara to her as Maria waved hello. Virginia said, "Wow, Maria, you look great!"

Maria said, "Yup, that's all I hear around my house! God is good."

"Well, you're living proof." They all smiled. Virginia said to Libby, "Hey, I picked up this makeup kit at Macy's on sale. When I saw it, I thought of you." Libby thanked her and gave her a big hug. Virginia asked, "Where is your dad?"

Libby said, "He's vegging out on the back deck."

Virginia went out there, and Jim looked over and smiled. "What's up?" He was trying to sound like nothing was bothering him, hoping she wouldn't bring up the topic of Peter. But she saw right through him.

"Can I talk to you about you and your brother?" Jim went right into his rehearsed side of the story. Virginia paid no attention to him. As she pulled up a chair, she interrupted. "Jim, I don't know what happened between you and Peter, but I do know that when you or Libby mention his name, I see your whole expression change. It's not anger. It's more a look of deep sadness." Jim just lowered his head and shoulders. He looked like all the fight had been taken out of him. "Jim, I want to tell you a story of when I was a little girl. I was just about Libby's age." Jim sat there motionless. "I want to tell you about my mother and my aunt Virginia. She was my godmother, and I was named after her. My mother and my aunt were twins. I remembered them always being together. They were so close. They did everything together. I can remember them at our kitchen table drinking coffee and always laughing. God, they always were laughing and carrying on like a couple of schoolgirls.

"One Christmas, all our relatives were over at our house. All the women were in the kitchen, and all the men were in the living room. I remember hearing a scuffle going on in there, and then I saw my dad and my uncle having a fistfight. I wondered, *Why would anyone want to fight on Christmas?* I was too young at the time to realize that the both of them had been drinking. Well, the longer they fought, the more people got involved and took sides, including my mother and my aunt. It escalated to the point where there were hurtful insults being thrown around. I'm talking about the kind people will never forget. When it ended, my uncle and aunt left, vowing never to set foot in our house again. Jim, in a couple of weeks, my dad and uncle were the best of friends again, like nothing ever happened. But my mother and aunt never spoke again. I remember how before she would attend any functions, she would have to find out whether my aunt was going or not. If she was, my mother wouldn't go. I remember being very confused. As a child, whenever I would get in an argument with one of my cousins, my mother and aunt would make us make up with each other, saying, 'You guys are cousins. You shouldn't be acting like this.' Then we would make up, and in a few minutes, it would all be forgotten. Why couldn't they do that? Jim, it's called pride, and that's why they call it the worst of the seven deadly sins. Pride creates a heart of stone.

"About five years later, I remember being in the kitchen baking bread with my mother. The phone rang, and when my mother answered it, I watched her almost collapse, holding on to the counter top. She immediately hung up and grabbed our coats as she pulled me out of the house. We didn't own a car, so we ran down to the bus stop. I never saw my mother run so fast. I could hardly keep up. I kept asking her what was wrong, and all she said was 'There's been an accident, and we have to get to the hospital right away.' All I could think of was that my dad must have got hurt at work. When we got off the bus, we still had to run about three blocks."

Jim still hadn't said a word. Even if he wanted to, he couldn't have.

"It wasn't until we got to the front desk that I heard my mother ask about her sister. They pointed in the right direction. When we got off the elevator, she searched for the emergency room. My mother was the most polite person I ever knew, but she was knocking people over everywhere. I remember turning down a hallway and seeing my uncle with his hands on his face, crying out, 'She's gone, my God, she's gone.' I can still see my mother just falling to pieces. I'll never forget the sound of a broken heart."

Jim asked, "What happened to your aunt?"

"She had a cold that day and decided to take the day off of work. She got up in the morning and made a cup of tea. Back in those days in Lithuania, we didn't have gas stoves. All the rooms had fireplaces, including the kitchen. Whenever you needed to heat up a pot of water or cook something on the cast-iron wood-stove, you would have to build a fire. Apparently, my aunt must have left the door on the woodstove open, and the flames spilled out onto the floor, catching it on fire. Eventually, the house filled up with the smoke. Because of her cold, my aunt never smelled anything. By the time the fire reached her room, it was too late. We found out later that she was already deceased when she got to the hospital.

"Jim, I never saw a person be so angry at someone and an hour later would have given her own life for her instead. My mother never had the chance to say good-bye or tell her sister how much she really loved her. I must have visited her grave a thousand times with my mother and heard her say she was so sorry. No matter how many times my mother said it, I don't believe it ever helped her with the guilt and remorse she felt. They say that time heals all wounds. I can tell you it was not true for her. In fact, as the years went on, it got worse—almost to the point where she had no joy in her life. Yeah, I saw her laugh here and there, but after she did, she would get real quiet, like she didn't deserve to be happy. Jim, I never saw her laugh again like she used to with my aunt. I prayed to God that you would never experience this. It's an awful thing to witness someone dying from an emotional tragedy years before your physical body does. God has given you so many blessings. Please don't lose the peace He has given you. No matter how much you believe you are right. Just ask this question: would you rather be right, or would you rather be happy?"

By now, both of them had tears coming down their faces. Jim just nodded his head yes, and they embraced each other.

77

It was now Friday morning. Jim was sitting out on the deck, having his coffee. He'd been in sort of a funk all week. He couldn't figure out what was bothering him. Things were now pretty good in his life, but he couldn't seem to enjoy it. Something was holding him back. Everything on the outside looked like it was good, but he didn't feel right on the inside. He thought, *Is this what sobriety is all about?* He had no desire for a drink, but he did have a desire to be someone or somewhere else. He suddenly remembered that George had called the other day. He had forgotten to call him back. Maybe Jim could talk to him now about what was bothering him. So he picked up the phone.

George said, "I don't know, Jim, I'm not feeling the love here."

Jim laughed and said, "I know, I totally forgot to call you back."

"That's OK, I have an in with the governor. I'll have him grant you a stay of execution."

"Thanks...it wouldn't have been the only one in my life."

George said, "You and me both, brother. So what's going on?"

"Oh, just getting ready for Nana's wake tonight."

"Yeah, I'll be there. I bet it will be mobbed. It will be good to see some old faces from the neighborhood. Some friendly, some not so friendly..." They both chuckled. "What's up with you, everything OK?"

Jim said, "Yeah. You know my brother, Peter, is coming in from California." Jim had already told George the whole situation with Peter and him.

"You nervous about it?"

"Yeah, sure, I don't know how it will go, but I already asked God for help on it."

There was a moment of silence, and George said, "You still there?"

"Yeah, sorry. There's just something else that's really bothering me that I can't seem to figure out."

"What's that?"

Jim said, "Well, three months ago, my life was a mess. I relapsed once again, I was out of work, the bank was foreclosing on my house, and so on. Then I get sober with your help. Libby gets this spiritual gift bestowed upon her. I have a beautiful, kind woman in my life. I get an unbelievable job opportunity. So why am I not ecstatic about everything? Why do I feel like there's no joy in my life? Am I crazy or something?"

"Wow, it's about time. You actually held out longer than I thought."

Jim didn't expect that kind of response. "What's that supposed to mean?"

"Listen, do you want to know why you feel this way? Because you won't allow yourself to feel any other way. You see, you have programmed your mind not to see yourself any other way. You can only see the past failures in your life, either with what you remember and focus on, or how other people see you and still like to remind you of. Jim, you are not the person you used to be. The Bible said in Romans 12:2, 'Be not conformed to this world: but be transformed by the renewing of your mind, that you may prove that what is that good and acceptable and perfect will of God.'

"You see, Jim, once you accepted Christ and turned your life over to His care, you belonged to Him. He said that the old you is dead, and you have been born again, and you should live your life according to His will. You have to let go of your old self and focus on who you are today. Your eyes can only look in one direction. They can't look back and forward at the same time. That doesn't mean you can't learn from the past, just don't be stuck in it. The old Jim is dead. I only see the new Jim. A kind, gentle, thoughtful, generous man who loves his daughter." Jim didn't respond right away. So George said, "Let me ask you a question."

Jim knew that every time George asked that, he got hit right between the eyes with a profound answer. So he said, "OK, go ahead."

George said, "Let's say Libby was in your situation. What would you tell her?" Before Jim could answer, George continued. "Would you want her to constantly look back at the mistakes in her life, or would you want her to look at the remarkable changes she made and have her focus on them?"

Jim said, "Yeah, you're right, but why is it so hard to do that?"

"Look, you live your whole life with an image of what other people think of you. You know God loves you. You know He has a purpose for your life. Having said that, are you going to walk out in the middle of the sidewalk announcing you're a candidate for the Nobel Peace Prize?'

Jim laughed and said, "No, not today."

"That's right. Because it's not going to happen overnight. It takes constantly staying close to Him by reading the word of God and praying daily. If there are people in your life who want to continually remind you of what you used to be like, well, remove them from your life and surround yourself with people who will encourage you, not discourage you. Jim, give yourself a break.

I've only known you a short time, but I tell you that from what I see, you are truly blessed. Enjoy the blessings God has given you. Use one of the suggestions in the program. Make a gratitude list and put it somewhere you can see it every day. You may not think that list is very long, and right now it may not be, but if you stay in fellowship with God every day, you'll feel that close relationship develop. The more you work on it, the more your heart and eyes will be able to see."

"All right, yeah. Thanks, George. I'm going to start making that list right now."

"OK, my friend. I'll see you tonight."

"Hey, George, can you give me a heads-up on the next thing I'm going to go through in this sobriety thing?"

"I could, but it won't benefit you as much because you still have to go through it and feel it to conquer it."

"Just thought I'd try."

"It's been tried on me a hundred times, so you're not unique. Tell Libby I said hi and that I'll see her tonight."

"Thanks again, George."

78

C harlie called Jim to see if he and Lucky could come by and carpool with them. The parking in Southie is at a minimum; it's the only place in Boston where double parking is normal. People just accept it.

They all met at three thirty and drove over. There was already a line out the door, even though the event wasn't supposed to start until four. They drove a couple of streets over and they got lucky—someone was just pulling out of a space. On the walk back to the funeral home, Virginia noticed Jim looking around. She said, "Jim, don't worry, everything will be OK."

Jim immediately responded, "No, I'm not worried."

Virginia looked at him and said, "Really, I just know it will be OK." Jim just nodded.

Once the line got inside, it was like going down memory lane. There were friends Jim hadn't seen in years. He proudly introduced Libby and Virginia to them. He saw people being reunited and telling stories of the old days. When he was growing up, there were several different neighborhoods of kids. You never drifted out of your own, at least not by yourself. But tonight, it was all different. Guys who had been arch-enemies growing up were laughing and hugging each other. Jim looked around and then looked at Virginia and said, "This is amazing. Even in Nana's death, she is still bringing people together." Then he saw Mrs. O'Toole. Jim had hung around with her son, Billy. Billy had a troubled life. He had basically been a real good kid; he'd just always had a knack for getting in trouble. It was never anything mean spirited; it was more stupid stuff than anything. Billy was finally sent to prison, but nothing changed in there for him. He got mixed up with the wrong crew. He would call Jim from there collect, and Jim would keep telling him just to mind his own business in there and do his time. Jim would often give Billy's mother a ride to visit him. One day, he got a call from her, and she told him that Billy had been murdered. Apparently he had been accused of moving illegal contraband in. The person running the organization was afraid he would talk and had him killed. Jim remembered thinking of how insane it was to get killed over a carton of cigarettes.

Jim wondered why Mrs. O'Toole was at Nana's wake. He knew they hadn't known each other. He walked over and said hi. She was so surprised to see him and gave him a big hug. Jim said, "I didn't know you knew Nana."

"I didn't, Jimmie. I just thought I had to come and pay my respects. I know how many times she tried to talk to Billy and help him change his ways, and I'm here just to show my gratitude toward her."

Jim remembered all those talks and sit-downs Nana had had with him. Jim said, "She sure did care about all the kids."

"There's absolutely no doubt about that. She surely was a saint."

"Amen."

When Jim turned away, he saw Peter coming in. He suddenly felt ill, just like before the first hit on a football field or in a boxing ring. Virginia had never met or even seen a picture of Peter, but she knew who he was by Jim's expression. She took his hand just to let him know she was there.

Peter was like a celebrity. Everyone was going over and shaking his hand. Jim didn't notice his wife at first, but then she appeared from behind him. She was extremely beautiful, with long, dark hair and a smile that lit up the room. Then he heard Libby call out, "Uncle Peter!"

Peter turned and said, "Oh my God, Libby, is that you? I can't believe how big you've gotten." Peter's wife came over and leaned down to greet her. Peter said, "Libby, this is my wife, Debra."

Libby shook her hand, and Debra said, "Peter, you're right, she is so cute."

As Jim watched this, Virginia tugged on his hand as if to say, *Go on*. He walked over to them, and as Peter stood up, he saw Jim. He reached out his hand to greet him. Jim also reached out, and they shook hands. The ice had been broken. They introduced Debra and Virginia to each other, who seemed so happy to finally meet. As the women exchanged greetings, there was obvious joy in their eyes. They knew how much this broken relationship had affected Peter and Jim. They didn't actually say it, but they both knew that their mission had been to help fix it.

As the women made small talk, Jim and Peter stood quietly by. Libby felt it was her time to do what she had been gifted to do. This wasn't a spur-of-the-moment thing. She had been planning this since she'd found out that Peter was coming. She walked in between the brothers and took each one by the hand. Then she closed her eyes. When Jim saw this, he knew right away what she was doing. His instincts told him to pull away. Then he remembered the story Virginia had told him about her mother and her aunt, so he held on.

The brothers felt themselves going back to their childhoods. The scene was Carson Beach. All of a sudden, Jim felt terrified and so alone. He could feel himself choking on water. He had been swimming and had fallen into a sinkhole. He remembered the panic he'd felt, sinking to the bottom. When his feet hit the bottom, he bent at the knees and pushed as hard as he could, propelling himself to the surface and gasping for air. Then he immediately sank back to the bottom. He did this over and over again. He remembered the feeling he had when he broke the surface and caught a glimpse of everyone laughing and having fun. He had thought, *Nobody even knows I'm drowning.* It was the ultimate feeling of abandonment.

Then, just as he thought he couldn't do it anymore, he felt two hands grabbing him and bringing him to the surface. He didn't know who it was until he reached the beach and finally caught his breath. A small crowd had gathered, and then he saw Peter leaning over him, asking, "Jimmie, you all right?" In just a few seconds, he went from feeling so scared to feeling so safe.

Peter started to feel some old feelings. Everyone knew Peter had been the strongest kid on the block and the obvious leader, but nobody really felt what he often felt. He remembered questioning God why his parents had to die. He had always been haunted by this question. Every time he had felt this way, especially on the worst days when he was at his bottom, he remembered God sending Jim to him to tie his shoes, make him dinner, or bail him out of something. That was when he knew what God needed from him. Not just to take care of Jim, but to know and feel that Jim's life was totally in his hands. That would be enough to keep him going for another day.

When they came out of this epiphany, they both were close to tears and full of compassion for each other. They both realized how much they had missed each other and knew that this moment would be life changing for them. When Libby spoke, they both snapped out of it. "Dad, can Peter and Debra come over to our house after the funeral tomorrow?" Jim told her yes, if they would like to.

Before Peter answered, both Virginia and Debra said, "Yeah, that would be great." Everybody chuckled a little and seemed relieved.

79

The next morning, Virginia, Jim, and Libby were walking down the church aisle looking for seats when suddenly they heard a very soft voice saying, "Virginia, over here." There were Debra and Peter. Debra had put their coats on the pew to save some spots. Jim thought the ladies must have made a plan yesterday to do this; he was sure they were working together.

When Jim sat down, he realized that he was less nervous than the day before. He thought, *Could this be possible?* Could the brothers' relationship be restored? The idea brought a smile to his face. They made small talk for a few minutes, and then the service started.

The pastor came out to the pulpit. Nana's favorite pastor was Fred, but this was not Fred. Everyone was a bit surprised. He was a tall black man maybe about Jim's age. The women in the congregation looked at each other; he was extremely handsome. The pastor greeted everyone. "Hello, my name is Pastor Norman. Pastor Fred is very sorry he couldn't make it here for the funeral. He's home with the flu, so he asked if I could fill in for him." Different people spoke of Nana and how she had changed their lives. Grace gave the most beautiful, heartwarming eulogy.

When the service was over, everybody thanked the pastor on the front stairs, especially the women. When Grace approached him, she also thanked him. He didn't respond right away; there was a moment of hesitation. He just kept staring at her, and then he realized why. He said, "I'm sorry, Grace, but I just have this strange feeling we have met somewhere before, but I can't figure it out." To Grace, this was the oldest pickup line in the book, but she was sure he didn't mean it that way. He quickly apologized but still kept looking at her, trying to figure it out. When they finished saying good-bye, they shook hands. Then, without warning, the pastor blinked his left eye at her, exactly the way her father used to. Grace stopped and looked stunned. The pastor apologized again, not even knowing why he had done that.

Grace stopped him and said, "Please, that's quite OK." The pastor, still looking embarrassed, said nothing. Graced looked up at the sky and said, "Thank you, Daddy." It was the signal that he would always be looking out for her. The pastor looked up as if he was going to see something. Graced turned and walked away. She smiled when she pictured her dad with Nana right behind him, urging him on to send that blink. When Grace looked back, the pastor was still looking bewildered. Grace thought that the pastor was even more handsome in person than when Libby had showed him to her in the vision at the hospital.

80

When Jim, Peter, and all the girls got outside, Libby spoke up before anyone had a chance to and said, "Uncle Peter, are you guys coming over?" Jim felt a little embarrassed for not inviting him first.

Peter seemed to have anticipated the question, and he and Debra said, "Sure," right away. Peter had only been to Jim's once, at Susan's funeral. They never had a chance to speak alone that day. Debra said, "We have to pick up the baby; he's with a friend of ours."

Virginia and Libby looked at Jim as if to say, *Why didn't you tell us they had a baby?* Jim had totally forgotten to tell them in all his worrying. Virginia quickly recovered and said, "Sure, take your time," like she already knew.

Libby started to say something, but Jim quickly grabbed her hand and said, "OK, we'll see you there." As they walked away, the hand gestures said it all. He looked like he was being scolded and on his way to the principal's office.

When Peter and Debra got to the house, Libby swung the door open. All Virginia's and Libby's attention swarmed over the baby. Libby asked, "Can I hold him?" Jim was unsure, but Debra said she could and handed him to Libby, who cradled him like he was her favorite doll. "What's his name?"

Peter and Debra glanced at each other and said, "Jim. His name is Jim."

Virginia looked at Jim, who looked like he had just seen a ghost. He said, "Wow."

Libby said, "Dad, he has your name." Any ill feelings Jim had about Peter just melted away. He thought, *What an honor.* Virginia discreetly grabbed Jim's hand and squeezed it as if to say, *See, I told you everything would work out.*

Things settled down, and the girls were playing with the baby. Peter looked at Jim and said, "Hey, can I talk to you for a minute?" They went into the kitchen, and Peter pulled out a big, faded manila envelope. He gently pulled out some papers and handed them over to Jim, who wondered what they could possibly be. Even when Jim looked at them, he still didn't know what they were. Peter said, "Jim, this is a college fund. I started it ten years ago when we sold Mom and Dad's house. It was for your future kids. I put ten thousand dollars into it." This was the same amount of money that Jim thought Peter had shorted him.

Jim was pessimistic at first. He thought, *Peter must have started the fund because he felt guilty.* Then he saw the date it had been opened, and it was the same day they'd sold the house. It had the name of the lawyer who had been a friend of their parents. Jim looked really confused. "Why did you do that?"

Peter looked down and then up at Jim, not really wanting to explain, but he knew he had to. "Jim, you were eighteen years old. You were running amuck all over town. I knew you would more than likely blow all the money, so I put this away for you."

Jim took a deep breath and nodded his head, acknowledging that back then, he had indeed blown any money he ever got. He looked at the current value of the fund and realized that by the time Libby went to college, it would be more than enough. Peter was very smart and had invested it well. Jim asked, "Why didn't you tell me that when I accused you of cheating me?"

"Jim, I tried, but you were really drunk and obnoxious that night, and the more we argued, the more hurtful things we said. You were pissed, thinking I stole the money, and I was pissed that you accused me." Jim couldn't believe it. It looked like he was about to cry. Peter saved him the humiliation and said, "We were both stupid to let this go for so long, so what do you say? Do you want to put this behind us and move on?" Jim tried to agree but could not speak. After two attempts, he just nodded yes, and they hugged for the first time in ten years.

Jim couldn't help but think, *How could a simple misunderstanding take ten years out of our lives?* He vowed never to let it happen again. He remembered his mother's favorite scripture. She would say, "Never let the sun go down while you are still angry."

81

When they got back into the living room, the girls were still in their own little world with the baby. After a few minutes, Peter asked Jim what he was doing for work. Was he still in the carpenters' union? Jim actually couldn't wait to tell Peter about his new job. He figured Peter would be impressed with the position that he had with Parsons Development and the story of how he got it. When Jim was growing up, he always looked for Peter's approval and recognition. And Peter was really excited for him when he heard about Parsons.

Jim knew that Peter also had a big position and asked if he had gotten any new promotions. Jim fully expected him to say yes. Instead, he saw a look come over Peter's face that he didn't ever remember seeing before. It was the look of a lack of confidence, or possibly even a look of failure. Jim knew something was really wrong. Peter had always been positive and took everything as a challenge that he knew he would conquer. Peter now spoke very slowly and methodically, choosing his words very carefully. This was very difficult for him. He just looked defeated. He told Jim that his company had been bought out by a larger, international company in Canada. He said that they were going to bring in their own people and downsize. Jim asked, "Do you mean you're going to lose your job?"

Peter put his head down, then looked up and said, "I already did, a few weeks ago. I'm in the process of looking for another one. Debra took some time off for the baby, but it looks like she'll have to go back to work sooner than expected." Jim just felt horrible. He never would have told Peter about his good fortune if he had known about their situation. Jim tried to encourage him, but it was hard. It was something he had never done before. Peter was always encouraging *him*. Jim asked when he was going back to California. Peter said, "I think in about a week. We actually talked about relocating back here. It seems the East Coast is doing much better than the rest of the country." Jim insisted he stay with them instead of a hotel. Things really felt like they were getting back to normal, except for Peter's situation.

Jim was trying to get a better relationship with God and found himself praying more often. That night, he said a heartfelt prayer, asking God to intervene someway and help Peter secure a job. He was amazed how easily the words came out. Then he remembered what Charlie once told him: if you're searching for words when you pray, it's because you're praying with your mind and not your heart. This couldn't have been truer, because that night, he could not sleep a wink.

82

I t was eight in the morning. Sam was awaiting a call from Ed, who had told him the night before that he needed Sam to drive Olivia, the twins, and himself to the airport. The twins' cousins were flying in from out of state to stay with them for a week. They were about the same age, one boy and one girl. The van would bring them all back, along with their luggage. Sam thought about his own children and how much he missed them.

Ed called and said they were ready, so Sam pulled the van around to the front entrance of the estate. The twins were giddy with excitement. When they all got situated, their mom and dad told them to behave on the ride to the airport, and Olivia asked them, "Well, what kind of plans do you have?" They both blurted out a slew of things they wanted to do. Olivia said, "OK, OK, you can only do one thing at a time." The girls giggled and said how excited they were to see their cousins.

Sam just smiled. "When was the last time you saw them?"

Ashley looked at Olivia and then quickly said, "It was last Christmas."

Sam and Olivia were asking where they would sleep as they rolled down the Mass Pike. Sam looked at Ed, thinking, *You're a lucky man. You got a second chance to make things right.* Although Sam loved to see this family reunited, he got depressed thinking about his own family. Were they angry with him? *Do they think*

I failed them? Would they ever be together again? It ate at his soul.

Olivia asked Sam to drop Ed off in front of the terminal, but Ed objected. "I can walk from the parking garage."

Olivia quickly answered, "You know what the doctors said, slow and easy. Who do you think you are, Superman?"

There was tension in the air. The old Ed would have reacted angrily, but instead, he said, "Honey, all these years we were married, you never knew I was Superman?" He looked at the twins, and they had their mouths covered with both hands, hiding their big grins. Ed looked at them and said, "You guys believe me, don't you?" Still covering their mouths, they both nodded yes. Ed looked at Olivia and said, "See, they even know." The girls couldn't hold on anymore and broke out in laughter. So did everyone else.

When they got to the arrival terminal, Olivia passed Sam a sign that said "McGuire" and asked that he hold it up so the cousins knew where to go. She said that their mother had asked her to do it and that the cousins were being escorted by someone from the airline. Sam said, "Sure, no problem." The twins got excited again and asked if they could take turns holding up the sign.

As they waited, people filed out of the gate with their luggage. It seemed like most of them had arrived, all walking to their waiting loved ones. Sam thought, *I hope they made it.* The twins looked so nervous, thinking that they might not have, and he didn't want them to be disappointed. Sam looked at Olivia and shrugged his shoulders as if to say, *I don't know.* But when Sam turned back to look at the gate, he saw a young boy and girl coming through. He was so relieved. It had to be them. He held up the sign.

The kids were looking all around—everywhere else but at him. He waved his hands to get their attention. When they saw him, they started running toward him. Sam was relieved again.

As they got closer, he looked into their smiling faces. It couldn't be true. He shook his head and blinked his eyes, and he shook his head again to clear his vision. He looked at Ed, Olivia, and the twins. They were completely ecstatic. Then he heard a word he hadn't heard in so long. A word he had wondered if he would ever hear again. "Dad, Dad!" There they were: his own children!

Sam ran toward the post that held the ropes separating the arrivals from the waiting area. He unhooked the chain and threw the rope aside. The airport workers would normally have stopped him, but they saw what was going on. They just smiled and hooked it back up. When Sam reached the children, he slid down onto his knees along the shiny wax floor with open arms and grabbed them. He squeezed them, looking up at them to make sure he wasn't seeing things, and kissed them. He had one in his left arm and one in his right. When he looked between them, he saw his wife coming around the corner with her luggage. He stood up slowly, looking back at everyone else again. It finally dawned on him. There were no cousins coming in from out of state. They had made it all up. They were giving each other high fives. They had pulled it off. Sam never had a clue. They all deserved an Academy Award, and they knew it.

Sam didn't run over to his wife. They both just stood and looked at each other. Then he saw tears in her eyes, and he knew they were tears of joy. They walked slowly into each other's arms and embraced. They just held each other for a long moment. Their children came and hugged them both around the waist. Olivia looked at Ed and saw that he was crying. She leaned over and kissed him. She whispered in his ear, "See? You're not Superman."

He smiled and said, "You did it, Olivia; you pulled it off." Ever since the day she had seen Sam crying while looking at his photos in the guesthouse, she had known what her mission was. She had contacted Sam's wife to plan this reunion.

Sam and his wife came over to greet them, saying over and over again, "Thank you, thank you." Ed said that they were truly welcome and that if they wanted to, they all could move back there and live in the guesthouse. Sam tried to show his appreciation but could not get the words out. Finally, he just leaned over to Ed and embraced him. Ed said, "This is a new beginning, a new beginning for the both of us. When you unhooked that chain over there and threw it aside, it meant the chains that bound you were gone."

Even though Sam was a Christian man, he had never understood it when someone said, "God has a plan for you." He questioned why God would let him go through what he had gone through. What kind of plan was that? Now he looked back at it. He had lost everything. He had been in debt, his marriage had suffered because of it, and he had been doing a job that he had no passion for anymore. He knew he had just been a number to that company. Now he was reunited with his family, which was once lost to him. He had a job that paid so much more and a position that he loved. He got to work with veterans and felt wanted and appreciated, and he lived in a beautiful home. He now understood God's plan and vowed to himself that he would never not trust in Him again.

83

It was a busy morning in the Davis household. Peter and his wife had taken the baby and had gone to meet some friends on Newbury Street, where Debra had wanted to go for the longest time. Libby and Maria were on their way over to Sara's house, and Virginia was working. Soon the house was empty, just Jim and Brutus. Jim decided to call George and let him know how things had gone with Peter and him.

When George answered, he said, "Hold on, Jim, I have someone on the other line."

"Oh, I can call you back."

"No, hold on, I'll be right off." A few seconds later, George came back on.

Jim said, "I just wanted to call and thank you for your advice about my brother Peter and me." Jim filled him in on the details of what had really happened, the huge misunderstanding, and how Peter had put that money away for Libby.

George said, "Wow, there couldn't have been a better outcome if you wrote it yourself."

Jim said, "I know."

"I told you about the promises. It looks like they're coming true for you."

"I know. I would never have believed it if you told me that last week."

"Good, I'm glad. You deserve it. Hey, what are you doing right now?"

Jim said, "Nothing, everybody's out. Just me and Brutus."

George said, "Why don't you take him down the island? I'm going to meet a guy I sponsor down there in a half hour. Do you remember Eddie Callahan from the Old Harbor projects?"

Jim said, "Yeah, he married Lisa Collins."

"Yeah, right. Well, they got a divorce a few years ago, and he's having a rough time with something. He's about a year sober, and like you, he's struggling with some guilt and can't seem to let go of it."

"Sure, I'll meet you down Sully's."

"Great, I'll see you then."

Jim looked at Brutus and said, "Brutus, do you want to go down the island and walk around the Sugar Bowl?" Brutus ran to the kitchen, grabbed his leash, and came running back with it in his mouth. Jim said, "Brutus, I swear, you're smarter than you let on. When I tell you to do something and you don't want to do it, you look at me like you don't understand." A blank stare came from Brutus. Jim said, "Oh, forget it. Now I'm arguing with a dog. I got to get out of the house more. Come on, Brutus, let's go. We got half an hour, let's walk down." Brutus seemed to understand, because if they drove there, he ran to the back door, but if they were going to walk, he ran for the front. Jim pointed his finger at him and said, "See? See what I mean?"

When Jim reached the bottom of L Street, he paused and looked right at the L Street Bath House. Seeing all the kids running in and out, he reminisced about all the time he'd spent there with Peter growing up. They hadn't had the material things kids have today—computers, smartphones, tablets, and so on. Instead of feeling like he'd missed out, he was glad those things hadn't been around then. He wouldn't have changed anything. Southie had been a great place to grow up. Looking back, he couldn't remember ever being bored or wanting to be anywhere else.

When he reached Sully's, he saw Eddie and George sitting at a picnic table. Jim thought he would just take Brutus for a walk and let them talk. He hadn't seen Eddie in many years, but he'd always liked Eddie. He was the type of guy who would give you the shirt off his back—or his last quarter, so you could buy an ice cream with all the other kids. Jim remembered how, when they used to walk down to Sully's with all the guys, Eddie would always look around for anyone who didn't have any money, and he would buy it for them.

When he got to the table, Eddie looked up at Jim. He stood up with a big smile and gave him a hug. It was always great to see someone from the old neighborhood. It always brought memories of a simpler time. They chatted for a few seconds and heard someone calling out for George. That wasn't unusual. Whenever people were around him, they realized how giving George was. He always had a hand out for anyone who needed it, and those people were always grateful. When George turned around, he saw that it was a guy who worked with him at the prison. George said, "Excuse me, guys, I'll be right back."

Jim and Eddie caught up on what they were doing with their lives. Eddie said how sorry he was to hear about Jim losing Susan. Eddie said, "Not that I ever lost someone so close to me, but you probably heard I got divorced a while back."

Jim said, "Yeah, I heard. And I'm sorry about that."

Eddie nodded and said, "I can accept it. I played my part in it."

"Are you still able to see your kids?"

Eddie said, "Yeah, I never miss a visit with them. And today, we're closer than ever."

Jim patted him on the shoulder and said, "See, that's what really counts."

Eddie said, "Yeah, I know, but..." He paused.

"But what?"

"I know all that, but I can't forgive myself for not being there for them. I was always there physically, but not always emotionally."

Jim said, "Eddie, nobody knows that more than me, believe me. I just had a talk with George a few weeks ago about the same thing. I told him the better my life was getting, the worse I started to feel about myself." Eddie jumped right up and told him, almost word for word, what he himself had been feeling. Jim said, "Listen, addiction is pure evil. It wants to rob us of everything that is near and dear to us. It beats us up and kicks us when we're down, telling us that we're good-for-nothing lowlifes, and it won't stop until we're dead."

They were really identifying with each other. They didn't even notice George until he said, "Sorry, guys." They both said he shouldn't worry about it. "You guys want to walk around the Sugar Bowl?"

Eddie said yes, but Jim said, "I'll let you guys walk. I'm going to take Brutus over by the pier."

Eddie said, "No, Jimmie, come with us." Jim had figured he wanted to be alone with George so they could talk privately, but he could see that Eddie had gotten a lot out of their short conversation and really wanted him to be a part of it. So Jim agreed, but he still walked a bit behind them so they could have some privacy. He was still close enough to hear a few words. Ed told George that he felt like a failure because Lisa had remarried to a guy who was very well off. They had a huge house in the suburbs and were always going on expensive trips around the world. "I'm not making any excuses for the bad choices I made," Eddie said, "but I felt like I couldn't measure up to him. That my kids had anything they wanted. Then one day, I took some painkillers when I threw my back out, and not only did it take care of my physical pain, but it took care of my emotional pain. It took all the guilt away, and it felt good. The problem was, now I always wanted to feel that way. Today, I realize it was only a temporary cure for a permanent problem."

Jim thought George would have responded to what Eddie was saying, but he didn't. He just let him talk until he was done. Jim figured he would give Eddie the same advice he had given to Jim a few weeks ago. Then very quietly, George said, "OK, well, is he good to your kids?"

Eddie said, "Oh, yeah, he's great to them."

"Do you like him?"

Eddie said, "Yeah, that's the thing. You wouldn't think I would. You know, someone else raising my kids when I'm not there. But the crazy thing is, I do like him. We get along great. Whenever plans have to be made, I talk to him instead of my ex-wife."

George stopped in his tracks. Both Jim and Eddie almost bumped into him. He looked at Eddie almost like he said something wrong. Then he said, "You don't even see it, do you, Eddie?" Jim and Eddie looked at each other, and then they looked at George.

Eddie said, "See what?"

"You don't even see how much God loves you."

"What do you mean?"

"God took care of you when you couldn't take care of yourself. He loved you so much, He put a wonderful man in your kids' lives to watch over them while you got better. Could you imagine if your kids grew up with another man who treated them badly, or if they grew up struggling for the necessities of life, food, shelter, and clothing? No, they needed nothing. This man provided everything for them. You were sick and needed help, and now that you're better, you can provide those things. You should be so very grateful."

Eddie thought for a minute and said, "You know, I never thought about that. He was looking out for me and my kids."

George said, "When you go to bed tonight, you should get on your knees and thank Him for everything He did for you."

Eddie smiled and said, "You're right." Then he started laughing and said, "You're absolutely right." You could almost see the guilt and shame lift off him and into the clouds over the harbor. Jim thought, *Wow, even though Eddie and I felt the same guilt about our pasts, there's not always the same answer for the same problem. Everybody's story is their own.*

84

J im arrived home hoping that someone would be there, but the house was still empty. He ran through all the channels on the TV, but nothing interested him. He looked around for something else to keep him occupied but couldn't find anything. Brutus was already hunkered down on the couch for his afternoon nap. Then he looked over at the computer. He hadn't checked his e-mail in a long time because he always needed Libby to help him. No matter how many times she showed him, he couldn't grasp it, or he didn't want to.

He thought, *This is dangerous territory*. He had always stayed away from it like it was the plague. For some reason, he decided to catch up with the twentieth century today and walked toward the machine with all the determination of an ancient warrior entering the arena before a life-or-death battle. He stood over it, talking to himself, convinced he was ready. He sat down and pushed the power button. To his amazement, it turned on. Remembering Libby's instructions, which he had heard a thousand times, he followed them step-by-step. Before he pressed the final button, he paused, and then he clicked on something. Bingo, right before his eyes, he had an e-mail. He pumped his fist, saying, "Yes, yes!" It took all of Brutus's effort to look up at Jim. Unimpressed, he went back to his nap.

In Jim's excitement, he hadn't noticed the e-mail was from Parsons Development Company. It quickly got his attention. The e-mail was very brief. It said that they apologized for the short notice, but they had some urgent matters to attend to and had scheduled another meeting for Friday afternoon at one o'clock. It had requested a confirmation that he would be available. Jim was excited to hear from them, hoping the project was about to get underway. Then he realized the e-mail had been sent five days ago, and it was already Thursday. Panic set in. He started to respond but couldn't remember how to do it. *Libby—where is she?* Then he wondered, *Should I call the office and tell them that my computer was down?* Or maybe he should drive down there and tell them himself. While he dwelled on this, Libby walked in. Jim jumped up and said, "Libby, boy I'm glad you're home, I need you to help me."

Libby interrupted him and said "Dad? Why did we get a letter addressed to the parents of Elizabeth Davis? It says it's from the mayor's office."

Jim said, "What? Let me see it." Jim looked at the letter. "You're right. It is from the mayor's office."

Libby asked, "Am I in trouble or something?"

Jim said, "No, no, honey, let me open it." As Jim read, the concern on his face turned to relief. "Wow, I can't believe it."

"Dad? Dad?"

Jim snapped out of it and said, "It says that you and Maria are getting an outstanding community citizens award for starting the Kids for Seniors program."

Libby jumped up and said, "What, me and Maria?" She quickly read the letter to verify it. "It says they're going to give it to us on Labor Day down at Castle Island. I have to call Maria." But the phone rang. Libby picked it up and said, "I know, I just got the letter too!" They went back and forth with each other.

When Libby got off the phone, Jim said, "Libby, I'm really proud of you."

Libby said, "Dad, I'm so excited!"

"You ought to be proud of yourself, too."

Libby said, "Dad, really, I'm so excited about this. Do you know what's the best thing about it?" Jim thought for a second, figuring it would be good on her future college and employment applications. Libby said, "The best thing about this is that we'll get so much publicity. It will probably be in the newspapers or even on the news, and when it is, the program will only get bigger and bigger, and it will really help the seniors!" No matter how many times Libby amazed Jim with her endless compassion for people, she always reminded him what was really important in life: love for others.

85

After Libby e-mailed Jim's reply, she looked out the window and saw Charlie and Lucky coming up the driveway. Jim hadn't seen them in a while. He had been used to seeing them every day when they worked together. He met them at the door. Charlie was ahead of Lucky, who lagged behind, apparently limping or in some sort of pain. Charlie said, "What's up, Jimbo?" He had a big grin on his face. They hugged, and Lucky just nodded at him and pushed past them into the house.

Jim leaned over to Charlie and whispered, "Is he OK?"

"I don't think so," Charlie answered as he burst out laughing.

Lucky turned around and said, "Oh, shut up." Jim had no idea what was going on.

It couldn't have been too serious, the way Charlie was laughing. Lucky walked over to the couch and sat down very slowly, letting out a big sigh. Charlie said, "You got to listen to this."

Then Libby came out of the kitchen, saying, "Listen to what?" Lucky threw up his hands, knowing he couldn't stop Charlie from telling the story.

As soon as Charlie started talking, Virginia knocked and opened the door. "Anybody home?"

Jim said, "Yeah, come in." She said hi to Charlie and gave Jim a hug. Libby was right there by her side, hugging her waist.

Then she said, "Hi, Lucky." Lucky didn't even look over. He just raised his hand to acknowledge her.

Charlie, trying to control himself, told Virginia, "I was about to tell what happened to Lucky today." Finally, when he thought he had it together, Peter and Debra came in. After everybody greeted each other, the process started all over again.

Charlie began, explaining that Lucky had had a scheduled colonoscopy today, so his doctor had told him to take a laxative yesterday. Charlie could barely get the words out without laughing. He continued, "So he went to the pharmacy and bought some laxative pills. The doctor's instruction was to take two of these tablets by mouth, one at noontime and the other at four o'clock. So he did. Then his sister stopped by. When she saw the packages, she said, 'What did you do?' Lucky told her the instructions, insisting he followed them correctly." By now, Charlie could barely even speak. Everybody kept looking at each other like, *What was so funny?* "His sister said, 'Lucky, you idiot. These are suppositories.'"

Everybody in the room just lost it. The laughter went on for several minutes. Lucky paid no attention to it.

"When his sister left the house," said Charlie, "still not knowing the difference between laxative tablets and suppositories, he takes two more the way they're supposed to be taken. And now he was on the toilet all night. He bought the suppositories thinking they were tablets. I said to him, 'How did you swallow the suppositories? They're huge.' He said they were shaped like a bullet. That was it. They were all out of control. Virginia, being a nurse, was laughing so hard. She said, "I think I'm going to pee my pants," which made everybody laugh even harder.

When the laughter subsided, Charlie said, "That's not even the funny part." Everybody's eyes opened wider with disbelief.

How can this get any funnier? By now, as hard as Lucky tried to stay mad at Charlie, he started laughing too. Charlie finally caught his breath and said, "When he got to the doctor's office, they told him his appointment wasn't until next month. He got his dates mixed up and had the dentist appointment confused with his colonoscopy."

"That's it!" Virginia ran to the bathroom holding her legs together, and everyone was either hunched over holding their stomachs or rolling on the floor. Lucky was right along with them now. He always wanted to be the center of attention. Well, today, he was the star attraction.

86

After everything settled down, Jim announced the news about Libby and Maria getting their award. They embraced Libby, telling her how proud they were. When Debra put down the baby to congratulate Libby, he immediately started to cry. When she picked him back up, he stopped and even gave a little smile. The longer Jim stayed sober, the closer he seemed to be getting in touch with his feelings, good or bad. He couldn't take his eyes off of little Jim. Virginia asked, "Is everything OK?"

Jim looked at her and said, "Yeah. You know, all the thousands of times I've witnessed a child either crying or laughing, I never gave it any thought."

Virginia asked, "Give what any thought?"

"You know, kids may not know about many things because they're so young, but children know one thing, and that's how they feel and what they need. What they do know, most adults don't know—or for whatever reason, can't express. Kids know nothing except the truth. I just figured out why Jesus said that in order to enter the kingdom of heaven, we have to be like children. Could you imagine if all adults could say what they feel without feeling they'll be judged? If they could talk to each other without pride or selfishness getting in the way."

Virginia nodded and said, "You're right, the world would be a much better place."

Peter said, "Hey, Jim, you feel like hitting some balls at the range tomorrow?"

Jim said yes, but then he remembered about the meeting with Parsons Development. He said, "Oh, shoot, I can't. I just got an e-mail today about a meeting tomorrow at the office."

Peter said, "Oh, OK," and his expression went from enthusiastic to somber.

Jim felt bad for him. He knew that Peter was a very proud guy, and being out of work was killing him. Then Jim had an idea. He said, "Pete, why don't you take a drive with me tomorrow to the office. The meeting should only be about an hour or so. But you can give me some suggestions. I feel really out of my element in there. It's an environment that's more your profession than mine, and sometimes I just don't know what to say. Come on, take a ride and give me some pointers."

Peter's enthusiasm came back. He said, "All right. And maybe we can hit some balls afterward."

"Sounds good." Jim had done this to make Pete feel better, but he soon realized that Peter could really be valuable to him.

On the ride over to the meeting the next day, Peter had a notebook full of things to go over with Jim. It might as well have been in Chinese. Jim had no idea what Peter was talking about. He just kept nodding his head up and down like he was absorbing it all.

Peter was telling him when to speak up and when to listen, how to make facial expressions in agreement or disagreement of other people's opinions. He was more confused than ever, but he didn't let Peter know. He knew he felt like he was helping Jim out, and he was, just by being there.

In the parking lot, Peter told Jim to pull up to the front door and said he would take the truck because he wanted to walk around for a while. He said everything around there had changed, and he wanted to check it out. As they got out, Jim almost bumped into Mr. Parsons, who was walking into the building at the same time. Jim apologized. Mr. Parsons said, "Don't worry about it, Jim. I'm glad you could make it."

Peter was standing right there, so Jim quickly said, "Oh, excuse me. Mr. Parsons, this is my brother, Peter."

Mr. Parsons reached out his hand and said, "I'm glad to meet you, Peter. You must be very proud to have a brother like Jim."

Peter said, "I am. More than he knows." It brought a smile to Mr. Parsons's face.

"All right, Jim, I'll see you upstairs."

As Mr. Parsons went in, Peter said, "Wow, he knows your first name. You must be a big shot. My CEO didn't know mine for six years. Mr. Davis, just call me when you're ready to be picked up." Jim laughed and gave him a light punch in the arm.

The meeting got started. All the concerns they covered were pretty much the same as before with only a few minor differences, so people looked at each other, wondering why this meeting had been so urgent. When Mr. Parsons was about to wrap it up, he said, "Now I need to discuss why I had you all come today. I regret to inform you that our chief financial officer, Joe Reagan, has resigned from our company." A hush came over the room. "As you know, Joe has been with this company since its inception. Unfortunately, he has come down with a serious illness and will be in treatment for a while. He was only a few years away from retirement and decided he wanted to spend some quality time with his family. Having said that, we just wanted to let you know that we will be aggressively seeking a replacement. We will keep everyone posted. We just ask you to keep Joe in your prayers. Thank you all for coming today."

Jim's wheels were already spinning. He thought that this would be an unbelievable opportunity for Peter, but he didn't know how to go about pursuing it. He didn't know whether asking Mr. Parsons about the position would be appropriate. He waited for the last moment before Mr. Parsons left, but he decided he didn't feel right about it. At the very last second, Jim had an epiphany. He thought about what Peter had done for him all of his life—protecting him, saving him from drowning, sacrificing his college career and putting his future on hold to be his legal guardian. Suddenly, he felt ashamed for not speaking up. He followed Mr. Parsons into the elevator; thankfully, they were alone. He asked about the process of hiring a CFO. Then he mentioned Peter and his company's buyout situation. He told Mr. Parsons that he didn't want any preferential treatment for his brother. Mr. Parsons took out his pen and wrote something on a business card. Jim thought he had made a mistake.

When the elevator opened, Parsons handed Jim the card and said, "Have your brother call this woman on Monday morning. She's the director of human resources. I'll e-mail her that Peter will be contacting her."

Jim said, "Mr. Parsons, I really appreciate it."

He said, "Jim, family is the most important thing we have. Remember, have him call first thing Monday morning."

"I will, sir. Thank you, thank you."

The meeting had run a little longer than expected. When Jim came out of the building to call Peter, he noticed that he was already in the parking lot, waiting for him. Jim walked toward the truck with a big grin on his face. Peter assumed that all the pointers he had given Jim had really worked. Jim jumped in and said, "Pete, you won't believe it—"

Peter interrupted him. "I told you they would work."

Jim said, "No, listen. The meeting was really about the announcement that the chief financial officer was retiring, and they were going have to replace him as soon as possible. Pete, after the meeting adjourned, I asked Mr. Parsons how you could go about applying for the job."

Peter started laughing and said, "Jim, that position is for someone who has a lot more experience than me. I don't think I could qualify for that."

Jim stopped and looked at him and said, "Peter, do you remember when I was a junior in high school and went out for the football team?" Peter nodded. "Do you remember when I came home and wanted to quit because I thought I wasn't good enough?"

"Yeah."

"Do you remember what you said to me?" Before Peter could say anything, Jim said, "I wanted to play middle linebacker, like you. Do you remember the day you were in the stands watching our practice?"

Peter said, "Yeah, I already told you, I'm sorry about that."

Jim said, "I know. That's not what I'm saying. I was a junior and was intimidated by the seniors. I wasn't playing as hard as I should. I was letting the offensive lineman push me around. Then you came running out of the stands and tackled me, knocking my helmet off and screaming, 'What are you doing? Play hard like I know you can.' After I put my helmet on and wiped my bloody nose, from that moment on, I never lay down to anyone. My senior year, I was the starting middle linebacker and made the all-star team. I said to myself that if I can get hit by you and stand up, well, then there's nobody else who can hurt me, and I'm never going to let anyone take that starting position away from me."

Peter nodded and said, "I taught you well."

"That's right," Jim said. "Mr. Parsons gave me the number of a person to call in human resources."

Peter asked, "He personally gave you a number for me to call?"

"Yup, first thing Monday morning."

"Jim," said Peter, "could you imagine if we ended up working for the same company?"

"You would have to sell your house and move back here. You guys could stay with us until you find something."

Peter said, "Are you kidding me? If I got this job, I would live in a tent if I had to. OK, I'll give it a shot."

"All right, now let's go to the driving range, and I'll give you a golf lesson."

"Hold on, little brother, I didn't show you everything I know. Have your money ready." They gave each other knuckles and drove to the range.

87

That Saturday, everyone was scrambling. Jim and Libby were to give Peter and Debra a ride to Logan Airport for the flight home to California. The thought of them leaving weighed heavy on Jim. He said a silent prayer asking God to help Peter land the job so they could be together again. Then he realized what God had done for him in just a short time once he put his faith in Him. He got on his knees and prayed out loud in his room. Peter walked by, thinking Jim was on the phone. When he peeked in, he saw Jim on his knees asking God to help Peter and Debra to have a safe flight home. He then prayed for their safe flight back to Boston when Peter got his new job with Parsons Development. When Jim finished, he caught sight of Peter out of the corner of his eye. Peter was so moved by all this. He said, "I don't even have the job yet. Why were you praying for us to have a safe return to Boston?"

Jim said, "Because I have faith that you'll get it, and faith is believing in things that are not seen but hoped for" Peter didn't say a word. He just reached out and gave Jim a hug. Jim didn't realize how much he had missed this. His pride would never have allowed him to remember that feeling because of the resentment he felt Peter had had toward him.

After dropping Peter, Debra, and little Jim off at the airport, Jim and Libby decided to go to the Halfway Café for lunch. When they got there, Libby jumped up and said, "Oh my gosh, there's Mrs. Stanton from school." Jim had hardly stopped the truck before Libby jumped out. She ran over to the table where Mrs. Stanton was sitting with her husband. She was just as excited to see Libby and introduced her to her husband.

She said, "Tom, this is Libby, the student I told you about." Mr. Stanton was used to bumping into his wife's students all the time, but when she said, "Libby," his whole expression changed.

He got up from his chair, shook her hand, and said, "Libby, it's so good to finally meet you." Jim was standing over to the side, not wanting to interrupt. He thought it was odd how excited they were. Jim just figured that this was about how kind and helpful Libby always was. Libby introduced her dad, and they exchanged greetings.

Libby looked down and noticed that Mrs. Stanton had really put on some weight over the summer. Seeing Libby notice, she said, "Well, I have some good news. I'm going to have a baby. In fact, I'm going to have twins."

Libby and Jim both said, "Wow."

Jim said, "Congratulations."

Libby asked, "Are you still going to teach at the school?"

"Yes, probably only up to Christmas. Then I have to take some time off." They talked some more, and when it was time to say good-bye, the Stantons both stood up and shook Jim's hand, but when they turned to Libby, they gave her a big hug. Mrs. Stanton had tears in her eyes. "We were so glad to see you."

Libby said, "Me, too. See you back in school!"

As they drove away, Jim turned to Libby and said, "Wow, I guess you were her favorite." Libby never mentioned to Jim what happened in school that day. He never knew what Libby had told her.

That's what God can do for you. Once you ask for forgiveness for your mistakes, He will pour blessings upon you. Mrs. Stanton asked God for another baby and His answer was "I will not only give you one child, but two." His promise is to give us abundantly more than we ask for.

88

After the Fourth of July, the summer seemed to fly by. It was now the middle of August. The nights were getting cooler, and there weren't as many people at the beach. Most of them were wearing sweatshirts and taking long walks around the Sugar Bowl.

The Kids for Seniors program that Libby and Maria had started was really getting some notoriety. The word spread, and people came from all over. Many who had moved into the suburbs years ago heard about the program and decided to check it out. Unbeknownst to them, they would meet old friends that they hadn't seen since they were in school. You could see them sharing old and new photos. One couple who had dated in high school were reunited and subsequently married at the age of seventy-six. They had the ceremony right there in the park.

Peter had called earlier in the week and told Jim that he had had an interview via Skype. He said he felt it all went very well. Jim told him he would pray that God would intervene and give him favor. Today, Jim came into the living room to do his routine channel surfing. When he sat down on the sofa, he noticed a flier from a local jeweler. It was open to the engagement ring section. A few of the rings were even circled. He thought, *No way. Why would Libby be looking at rings?*

Just then, Libby came down the stairs with Brutus following her. Jim asked Libby, "Can you come here for a minute?"

"What's up, Dad?"

Jim said, "Libby, you're not thinking about eloping with Smitty, are you?"

"Why are you saying that?" Then she noticed the flyer Jim was holding. Libby looked a little embarrassed and said, "Oh, that." Then she got real quiet, and it dawned on Jim that she was picking out an engagement ring for him to give to Virginia.

Jim compassionately said, "Libby, I know you would want that, but—"

"But what?" Libby said. "Dad, she's perfect for you. You're not ever going to find someone like her. Dad, I know these things. I can feel it. I don't know how or why, but I just know you're supposed to be with her."

"How do you know that?"

"I don't just see it, I feel what you guys feel when you look at each other. You know what happens to me. I feel things inside of me, and most of the time what I feel when I look at people is that they are so scared of everything. That's the way you guys are when you're by yourselves. But when you see each other, I feel that fear leave both of you. Then you feel that everything is OK. It's the same feeling we get when we know that God is protecting us all the time. You and Virginia both feel safer when you're with each other."

Jim couldn't say a word; he just held out his arms. After a long hug, he finally said, "I don't know why God has been so good to me after all the mistakes I've made."

Libby looked up at him and said, "Dad, He rewards people who are faithful to Him. Once you ask for forgiveness, He will bury your sins at the bottom of the sea, never to be brought up again."

89

Jim was looking out the kitchen window, sipping his coffee, when he remembered that he still had to stain his new deck. He tried to think of a good reason to put it off. Then he remembered when he had prayed to God to help him with his procrastination problem. So he said, "OK, God, I hear ya." He called Tommy next door and asked him if he wanted to take a ride to Home Depot to pick up some stain.

Tommy said, "Sure, do you need help with the staining?"

"Yeah, I do. Do you want to help?"

Tommy asked, "Are you paying me union wages?"

"No, but I'll give you a baloney sandwich."

"With cheese?"

"Only if you don't take any breaks."

Tommy said, "Sounds like a deal."

As they made their way to Home Depot's paint department, suddenly they heard someone yell, "Hey, screwball!"

Tommy looked at Jim, and Jim said, "Don't look at me. I'm sure not over there calling you."

Tommy looked down the aisle and saw one of his elderly friends from the Dunkin' Donuts crew. He said, "Hey, Paul, what's up?" Tommy laughed and told Jim he'd be back in a minute.

Jim was looking at stain colors when he bumped into some-one. He turned and said, "Oh, I'm sorry." Then he had to look twice. It was Ted Wright from the bank. He hadn't recognized him at first because he had lost so much weight.

The men greeted each other, and Jim said it was funny that he'd bumped into Ted, because for some reason, he had been thinking about him lately. He remembered that Ted had lost his job a few months ago and had had to sell his house. The way he had treated Ted in the bank the day he went in to discuss his own mortgage had bothered Jim. Jim said, "Ted, you lost some weight?"

"Yeah, I had surgery to remove a malignant tumor on my lung."

Now Jim felt even worse than before. He said, "I'm really sorry, Ted. You know, I owe you an apology for the way I treated you at the bank the day I came in. I wanted to apologize when I saw you in the Sidewalk Café."

Ted said, "Jim, you don't owe me an apology. In fact, I have to thank you for saving my life."

Jim looked puzzled. "How in the world you figure that?"

"I'll tell you. After the bank let me go, I took a job in a nonprofit company that helps single moms get on their feet. I didn't want to take it. I felt it was below me. I felt with my credentials, I should have something else, something more prestigious. Then I remembered our conversation in the bank that day and couldn't get some of the things you said out of my head. It really made me rethink my life and what I wanted to do. I still had to make ends meet, so I took the job. I did everything from helping with their paperwork and cleaning the building to moving them in or out. Jim, it's the most rewarding job I ever had. I can't wait to go to work in the morning, and I don't look forward to leaving at night. There's nothing in the world like making a difference in someone's life.

"One day we were moving a mom into transitional housing. We were carrying a sofa down a flight of stairs. One of the stairs treads cracked, and I fell down, with the sofa landing on my chest. I could hardly breathe, so they took me to the hospital. They did X-rays on me. When the doctor came into my room, he had a very serious look on his face. I figured, how bad can it be, a few broken ribs? That's when he told me that he had found this mass in my chest. After the biopsy, we found out it was cancer. I went into surgery the next day. They ended up getting all of it, and so far, I have no other trace of it. The doctor told me he figured it was probably in there for six months to a year. So the day you were in my office, I had it and didn't even know it. He said that they got it very early, but if it wasn't discovered and went too long, it would have probably killed me. So that's how you saved my life. It was by God's grace that you came to my office that day. There is no other possible reason that things happened the way they did. The older I get, it never ceases to amaze me that what we sometimes think is a tragic situation, God can turn into a miraculous blessing."

"Ted, I got to tell you, I'm finding out myself how true that really is."

On the ride home, Jim told Tommy about the award that Libby and Maria were getting for creating the Kids for Seniors program. It brought a smile from Tommy, and he said that was great. Tommy loved hanging out with the older folks. Jim told him he was invited to attend the ceremony.

"When is it?"

"The Saturday on Labor Day weekend." Jim said, "Everybody's coming: Charlie, Lucky, Pastor Pete, Big Ben, Libby's friends, Virginia, Grace, Nathan, Carlos and his family, and several people from the congregation."

Tommy said, "Yeah, that will be cool."

"We've decided to have a big cookout afterward."

Tommy said, "Then I'm definitely coming."

90

After they finished the deck, Jim went upstairs to take a shower. When he got out, Libby and Virginia came home. They had been out shopping for some clothes for the award ceremony. Libby asked, "Dad, can we go down to Sully's for dinner?"

Jim was exhausted, but the thought of a Sully's double cheeseburger was too tempting to turn down. He said, "OK, you talked me into it."

Libby turned to Virginia and said, "See, he never turns down going down to Sully's."

Jim looked at both of them and said, "Oh, you guys already planned the whole thing."

They laughed and said, "How did you figure that out?"

Jim said, "Come on, let's go before I change my mind."

When they got there, Jim asked Virginia what she would like. He didn't have to ask Libby; he already knew—two hot dogs with mustard and relish, a large french fry, and a Pepsi. Virginia asked, "What do they have here that's not fattening?"

Jim looked at Libby, who started laughing. Jim said, "The only thing they have here that's not fattening is the bottled water. When you come to Sully's, the last thing you worry about is gaining weight."

"OK, I'll have a bottled water and a fish sandwich with no tartar sauce."

Jim said, "No tartar sauce! That's like having peanut butter with no jelly."

Virginia said, "I told you, I don't want to get fat."

Jim shrugged and said, "OK, you got it."

When they got their food, Libby had picked out a table. "Dad, over here!"

Jim said, "Good looking out, kiddo." Jim dove right into his double cheeseburger. Then he noticed Virginia taking the bread off her sandwich and feeding it to the waiting pigeons. She slowly picked up the piece of fish and daintily started to peck at it. When she looked up at Jim, she started to say something, but Jim quickly raised the palm of his hand toward her and said, "I know, I know, you don't want to get fat." Virginia laughed, and they both looked at Libby. Except she had her eyes fixed on the next table, where a mom was sitting with her two young kids, the cutest, Irish-looking boy and girl. They were probably about five or six years old.

Libby had a very serious look on her face. Jim knew that when she looked like this, something was really bothering her. Jim asked, "Libby, what are you looking at?" Libby didn't respond. She just kept looking at the mother.

Jim watched the family. The kids were asking her for help putting ketchup on their french fries, but the mom wasn't paying any attention to them. When they asked again, she said, "You guys, stop bothering me." Then Jim noticed that her eyes were fixed on her cell phone as she constantly texted someone. He knew that Libby was upset. She could just sense what those kids were feeling at that time. She knew they felt like they weren't important enough for their mother to shut off her cell phone and give them some attention. Libby knew how these kids could be affected by constantly being ignored. Not just then and there, but if it continued, it could affect them for the rest of their lives. She knew that they didn't deserve that.

Jim knew what was about to happen next. Libby got up and went over to the family's table. She opened up the ketchup packets and put them on the kids' fries. They smiled and said thank you. Amazingly, the mom never even noticed her. Libby said to her, "Here's some extra packages in case they want more."

The woman looked up at Libby and then looked at the kids eating their fries. She seemed confused. How had the ketchup gotten on their fries? Libby reached across the table to hand her the packets. When the woman reached out for them, Libby grabbed her hand. The woman immediately froze. "What's happening to me?"

Then the visions started coming. The kids were now teenagers. She was divorced, and the kids had chosen to live with their father. They seemed different—very happy and content. She could feel the love and attention that they were getting from their dad. Then she was on the phone with them, feeling that everything they talked about was just superficial. The weather, their classes. She realized how difficult it was to talk to them. It seemed like they just wanted to get the phone call over with. The woman started to cry. Now both kids were married and had chosen to relocate across the country where their dad had his new career. The next thing she saw was her grandchildren; both had girls. She now could feel how terribly sad she would be, not being a part of their lives. She felt so remorseful that she hadn't cherished the days when they were very young and hadn't been more nurturing to them. She felt how she was responsible for it all. She knew that God had given her the most beautiful gift of children, and she remembered now how she thought it was a burden rather than a blessing.

Libby let go of the woman's hand, and she now could see her children through the tears in her eyes. She lunged for them, grabbing both and pulling them to her chest, squeezing them continually and saying, "I'm so sorry. I'm so sorry, kids." Then she noticed that she still had the cell phone in her hand. She looked at it and then threw it on the ground, pulling her children to her again. After she wiped her tears, she looked at Libby and said, "Thank you, thank you so much." Libby just smiled at her and nodded. Then Libby sat down to eat her hot dogs, never missing a beat. She just knew when God was directing her to intervene in someone's life. Jim and Virginia just looked at each other with their hands over their mouths, knowing they had just witnessed firsthand the future relationship of a mother and her children.

On the ride home, Jim's phone rang. It was Peter. "How's my little brother doing?"

"Yeah, we're doing good. Me, Virginia, and Libby just left Sully's."

Peter said, "Tell me you didn't get the double cheeseburger."

Jim said, "Yup, and with everything on it."

"Oh, you're killing me."

"I would have bought you one if you were here."

"OK, I'm going to hold you to that. I'll be there next Thursday."

"Whatta you mean?"

Peter said, "I got the job."

Jim stopped in the middle of the road. The driver behind him beeped his horn. Libby said, "Dad, what are you doing?"

Jim pulled over to the curb and said, "Say that again."

"I got the job. They just called me and offered me the position. I'm flying in next Thursday. I have to meet with them and sign all necessary paperwork. We're moving back to Boston!"

Jim yelled out, "Wahoo! I can't believe it." Virginia and Libby kept asking what was going on. Jim said to Peter, "That will mean you'll be here for Libby's award on Saturday. Are Debra and the baby coming?"

Peter said, "No, it's too short of a notice. The baby has doctor's appointments already scheduled."

"When are you starting?"

"They want me there by October first."

Jim said, "Yeah, that's when they want me to start full time, too. What about your house? You have to sell that right away."

Peter said, "Jim, you're not going to believe it. They're relocating me."

Jim asked, "What does that mean?"

"They're buying my house so I can look for another one there. I just got off the phone with a real estate agent. We're going to look at some houses when I get there."

Jim said, "Wow, I can't believe how this all worked out."

"This would have never happened if it wasn't for you. I'm sure of that. I'm sure that Mr. Parsons personally had something to do with this. When I talked to human resources, they told me they had over one hundred applicants, and I'm sure most of them were more qualified than I was. Debra and I are so grateful for your help. Things were really getting stressful for us."

Jim said, "Well, it was all part of God's plan."

Peter said, "You're right, what else could it be? You couldn't write a better ending for the situation."

"Amen. I'll pick you up at Logan, and you can stay here."

"OK, thanks. I'll call you later with the flight schedule. Jim, thanks again, I really mean it."

Jim said, "No problem. I'm glad I could help. Talk to you soon."

Peter said, "OK, my brother."

When Jim hung up, Virginia and Libby jumped on him, wanting to know what was going on. He filled them in on the details, and they were as excited as he was. Jim drove off with a feeling he had never really experienced before. All his life, it was always Peter helping him, always getting him out of jams. Now it was Jim helping Peter. He thought how it would never have been possible if it hadn't been for Libby. She showed him what his life would have been like if he didn't change his ways. He wished everybody going down the road had someone like Libby in their lives to help them make the right choices. As he was thinking this, he turned and looked at Libby, who was looking at Jim with a big smile on her face. She said, "Everyone already has someone, Dad, if they want Him. His name is Jesus, and He's been waiting for them to ask."

91

It was Saturday morning of Labor Day weekend. Everyone was getting ready for Maria and Libby's award ceremony for the Kids for Seniors program and the big cookout afterward. Jim had picked up Peter at the airport on Thursday. He was on Skype with Debra and the baby. Libby was on the phone with Maria, Virginia was preparing food for the cookout, and Jim was having a deep conversation with Brutus on what to watch next on TV. Libby said, "Dad, come on, you're going to be late."

He just looked at Brutus and said, "OK, Brutus, no more cartoons for you, let's go."

They all piled into two cars and drove down to Castle Island, but the traffic was all backed up on Day Boulevard. Jim said, "Well, what else can we expect? It's Labor Day weekend." By the time they got to the parking lot, they realized why things were really backed up. There were news vans and television cameras everywhere. Not only that, there were different buses from all kinds of senior centers there. Most of them were from places that had heard about the award and wanted to check it out the program.

A representative was there from the mayor's office. When Libby and Maria went up to meet the rep, the cameras followed. People from the mayor's office pushed the media back and told them to give the girls a little space. All of Jim's friends came up to greet them. Close to fifty of their friends and people from their congregation were there. When things settled down, the ceremony started. The representative started it out by thanking everyone for coming. After praising Libby and Maria's vision for the program, he called them up to the podium. Jim and Carlos escorted them. When they actually got up there and turned to face the crowd, they were amazed. There must have been a couple of thousand people there. The representative awarded Maria and Libby plaques and a letter from the mayor praising them for their contribution to the elderly.

After the ceremony finished, several seniors came up and thanked the girls from the bottom of their hearts. They told Maria and Libby how it had been the best summer they'd had in years and were looking forward to next year. Then the couple that had been reunited and got married came up to personally thank them. They told them they had been boyfriend and girlfriend at Southie High, spending three years together inseparably, when the Korean War broke out and he was shipped overseas. Then she had had to relocate to the Midwest with her family, and they had lost contact with each other. They both had married others and had many children and grandchildren. They had wonderful marriages, but both of them had lost their spouses within the last five years. The husband said, "Even though we had very fulfilling lives, we still often thought of each other. You never forget your first love, you know." Smitty was standing next to Libby, and both of them turned red. "Then we heard about this program and decided to come." He looked at his new bride and said, "The minute I saw her, I knew who she was. I can recognize her smile anywhere, even after all the years." They thanked Maria and Libby one more time and walked away hand in hand.

Jim looked at Virginia. She was wiping tears from her face. Jim helped her wipe and said, "Can you imagine if Libby had never spilled that drink on you? We would not be standing here right now."

Virginia laughed and punched Jim in the chest. She said, "I have to go to the bathroom. Wait for me."

Jim heard a woman's voice saying, "Excuse me."

When he turned, the woman introduced herself. "Hi, my name is Ann. I'm Sara's mother."

"Oh! I'm glad to meet you. Libby and Sara have become close friends."

She said, "That's what I wanted to thank you for. Before she met Libby, she was really isolating herself in her room. She missed her dad so much and felt all alone. Then when she met Libby, everything changed. She didn't feel so alone. Even though she misses her dad, Libby instilled something in her. She told her that the separation was only temporary and that they would be reunited in heaven. It really gave her hope that they will be together again, and that changed everything for her."

Jim said, "Libby has the gift of discernment. She can really comfort people."

Ann said, "I took Sara to many doctors and therapists, but none of them helped her like Libby did. So, thank you."

Jim said, "You're welcome. I'm so glad she's feeling better."

Everyone walked over to the park to start setting up for the cookout. Jim stopped and looked around at all his friends and thought, *Wow, I am truly blessed. None of this would ever be possible if I wasn't sober.* They fired up the grill, and the conversation and fellowship began. Libby looked toward the ocean and saw Ed Donlan's yacht on the water very close by. All of Ed's and Sam's families were on it, with Tommy and his crew piloting. Then she noticed several more people on the boat: Mr. Donlan's employees from his house. There were the maids and the landscapers. The most amazing thing was that Ed was waiting on them, serving food and drinks. Then she saw Marguerite, the head maid, holding up her glass and looking for a refill. Everyone on the yacht clapped and cheered her. Mr. Donlan got the biggest kick out of it.

Lucky was standing next to Pastor Pete and Big Ben. Then Lucky heard someone calling him. When he looked over, he saw the guys who were always harassing him. Standing next to Ben and Pete, he felt untouchable, and he wanted them to know it. When the guys came over, he said, "I thought you guys were supposed to be on a leash."

One of the guys said, "Oh, you're feeling a little brave today, huh?"

Lucky said, "Are you guys feeling a little brave, or just suicidal?"

The guy said, "Why, do you think you can stop us?"

Lucky laughed and said, "Yeah, me and my boys." The guys looked behind him at two five-year-old boys eating their ice creams. Lucky didn't realize that Pete and Ben had walked away a few minutes ago and that the kids had come over to sit behind him on a bench.

The guys said, "OK, Lucky, have it your way."

Lucky expected them to walk away, but instead, they came toward him. He smirked at them and said confidently, "Oh, boys," referring to Ben and Pete, "can you take care of this for me?" The guys just kept walking toward Lucky. One more time, sounding a little more concerned, Lucky instructed Ben and Pete to move in on the guys. When they were about five feet away and circling him, he looked back and saw the two little boys with ice cream dripping off of their chins. By now, Pete and Ben were way off in the distance. Panic set in as Lucky was grabbed and raised over the men's shoulders. Lucky's screams had everyone looking by now. They all knew who these guys were and knew they would never hurt him.

The guys walked over to the railing over the water and in perfect cadence, they counted "One, two, three!" and hurled him into the ocean. Everyone cheered and laughed, knowing full well that Lucky had instigated the situation.

When he finally climbed back up on the railing, he looked like a drowned rat. He kept saying, "This ain't right, it just ain't right."

After the main meal was finished, Jim announced that dessert was being served. Grace and her new pastor friend were in charge of it. The people lined up for cheesecake and ice cream. Jim told Virginia that he would bring hers and asked Libby to help him. When Grace put the three pieces of cake on the plates, he asked Libby to pick one out for Virginia. When she did, he said, "Libby, do me a favor. I have something in my jacket pocket. Grab it for me, will you?"

Libby reached in and pulled out a small, velvet box. Libby looked confused and asked, "What's this?"

"I don't know." Libby slowly opened the box, figuring that with Jim's sense of humor, it was probably a joke. Then she gasped. It was a one-carat diamond engagement ring. She started to scream, and Jim said, "Shush, be quiet."

Libby said, "Dad, is this what I think it is?" Jim proudly said yes. "When are you going to give it to her?"

Jim said, "Right now. Take it out and put it on the cheesecake." Libby placed it on the cake perfectly. Jim said, "Now place a napkin on it."

Libby said, "Dad, you did listen to me about getting a ring for Virginia."

Jim said, "No, I actually bought it before we talked about it. See, even with your gift, you didn't know. Who's better than me?"

As they walked over to Virginia, Jim put his poker face on. That was one of *his* gifts. That's why he was always able to pull off the best practical jokes of all time. Libby, on the other hand, had the worst possible poker face there ever was. As much as she tried, she could hardly contain herself. Libby put the cake down in front of Virginia. Virginia wondered what was so funny. She asked, "What is it?"

Jim said, "It's cheesecake and ice cream."

Virginia said, "No, I can't have any. I told you, I'm trying to lose weight."

Libby looked up at Jim as if to say, *What are we going to do now?* Never missing a beat, he said, "You have to at least try it, because Grace asked me to let her know what you think."

Libby looked at Virginia, who said, "OK, but just one bite." She picked up a fork and caught Libby looking at her. Then she said, "What's up with you guys?" She then took the napkin off and saw the diamond ring. She said, "Oh my God, whoever made the cake must have lost her ring!" Libby and Jim laughed.

Then Jim got real serious and said, "No, no one lost her ring. It's yours. I want to know if you'll marry me." Jim was so close to Libby that he had wanted her to be a part of this.

By now, Virginia was shaking. She looked at the ring for a very long time. She asked, "Do you really want me to marry you?"

Jim said, "No. I really, *really* want you to marry me."

She jumped up and said, "Yes I'll marry you."

Libby yelled, "Awesome!" Everybody turned to see what the commotion was. Libby screamed, "They're getting married!" which brought everyone running to the table. After everyone congratulated them, Libby said, "Virginia, you haven't tried the ring on!" In all the confusion, the ring was still in the cheesecake. Jim removed it and cleaned it off, and then slipped it on Virginia's finger. Everyone clapped. The pastor came over and gave them a special blessing and asked God to anoint them.

Virginia said, "My God, it fits perfectly. How did you know what size I was?"

"One day when you were preparing some dinner at my house, you had taken off your favorite amber ring you told me your mother gave you. That's the day I said I had to run to the bank, but I really took it to the jeweler's on East Broadway. I told him what I was doing, so he measured it for me. When I got home, I put it back in the same place. You never noticed it was gone."

Virginia said, "Wow, with all that creativity, you would think that you would have invented something by now that allows you to watch TV and go to the bathroom at the same time." Everyone laughed, and all the women came over and gave Virginia high fives.

Peter looked at Jim, patted him on the back, and said, "Welcome back to the club, my little brother."

As the cookout wound down, Peter said, "Hey, the summer's over. How about we all take one last walk around the Sugar Bowl?" Everyone agreed. They started out behind Sully's toward the Rowes Wharf side. They continued by the fishing pier, Deer Island, and Fort Independence, and then started around the Sugar Bowl.

Jim and Virginia were holding hands. Charlie came up to Jim and said, "Hey, bro, I'm really happy for you guys."

Jim stopped and said, "Charlie, thanks for never giving up on me. Even all those years I was angry at God."

"Hey, I had all the faith that He would reach you. But I will say you went down swinging. He blessed Libby with that gift so He could reach you through her."

Libby, Maria, Sara, and Nathan were walking way out in front of everybody. Jim said to Charlie, "Look at them. I don't know why, but I just got a strange feeling that they're planning something."

He yelled out, "Hey! What are you guys planning up there, how to find world peace?" The crowd all looked at them. When the kids turned around, they had looks on their faces that said, *How did you know that?* Jim said, "No, no, that's what they're really planning on doing!" All three girls and Nathan looked at Jim and smiled. Then they laughed as they turned away and started to run. Jim yelled, "No, no, Libby! My heart can't take it."

Charlie exuberantly yelled, "Hallelujah, praise God! We're going to the United Nations!"

Jim took off after them, saying, "Libby! Come here, come here, listen to me! Listen to your father!"

Made in United States
North Haven, CT
22 May 2024

52720070R00192